MURDER AT STANDING STONE MANOR

*The Langham and Dupré mysteries by Eric Brown
from Severn House*

MURDER BY THE BOOK
MURDER AT THE CHASE
MURDER AT THE LOCH
MURDER TAKE THREE
MURDER TAKES A TURN
MURDER SERVED COLD
MURDER BY NUMBERS

MURDER AT STANDING STONE MANOR

Eric Brown

SEVERN
HOUSE

First world edition published in Great Britain and the USA in 2021
by Severn House, an imprint of Canongate Books Ltd,
14 High Street, Edinburgh EH1 1TE.

Trade paperback edition first published in Great Britain and the USA in 2022
by Severn House, an imprint of Canongate Books Ltd.

severnhouse.com

British Library Cataloguing-in-Publication Data
A CIP catalogue record for this title is available from the British Library.

ISBN-13: 978-0-7278-5056-0 (cased)
ISBN-13: 978-1-78029-806-1 (trade paper)
ISBN-13: 978-1-4483-0544-5 (e-book)

All Severn House titles are printed on acid-free paper.

MIX
Paper from
responsible sources
FSC
www.fsc.org   FSC® C013056

Typeset by Palimpsest Book Production Ltd.,
Falkirk, Stirlingshire, Scotland.
Printed and bound in Great Britain by
TJ Books, Padstow, Cornwall.

Dedicated with thanks to
Graham Brack

ONE

Maria placed the hotpot in the Rayburn, washed her hands at the sink, then moved to the living room and gazed through the French windows.

She had never been in any doubt about their move to the country, and the past few days had confirmed her conviction that she and Donald were doing the right thing.

She had taken a fortnight off work to settle into Yew Tree Cottage and begin the laborious task of unpacking. The move from London had gone well, and on entering the property on Monday morning, Maria had not been beset with the second thoughts or despondency that had accompanied other house moves in the past. Mrs Ashton had left the place spick and span, along with a bottle of Bordeaux and a card wishing them well.

Added to that, over the course of the past few days Maria had greeted a procession of neighbours who introduced themselves and welcomed her and Donald to the village.

She looked down the length of the snow-covered back garden to the stream glinting beyond a stand of willows and elms. In the distance, she made out the imposing bulk of Standing Stone Manor, smoke rising vertically from one of its many chimneys.

Hugging herself, she turned and regarded the room. Not for the first time since the move, she felt a certain euphoria, a happiness she could only put down to the thought of her and Donald making their home in Yew Tree Cottage.

In the past, she had always preferred large, airy rooms, but over the course of the last few evenings, snuggling down on the sofa before the roaring fire, she had come to appreciate the long, low-ceilinged room, with its blackened oak beams and old-fashioned *fleur-de-lis* wallpaper. What was more, it was proving to be a warm house – dispelling Donald's prognostication that it would be an ice-box. The Rayburn heated a couple of radiators, one in the kitchen and the other in the room that would be his study, and open fires in the living room and master bedroom provided sufficient warmth if they were lit early enough.

They had managed to make four rooms habitable – the living room, kitchen, dining room and master bedroom. The others, including the study, were piled high with cardboard boxes and packing crates, many of them containing books.

From the mantelpiece, she took down a handwritten card that had dropped through the letterbox that morning.

Wellspring Farm, Crooked Lane

Dear Neighbours,
Wonderful to have new blood in the village. We're having a little dinner do on Friday night at eight. Do come.
Mr and Mrs Richard Wellbourne

The telephone bell shrilled, startling her. She plucked up the receiver and settled herself on the sofa before the fire. 'Ingoldby four-five-two,' she said. 'Maria speaking.'

'Darling,' Donald said. 'Why is it that, down the phone, your voice sounds so husky and sensual, like melted chocolate?'

'Donald,' she laughed, 'you're drunk!'

'And so would you be if you'd just undergone a liquid lunch with your editor and agent.'

'How is Charles?'

'On top form. Just back from a short break in Paris with Albert and singing its praises.'

'How did the editorial meeting go?'

'Good news in that department, old girl. I don't know how he did it, but Charles has secured a three-book deal from Worley and Greenwood, with an increased advance and higher royalties.'

'You clever man!' Maria said, smiling to herself. The previous week, Charles had told her that sales of Donald's latest thriller had exceeded all expectations, and that better terms were therefore in the offing.

'You're not working too hard, are you?' he asked.

'I've unpacked a few more boxes and made a hotpot for dinner. I hope you haven't eaten too much for lunch?'

'No fear. The portions at Greenwood's favourite haunt are minuscule. Look here, take it easy this afternoon. No more unpacking until tomorrow, and we'll do it together.'

'I think I'll go out for a walk. The sun is shining and the snow is so beautiful. Oh,' she went on, glancing up at the Wellbournes' card, 'our neighbours, the Wellbournes, have invited us to a do tomorrow evening.'

'Ah, the gentleman farmer. Apparently Richard Wellbourne is a bit of an eccentric. Plays the fiddle to his cows at milking time.'

Maria laughed. 'How do you know that?'

'Overheard some locals nattering in the Green Man the other night. Wellbourne swears blind that a bit of Bach increases his herd's yield.'

'Very odd.'

'We've moved to the country, old girl. They do things differently there. Right-ho, I'd better say toodle-pip. Old Greenwood's gesturing for me to get off the blower and have one for the road. See you tonight, darling.'

'Drive carefully,' she said.

She replaced the receiver, moved to the hallway and pulled on her overcoat, hat and gloves. There was another envelope lying on the welcome mat. She picked it up and pulled out a small postcard. The black-and-white photograph showed a tall standing stone; she turned it over and read the scrawled handwriting.

Standing Stone Manor

Langham,
Charles told me you'd moved to the village. I need to see you, pick your brains about something fishy going on here.
Professor Edwin Robertshaw

She tucked the card into her coat pocket and unlocked the front door.

'Something fishy . . .' she said to herself as she stepped out into the freezing late-January afternoon.

There was not a breath of wind in the air and the sky was bright blue. Sunlight bounced off the snow, dazzling her as she walked carefully down the garden path and turned left along the lane to the village.

It was on days like these that she realized how much she loved the snow. It transformed the landscape, turning hard angles soft, giving a fleece-like padding to buildings that might otherwise have been ugly. Not that there were any ugly buildings along the lane: a row of thatched cottages extended to her left, and on the right, beyond the hedge, white fields undulated to the horizon.

Her every footstep compacted the snow, creating a regular succession of squeaks. Not many people had been abroad today, judging by the lack of footprints. Hers were the only ones along the lane until she came to the village green, where she followed a line of dark prints like stunted exclamation marks leading to the row of shops on the far side.

One of the attractions of the village – other than the public house – was that it was well served with shops: a butcher, a baker and a general store-cum-post office. That morning a neighbour had informed her that the village hall held regular cake sales and that the vicar hosted afternoon teas at the church hall every second Tuesday.

She bought two threepenny stamps from the young woman behind the post office counter, who said, 'You must be the lady who's bought Yew Tree Cottage. How are you settling in?'

'Very well, thank you. I'm Maria. Maria Dupré.'

'Flo Waters,' the woman said. 'I don't think my mum thought about it when she christened me. But I never liked Florence or Florrie. If you need anything, just ask.'

'I was wondering if there was a local coal merchant. Mrs Ashton left a supply, but with this weather we'll soon be running out.'

'Ah, you need to see old Wicketts Blacker, you do,' Flo said. 'He works a couple of days a week for Hurst and Forshaw over at Bury. Wicketts'll see you right.'

The bell over the door tinkled and someone whom Maria took to be a schoolgirl breezed in, beaming under her brown beret. 'Hello, Flo!' The girl saw Maria and the intensity of her smile increased. 'Oh, hello, you must be . . .'

'Maria. My husband and I have just moved into Yew Tree Cottage.'

'Nancy,' the girl said, offering a mittened hand. Maria shook it. 'My uncle told me all about you. Your husband is a famous writer, isn't he? And you work in publishing.' She gave Maria a mischievous grin.

'Well, word does get around,' Maria said.

'The professor knows a friend of yours, Mr Elder from Bury way.'

'Would that be Professor Robertshaw of Standing Stone Manor?'

'That's right. My uncle knows just about everyone in the world,' the girl said. 'Can I send this letter to London, Flo?' she went on, sliding an envelope under the grille.

Flo licked a stamp and hammered it on to the envelope with her fist. 'Maria was asking about coal,' she said. 'Will you show her where old Wicketts lives, Nancy?'

The girl paid for the stamp, then turned to Maria. 'It's on the way back to the manor.' She hesitated. 'I say, would you like to come back for tea and cake? My uncle might be busy with his work, but I could entertain you.'

Maria smiled. 'That would be lovely.'

Wondering about the professor and the fishy goings-on at the manor, she said goodbye to Flo and followed Nancy outside.

A dog sat patiently beneath the green-and-white striped awning, its lead tied to the railings of the neighbouring house. Nancy praised the dog and untied the lead.

'What a handsome beast,' Maria said. 'What kind is he? A long-legged spaniel?'

The dog, a big red-and-white patched male, nosed Maria's hand in a friendly fashion.

Nancy laughed. 'Everyone asks me that. No, he's an Irish red-and-white setter. He's called Bill and he's very affectionate.'

The girl was older than she'd first assumed; closer to twenty than fifteen, Maria saw as they turned left and tramped away from the village green, Bill trotting obediently between them. Nancy wore a brown duffel coat and fur-trimmed boots, and her face beneath the beret was pretty in a fresh-complexioned, innocent way, with wide blue eyes, a snub nose and a spill of golden curls.

'I take it you live with your uncle at the manor?'

'He took me in two years ago when my parents died.'

'Oh – I am sorry.'

The girl stared down at the snow, her lips set in a determined line as she plodded along. 'The train crash at Barnes. You must have read about it?'

'Of course. How terrible.'

'But Uncle Edwin and Xandra were bricks. They made me welcome and said I could stay as long as I liked. Wasn't that nice? I'd finished boarding school in Cambridge that summer, and I was thinking of going into nursing, only . . .'

'You needed time to think about your future?'

Nancy turned to her and beamed. 'That's exactly it. I needed time. I didn't want to rush into nursing, and anyway, the thought of hospitals . . .' She gave a theatrical shiver. 'To be perfectly honest, by then I'd had enough of them. My parents were in St Thomas's for a week after the accident. I visited them every day . . .' She trailed off.

Maria said, filling the silence, 'Have you thought of alternatives to nursing?'

Nancy widened her eyes and smiled. She had an expressive face and an innocence that Maria found enchanting. 'Oh, I'd love to write. I'm considering journalism. At the moment, though . . . Well, Aunt Xandra is ill, so I'm looking after her. It's the least I can do, isn't it, after they let me live at the manor?'

They walked along the lane in silence for half a minute, until Nancy looked up and pointed to a tumbledown cottage set back amongst an overgrown tangle of hawthorn and blackberry brambles.

'That's where old Wicketts lives. You'll see him around, and you won't mistake him. He's about four foot high and looks like a goblin. He does a little odd-jobbing up at the manor, so if I see him, I'll tell him to drop by.'

They turned along a snow-filled lane, marked by a trail of

footprints Maria took to be Nancy's, along with Bill's paw prints. They came to the small humpbacked bridge that could be seen from the cottage, and Maria paused at its high point and gazed upriver. A hundred yards away, she made out Yew Tree Cottage, peeping through the trees on the right. Its snow-covered thatch came down to within five feet of the ground at the back, and a patch of snow around the chimney bricks, warmed by the open fire, had melted to reveal the blackened Norfolk reed. Next to the cottage was Wellspring Farm, a long, low house with several honey-coloured stone outbuildings set back from the lane.

Nancy pointed to the left. 'Standing Stone Manor,' she declared as if they were long-lost explorers in sight of land. 'We're almost there. I'll let Bill off the lead so he can run home. Now, take my hand, because this side of the bridge is beastly treacherous!'

She released the dog and it shot off, sure-footed, its nose to the ground.

Maria held the girl's mittened hand and together, tottering along the iced lane, they made their way to the manor.

TWO

'I'm afraid you'll have to excuse the mess,' Nancy said, kicking the snow from her boots and groaning as she pushed open the great oaken front door. 'Unc never tidies up after himself – he's something of a hoarder – and my time's taken up running after my aunt.'

Bill squeezed past Maria's legs as she followed the girl into the hallway. After the combined illumination of sun and snow outside, the interior of the manor was dim with gloomy tones of mahogany and tan. When her vision adjusted, Maria made out what she could only describe as an overstuffed hallway. She goggled at a moth-eaten grizzly bear, half a dozen dilapidated bookcases, hatstands, occasional tables and *two* grandfather clocks.

Nancy saw her staring at the latter and explained, 'Only one of them works. Unc uses this one,' she went on, marching over to the nearest and opening its door, 'as a cupboard.'

The weights and chains had been removed and shelves fitted in the narrow chamber. On these, Maria counted over two dozen pipes of various types.

'He has a rule,' Nancy said. 'Cigars in the house, pipes outside. He selects a different one every time he goes for a wander.' She peered more closely at the array of pipes. 'There's one missing – the cherrywood, I think. That means he's out. We won't be interrupted. This way – no, don't take your boots off. We don't stand on ceremony here.'

Maria wiped her feet extra vigorously and followed the girl along a sepulchral corridor.

They came to a room at the rear of the house, with French windows overlooking a long, snow-covered lawn. In the distance, on adjacent land beyond the lawn, a lone standing stone rose tall and stark against the winter blue sky.

'Would you prefer tea or coffee?' Nancy asked.

'Tea with a little milk would be lovely.'

'I'll be back in half a sec – and I made a ginger cake this morning.'

'You must have known it's my favourite!'

Alone, Maria looked around the room. A fire blazed in a vast hearth, illuminating a living room best described as shabby. As in the hallway, various hues of brown predominated, the walls and ceiling stained over the years with a patina of nicotine. Three great settees were arranged before the fire in a manner that suggested an encampment, or even a stockade. The pictures on the walls were not what she might have expected – an array of long-dead ancestors – but a series of black-and-white photographs depicting stone circles and solitary menhirs.

Bill had curled himself neatly on the rug before the fire, watching her with his big brown eyes.

She moved to the French windows, alerted by movement outside. In the distance, a small figure was pacing widdershins around the standing stone. The man appeared to be in his sixties, small and stout, attired in a Harris tweed jacket, plus-fours and a deerstalker. He carried a shooting stick and waved it about as if to illustrate something he was saying. Maria assumed he had company, but she soon realized that the man was quite alone and talking to himself.

Nancy entered the room with a tray. 'Oh, there he is,' she said, depositing the tray before the fire and joining Maria at the window. 'He talks to it, you know?'

Maria glanced at the girl to see if she was joking. 'No!'

'He does. He's obsessed. Standing stones are his abiding passion, and when the manor came on the market just after the war, he had to buy it. He has some theory or other about standing stones in general and this one in particular. And if you're unfortunate enough, one day he'll bore you to tears. I'm sorry; you must think me an ungrateful little wretch. Unc is OK, but he can be . . .'

'Yes?'

'Well, he can be an old grumps from time to time.'

They moved to the fireside, and Nancy poured two cups of strong tea and cut thick wedges of ginger cake.

Knees together, Nancy leaned forward, clutching the teacup in both hands, and regarded Maria with her large blue eyes.

'Now, you must tell me. Whatever made you leave London and settle in Ingoldby?'

Maria laughed and tried to explain why the attraction of London, after fifteen years, had begun to pall.

She realized, as they chatted, that she liked Nancy. It was not that she felt merely a natural sympathy for the girl, what with her having lost her parents and finding herself looking after a sick aunt miles from anywhere; Nancy Robertshaw was personable and outgoing, with an easy, friendly manner. Maria found herself wishing she could buy Nancy a new dress to replace the one she was wearing, which was patched and had been taken in. Even the collar of her scarlet cardigan was frayed.

'It's so good to have someone in the village I can talk to!' Nancy said at one point, taking a great bite from a slab of cake and munching. 'I mean to say, everyone is ever so friendly here, but there seems to be no one younger than Unc. Other than Roy, that is . . .'

She coloured instantly, and Maria received the impression that the girl regretted the pronouncement.

She said, 'Roy?'

'Oh . . .' Nancy stared into the flames. 'Just a young fellow who has a caravan in the Wellbournes' meadow. Roy Vickers. "One of war's casualties", as Unc says.'

Maria smiled to herself and congratulated Nancy on the quality of the cake.

'When Unc told me that your husband was a writer, I went into Bury and withdrew one of his books from the library. I must say, I was impressed.' Nancy beamed at Maria. 'I'm so glad you've moved into the village.'

Maria smiled and murmured something to the effect that she hoped Nancy would not be disappointed.

At that moment, the French windows banged open as if blown by a gale, and the squat, tweed-clad figure of Professor Robertshaw strode into the room. He pulled off his deerstalker, brrr'd his lips like a hypothermic horse and barged between the settees to the fire, where he proceeded to toast first his outstretched hands and then his buttocks.

He was even smaller than Maria had assumed at first sight, and oddly broad across the shoulders as if in compensation.

His face was grey and slab-like – not at all unlike his beloved standing stone – with a clipped military moustache and bushy eyebrows beneath a bald dome.

Nancy leapt to her feet and said somewhat nervously, 'This is Maria – Maria Dupré – our new neighbour at Yew Tree Cottage,' while twisting her fingers together as if worrying how her uncle might react to Maria's presence.

'You do have a tendency to state the obvious, Nance.' He turned to Maria and smiled. 'Your fame precedes you. I know your employer, Charles Elder. He told me you were moving in here. Nance,' he went on, 'go see how Xandra is, there's a good girl. Quick sharp.'

Nancy nodded, smiled ruefully at Maria and hurried from the room.

'Hope the gal didn't come on too strong,' the professor said. 'She does latch on to people somewhat. If she gets too much, just put her in her place as you would a young pup, you hear?'

Bridling, Maria said, 'I was very much enjoying our conversation.'

The professor sniffed, stepped over the dozing dog and collapsed into one of the settees as if pole-axed, his impact with the old cushions raising a vortex of ancient dust that swirled in the firelight. He stared across at a table bearing a decanter and glasses, then muttered something to himself. 'Don't suppose you'd oblige an old man and pour me a snifter, would you?'

Maria leaned over, selected the glass that seemed least dusty and poured the professor a generous measure.

He nodded his thanks and took a mouthful, closing his eyes and lying back on the settee. 'Dreadful state of affairs,' he said then, apropos of nothing.

At first, Maria assumed he was alluding to the fishy goings-on he'd mentioned in the note, but then he said, 'Xandra's dying. That's my wife. Nance doesn't know, so not a word to her, understand?'

Maria murmured, 'I'm sorry.'

'She had TB years ago, but the medication she was treated with . . . Well, the ruddy stuff played havoc with her kidneys.' He shook his head. 'Not that Xandra helps herself. Sometimes wonder if she doesn't have a death wish. My brother, Spencer – he has a private practice in town – gives her a few months.'

'I'm so sorry.'

'Well,' he said, opening his eyes and regarding her, 'nothing we can do about it, is there? You can't fight fate, what? Get the missive?'

The sudden change of conversational tack non-plussed her. 'Oh, you mean your note?'

'I'd like to see your hubby – Langham. Is he around?'

'He's up in London today, on business.' She hesitated. 'If you'd like to tell me, I could pass on the gist—'

He interrupted. 'I'd like to see Langham, if it's all the same. Is he free tomorrow?'

'I don't see why not.'

'Then send him round. Eleven will suit me. Does he like Scotch?'

Later, Maria wondered what had made her say, 'Actually, he's teetotal.'

If it was a desire to discommode the old man, it succeeded. He stared at her. 'He's *what*? Doesn't drink?' He harrumphed for a while as if considering the wisdom of admitting a non-drinker into his home.

Maria found herself colouring and was relieved when the door opened and Nancy entered, smiling. 'Xandra's just woken from a nice sleep, Uncle. I made her a cup of Bovril.'

'Vile stuff. Don't know how she stomachs it.'

'It does her good,' Nancy ventured, somewhat diffidently.

The professor waved this away. 'Our guest was about to leave,' he said. 'Show her out, Nance.'

Maria, somewhat surprised, stared at the professor, but he'd closed his eyes and slumped back on to the settee.

Nancy, standing behind the recumbent figure of her uncle, looked suddenly enraged and on the verge of tears. Maria climbed to her feet and looked down at the old man. 'It was nice to meet you, Professor,' she said, more loudly than normal.

He opened one eye, nodded, then took another nip of Scotch. 'The same,' he said. 'Don't forget to send your husband along, you hear?'

Without replying, Maria followed Nancy from the room.

'He's so rude!' the girl exploded when they reached the hallway. 'I can tolerate his treating me abominably, but I can't take it when he's rude to guests!'

Maria gripped Nancy's hand. 'I enjoyed our chat, and the cake was heavenly. Why don't you come round to the cottage one afternoon? We'll be at home all this week and next, and all we'll be doing is unpacking. It will be lovely to see a friendly face.'

Nancy beamed and lifted her shoulders in a quick, complicit shrug. 'I'd like that. I could even help you unpack.'

'Do,' Maria said, and squeezed the girl's hand once more.

As Maria was about to leave, Nancy said, 'If I see Wicketts, I'll tell him you were asking after coal. And if you want some logs,' she went on, 'Richard Wellbourne has some for sale in the meadow at Wellspring Farm, next door to you.'

'Speaking of the Wellbournes,' Maria asked, 'will you be going to their get-together tomorrow?'

Nancy pulled a face. 'If I can sneak off from nursemaid duty,' she said.

Maria thanked her again for the tea and cake and set off through the snow.

She left the grounds of the manor, turned left along the lane and negotiated the treacherous bridge. Another left turn brought her on to Crooked Lane. On the way, she passed Wellspring Farm, set back from the lane, and the enclosed meadow that Nancy had mentioned.

Sitting in the middle of the snow-covered square of land was a quaint gypsy caravan. She recalled what Nancy had said about the young man called Roy who lived in the meadow. For all that a part of her liked the idea of living fancy-free in a gaily painted gypsy caravan, she didn't envy anyone having to eke out an existence in sub-zero temperatures.

A short distance from the caravan was a pile of chopped logs, evidently recently cut as they were not yet covered in snow. She was about to approach the caravan and ask if she could send Donald along at some point to buy some wood when the door opened and a young man came down the steps. He carried a galvanized metal pail in his right hand, his left arm outstretched to counterbalance its weight. He stopped in his tracks when he saw Maria.

He was in his early thirties, with a starved-looking, hatchet face, a pronounced five o'clock shadow and ink-black hair. He wore a ragged Royal Air Force greatcoat, baggy corduroy trousers and hobnail boots. This, presumably, was Roy Vickers – 'one of war's casualties', as the professor had told Nancy.

She smiled. 'I hope you don't mind my enquiring . . .' she began tentatively, gesturing to the logs.

'What about them?'

'Well, I understand they're for sale?'

'Who told you that?' he asked. Before she had time to reply, he went on, 'Well, they're not. I've spent all morning chopping the soddin' things, haven't I?'

'In that case, I'm sorry I asked,' she said.

Vickers swung away from her, stepped away from the caravan and slung the contents of the bucket into a patch of nettles. Seconds later, the reek of urine reached her on the cold breeze.

What a rude creature, she thought as she hurried away. She recalled that Nancy had coloured when she'd mentioned the man's name, and hoped she might be wrong in assuming that the girl had anything to do with this 'casualty of war'.

She came to the gate that gave access to the back garden of Yew Tree Cottage. In the distance, the sun was westering over the spinney on the brow of the hill, igniting the bare trees with its molten light.

She hurried into the cottage and was met by the warmth of the fire in the living room and the appetizing aroma of the hotpot cooking in the kitchen.

THREE

Langham caught the three-thirty train from Liverpool Street and alighted at the country halt just after five, the only passenger to do so. It was dark and snow was falling, and he drove slowly along the winding lanes with the windscreen wipers working furiously and the Rover's headlights illuminating the ceaseless flurry.

A three-book contract and increased royalties! Bless Charles . . .

He was still euphoric from the drink he'd consumed at lunch and from the good news about the contract. The first book wasn't to be delivered until the end of the year, which fitted in well with his plans. He was due to take a month or so away from the desk while he worked on the cottage and settled into village life. He'd begin the next thriller in March and have a good first draft in the bag by June. Then he could work on the rewrite at his leisure until Christmas.

He had also taken a couple of weeks off from the detective agency. It was unfortunate that this first week coincided with his partner, Ralph Ryland, being called away from the office. Ralph's older brother, Patrick, had suffered a heart attack, and Ralph had dropped everything to be with his sister-in-law and her three children in Portsmouth. The agency was still open, with Pamela doing sterling work on the front desk, taking telephone calls and interviewing prospective clients.

It was almost five thirty by the time Langham reached Ingoldby-over-Water, rounded the village green and drove down the lane to the cottage. He parked in the drive and simply sat for a minute, staring at the warm orange light behind the mullioned window of the living room. A full moon hung over the snow-covered thatch and smoke drifted lazily from the chimney. He shivered and hurried inside.

Maria was curled up on the sofa before the fire, reading a manuscript.

'Mmm. What's the wonderful smell?' he asked.

'Chanel, *oui*?'

He kissed her. 'I mean the *other* wonderful smell.'

'Ah, that would be the beef hotpot, with those horrible things you insist I put in it.'

'Horrible? You're calling dumplings *horrible*?'

'Yes, *horrible*. Big, indigestible balls of flour and suet.'

'Just the thing to warm your cockles on a freezing winter's night, my girl.'

'Would you like a drink before we eat?'

'In celebration – why not? Scotch and soda, please.'

He watched her as she moved to the drinks cabinet and poured the Scotch, along with a gin and tonic for herself. They sat on the sofa before the blazing fire, and Langham raised his glass. 'To us, and life in Yew Tree Cottage,' he said. 'Anyway, how went the day?'

She sipped her gin. 'Actually, I've had a very interesting couple of hours. Oh – first, this . . .' She jumped up and took a card down from the mantelpiece.

He read it.

Standing Stone Manor

Langham,
Charles told me you'd moved to the village. I need to see you, pick your brains about something fishy going on here.
Professor Edwin Robertshaw

'What the Devil can he mean by "fishy"?'

'I don't know, Donald. But I found him very rude.'

'You've met him?'

'Thereby hangs a tale, as you so frequently say. I was in the post office when I met his niece, a sweet child called Nancy. I say "child", but she's probably about twenty. She moved in with the professor and his invalid wife when her parents died a couple of years ago. She invited me for afternoon tea, and I was so taken with her that I accepted.'

'In what way was he rude?'

'He was very brusque with me and more or less told me to leave a few minutes after I'd met him.' She regarded her drink, then looked up. 'And he treats Nancy awfully – has her running around after his dying wife.'

'Charming. Did he mention anything about this fishy business?'

'Only that he'd like to see you tomorrow at eleven.'

'I've half a mind to let him go hang,' he said, 'if he can't keep a civil tongue in his head.'

She smiled. 'But you won't, will you?'

'You know me too well. Dangle something fishy before my nose and I'm like a hound on the scent.'

She finished her drink and moved to the kitchen. He heard her open the oven and remove the hotpot. He switched on the wireless and found some music on the Light Programme. Doris Day's 'Que Sera, Sera' eddied from the speaker.

Over dinner, Maria told him more about Nancy Robertshaw. 'I hope you don't mind, but I invited her round to help with the unpacking.'

'Not at all,' he said. 'Excellent hotpot, by the way. The dumplings are exceptional.'

She smiled. 'The fact is I felt sorry for the girl. I think she never gets out, or very rarely, anyway.'

'She didn't give the impression that she might know what the fishy business was about, did she?'

'Not a word,' Maria said. 'Going by the professor's treatment of her, he wouldn't tell her anything anyway.'

After dinner, they moved back to the living room, and Langham poured more drinks.

'I asked in the post office about coal,' Maria said, 'and the nice woman behind the counter told me we need to see someone called Wicketts Blacker. What a peculiar name,' she went on. 'Nancy showed me where he lives – the tumbledown cottage on the lane just before you reach the manor.'

'I could pop in or leave a note when I go and see the truculent professor in the morning. We don't want to be running out of coal—'

He was interrupted by a hammering on the front door.

'Who the blazes can that be?' Langham said, lodging his glass on the arm of the sofa and moving to the hall.

He unlocked and unbolted the door to find a bedraggled, snow-covered young man in a greatcoat stamping his feet. He was without a hat but had turned his collar up to frame his blade-lean face.

'I owe you an apology,' the man said with a trace of a Norfolk burr, his dark eyes avoiding Langham's. 'Or, rather, I owe your missus an apology.'

'You do?' Langham squinted up at the tumbling snow. 'Well, you'd better come in, hadn't you?'

'Won't bother. I just wanted to—'

'Nonsense. In you come.'

The young man limped over the threshold, his sudden smile warming his hitherto sullen countenance.

On impulse, Langham said, 'Look, we're having a drink. Why not join us?'

He could see the debate going on behind the young man's eyes. He ran a hand through his jet-black hair and nodded finally. 'I will, thank you, but I won't stay long.'

'This way,' Langham said, leading the way to the living room. The young man followed, dragging his left leg.

'Someone who owes you an apology,' Langham told Maria as they entered the room. 'I'm sorry, I didn't catch . . .'

'Roy. Roy Vickers.'

Maria was standing before the fire, frowning at the newcomer. He hung his head and avoided her gaze.

Langham made the introductions and poured Vickers a whisky. 'Sit by the fire and get warm. You look perished.' He passed Vickers the tumbler and the young man limped to the armchair and sat down on the edge of the cushion.

He regarded Maria shyly through his flopping fringe. 'I was rude earlier. I didn't mean what I said.'

Langham looked from Vickers to Maria. 'What happened?'

Trying not to smile, Maria said, 'I was on the way back from the manor when I passed the meadow and the caravan. I understood that Mr Wellbourne had some logs for sale, and when I saw them . . . Mr Vickers told me in no uncertain terms that they were not for sale.'

Vickers said, 'I don't know what came over me. Look, I'm sorry.' He shook his head. 'I hardly slept last night, and I was in pain, and when I saw you eyeing the logs . . . Well, I'm not normally so rude.'

'It's good of you to come round and apologize, anyway,' Langham said.

'Apology accepted,' Maria went on.

'How's the Scotch?' Langham asked.

Vickers raised his glass. 'It's a drop of good stuff, right enough.'

'We were just raising a glass to the move,' Langham said.

As Vickers warmed by the fire, the reek of damp clothing and old sweat filled the room. Beneath the greatcoat, Langham made out a light-blue RAF tunic. He wondered if the young man had flown, or merely acquired the tunic as part of his down-at-heel, ragtag wardrobe.

Vickers took another mouthful of whisky and said to Maria, 'You said you were coming back from the manor. Friendly with the professor, are you?'

'I'd only just met him. His niece, Nancy, invited me in for tea.'

Vickers nodded. 'Well, a word to the wise. Be careful of Robertshaw. He might come over all posh and learned, with his Oxford professorship and letters after his name, but the man's a nasty piece of work.'

Langham sat back, nursing his glass. 'In what way?'

The young man flicked a glance from Maria to Langham, hesitating. 'Well, I don't like the way he treats Nancy, for starters. Has her running around after him and his wife like a slave.'

Maria tipped her head. 'Do you know Nancy well?'

Vickers looked away. 'Spoken to her once or twice. Can't say I know her that well. But anyway, the professor treats her like dirt – and that's not the worst of it.'

'Go on,' Langham said.

The young man stared into his drink. He looked up, skewering Langham with his intense gaze. 'Two things. I went up to the manor last summer, looking for a bit of work. He has a big garden, and I knew old Wicketts was all on to keep it in check.

I needed a bit of money to tide me over, so I decided to ask the professor if he needed a hand.'

'What happened?'

'What happened? He attacked me with his ruddy shooting stick before I could open my mouth. Accused me of trespassing and told me to get off his land. Ended up in a right slanging match – me calling him all the names under the sun . . .'

He touched his head just above the hairline, then leaned forward so they could inspect the scar. 'He did this, with that stick of his. Blood all over the place. Lucky I didn't need stitches. Harriet Wellbourne saw me staggering back to my van and she cleaned me up, bless her. They're good sorts, the Wellbournes. People think they're a bit odd, but don't listen to tattle. They're the salt of the earth. Unlike that Robertshaw. And another thing—' He stopped abruptly, staring at the dregs of his whisky.

Langham filled his glass. 'Go on.'

Vickers took a mouthful, then smiled. 'My old dad used to say that you shouldn't talk behind people's backs – but then I reckon it depends on who that person is, doesn't it?' He stared at the fire. 'Fact is the professor has a sick wife at the manor. She's dying, according to some people. Anyway, I reckon Robertshaw's just counting the days before she buys it, then he can . . .'

He fell silent again.

'Then he can what?' Langham urged.

The young man knocked back his drink and, as if emboldened by the alcohol, went on, 'I was up in Bury one day, in the Midland Hotel, having a quick one before I caught the bus back. And who should I see over in the dining room but the professor, all lovey-dovey with a blonde piece.'

'So you think Robertshaw is having an affair?'

'It certainly looked that way, Mr Langham. I'm no prude. People can do what they want as far as I'm concerned. But it just struck me as . . . as two-faced. You should hear Robertshaw in the Green Man, bewailing his fate to his cronies and weeping crocodile tears over his sick wife – and all the time he's running around with some tart behind her back. It fair stinks, in my book.'

'Does Nancy know about this?' Maria asked.

Vickers shrugged. 'No, I shouldn't think so. She'd be upset. She's a good, sweet kid, Nancy is.' He stopped suddenly, then climbed to his feet and lodged the empty glass on the mantelpiece.

'I'll thank you for the whisky and be making tracks. And I'm sorry again for what I said earlier,' he finished, dipping his head to Maria. 'That was well out of order.'

As he was showing the young man out, Langham said, 'Do you ever drink at the Green Man?'

'Well, I'm not a regular – can't afford it. But I like a pint when I can.'

'Then we should meet up for a beer at some point,' Langham suggested.

Vickers smiled. 'Yes, that'd be grand.'

'Well, goodnight, Roy. I'll see you around.'

The young man hesitated, then took Langham by the hand and shook it. 'Thanks again for the drink, Mr Langham,' he said, and ducked out into the freezing night.

Langham returned to the living room and refilled his glass. He joined Maria on the sofa. 'Well, the more I hear about the professor, the more intrigued I'm becoming. I must admit I'm rather looking forward to meeting him tomorrow.'

Maria pulled a face. 'I would be happy never to set eyes on him again,' she said. 'I pity poor Nancy, having to live under the same roof as the ogre.'

They sat in companionable silence, sipping their drinks as the embers settled in the grate and dance music played on the wireless.

'What did you make of young Vickers?' Maria said after a while. 'I must admit, I didn't take to him this afternoon.'

'And what do you think of him now?'

'Well, he's rather a pathetic fellow, isn't he?'

He nodded. 'I wonder if he injured his leg serving with the RAF?'

'He did, according to the professor.'

Langham drained his glass. 'Poor chap.'

Maria finished her drink and said, 'Bed?'

'Mmm,' he said. 'I think I'll make an early start in the

morning, unpack a few books and arrange things in the study. Then I have the prospect of the professor's hospitality to look forward to.'

He turned off the wireless, placed the fireguard before the hearth and followed Maria up to bed.

FOUR

After a breakfast of coffee and toast, Langham set to work in the room he'd designated as his study. It was next to the dining room and looked out over the back garden, and had the advantage of having fitted shelves on two walls. With the bookcases he'd brought from London, there would be more than enough shelf space for his library.

The bookcases arranged to his satisfaction, he began the pleasurable task of opening the boxes, pulling out his treasured volumes and slotting them on to the shelves.

It was another brilliant winter's day, and the sun dazzled off the snow in the garden. He heard Maria moving about in the spare room overhead, opening boxes and placing clothes in various drawers and cupboards.

Later she came downstairs and popped her head around the door. 'Time for a break? How about a cup of tea?'

'Love one.'

He looked at his watch. He was surprised to see that it was almost ten: he'd been working for a couple of hours.

Maria returned with two mugs and gazed around the room, looking impressed. 'My word, Donald. At this rate, you'll be finished by the end of the day.'

'Maybe, if not for the meeting with Robertshaw in an hour – oh, and the do at the Wellbournes' this evening.' He sat on the floor with his back against a box, sipped his tea and admired the books ranged along the walls.

'I'd forgotten about the Wellbournes' party,' Maria said, settling herself on a packing crate. She wore light-blue cropped canvas trousers and a blue-and-white hooped T-shirt, and looked rather like an attractive matelot taking a breather from swabbing the deck. 'We'd better take a bottle of wine.'

'If we can find which box they're in.'

Maria wrinkled her nose at him. 'I know exactly where they are, Donald.'

'I should have known you'd make that a priority.'

A quiet tap sounded on the door, and Maria said, 'Another neighbour come to say hello, no doubt.'

She jumped from the packing crate and hurried into the hall. Donald heard a low exchange, followed by Maria saying, 'We were just having a cup of tea. Come in.'

She entered the study and stepped aside, gesturing to their guest to enter.

A slim, golden-curled girl stepped diffidently into the room. He thought the best word to describe her would be elfin, and although he knew she was older, he thought she looked no more than twelve.

'Donald, meet Nancy Robertshaw. Nancy, my husband, Donald.'

He took her hand in a gentle shake, careful to exert minimal pressure lest he break her bird-like metacarpals.

'My word,' she breathed, gazing at the ranked hardbacks. 'I take it this is the library?'

'My study,' Langham said. 'Take a pew, or rather a packing crate.'

Maria popped into the kitchen and returned with another mug of tea. Nancy hugged it to her chest and smiled at him. 'I withdrew one of your books from the library last week, Mr Langham. I thought it was super. I've never read anything so thrilling.'

'You're that rare breed.' He laughed. 'A satisfied customer.'

'I'll *buy* the next one, and if you could sign it . . .'

'I'd be more than delighted.'

'I actually came round to tell you that my uncle is spending the morning at the site, Mr Langham. So when you drop by, don't knock on the front door. If you go around the house and past the standing stone, you'll find him.'

Langham said, 'The site?'

'Well, that's what Unc calls it. I call it a hole in the ground.'

'I thought the professor had retired,' Maria said.

'That's right – years ago. The stone is just his hobby. He has some theory about it, but don't ask me. He must have told me all about it a million times but it goes in one ear and out the other. Isn't that awful?'

Maria said, 'Not at all; each to their own, as Donald is so fond of telling me.'

Nancy smiled at Langham, swinging her legs so that her heels drummed against the packing crate. 'Do you mind my asking what Unc wanted to see you about, Mr Langham? Only he hasn't been himself of late, and this morning he was impossible.'

'Impossible in what way?'

'Even more tetchy than usual. I made him breakfast and nothing was right. The coffee was too hot and the toast too cold, and I hadn't put enough treacle in his porridge! He was like a bear with a sore head. I felt like tipping the porridge all over his head and walking out!'

'I hope you didn't,' Maria said.

Nancy lifted her chin in a mock-virtuous manner. 'I showed admirable restraint, if I say so myself.'

Langham laughed. 'Well, your uncle didn't say why he wanted to see me. I was hoping you might be able to shed light on the matter. I . . . I suspect he just wants to say hello to the newcomers.'

Nancy looked dubious. 'Unc isn't usually given to such social niceties, Mr Langham. It's more in his way to ignore people. Or run them off his land.'

Maria smiled. 'Ah, *oui*. We heard all about that from Mr Vickers. He called around last night.'

'Oh, he told you . . . It was awful, Maria. I saw it all from the kitchen window. I heard raised voices and looked out in time to see my uncle setting about Roy with his stick.' She stopped, looking from Maria to Langham with comically wide eyes. 'I felt sick. I wanted to go out there and help Roy, only . . . Well, I was too frightened of what *he* might say. When Unc's temper is up . . .' She left the sentence unfinished.

Langham sipped his tea. 'I understand Roy was in the RAF?'

'That's right. Bombers. He was a gunner, in the tail bit at the back of the plane.'

Langham grimaced. 'Ah, a tail-end Charlie. Hellish danger-ous. The casualty rate was frightening. I take it that's how he sustained his injury?'

'He hasn't said as much, but I once overheard Richard

Wellbourne telling his wife something about it. Apparently, Roy was shot down over France, and I suspect he was injured then.'

'Was he taken prisoner or did he manage to evade capture?'

Nancy shrugged. 'I really don't know. I mean . . . I've spoken to him a few times, but . . .' She hesitated. 'The thing about Roy is . . . Well, he doesn't do himself any favours, living like a tramp in that caravan.' She smiled at Maria. 'But I do think he's rather handsome, don't you?'

Maria returned her smile. 'I think he would be if he cleaned himself up a little and shaved,' she allowed.

Langham looked at his watch. 'Crikey. Ten to eleven. Time I was pushing off.'

Maria said to Nancy, 'Would you like another cup of tea? You could stay and help me unpack a few boxes upstairs. Unless you need to get back, of course?'

Nancy beamed. 'I'd love another tea, and I'd be delighted to help. I don't need to be back until noon, when I make Xandra's lunch.'

Langham made his farewells, pulled on his overcoat and gumboots, and left the cottage by the back door.

A low hedge separated the back garden from Crooked Lane. He pushed through the rotting timber gate in the hedge and made his way along the lane which followed the winding course of the stream.

Fresh snow had fallen during the night, giving the landscape a renewed, pristine aspect. Langham found himself squinting against the glare of the sun reflecting from the snow and taking high steps to negotiate the drifts as he came to the bridge and moved carefully over its ice-covered surface. He almost lost his footing on the other side, regained his balance and slowed his pace as he followed the lane to the manor house.

He saw a tiny, stoop-backed old man shovelling snow in the driveway and assumed this must be the chap with the strange name who did odd jobs for the professor.

He waved as he approached and said, 'I understand you deliver coal, Mr . . .'

The wizened old man pushed back his flat cap and scratched his brow. 'I be Wicketts and you'll be Mr Langham, I take it?'

'That's right. I hear you're the man to see about coal?'

'I be the chap, all right. Five bags every fortnight; leastways that's what ole Mrs Ashton had delivered, from September through till April. Six bob a bag, premium grade. Pay me when I deliver 'em next Monday. That suit?'

'Capital,' Langham said. 'And thank you.'

'You be seeing the Guv?'

'That's right. I understand he's at the . . . site?'

'The ruddy great 'ole in the ground, more like. Mind how you go.'

Langham nodded. 'I will. It is rather treacherous, isn't it?'

The old man gave him an odd look. 'No, I mean, watch your step with the Guv. He's in a hell of a mood.'

'I'll be careful. Thanks for the warning.'

Wicketts returned to his work, and Langham moved off down the drive and walked around the house.

In the distance, striking in its primitive asymmetry after the formal Georgian angles of the manor house, the standing stone stood in silhouette against the blue sky. Langham tramped through the snow, pausing before the menhir and staring up at its cold, grey length. Unlike the only other ancient standing stones he'd seen, at Stonehenge, this one was not squared-off at its summit but stepped, so that a higher nub of stone appeared to be knuckling the sky.

He reached out and laid a hand against its freezing surface, wondering who might have erected the henge, and how long ago, and why.

He moved around the stone and stared across the snowy ground.

A hundred yards away he made out a line of scaffolding planks laid alongside a trench to form a walkway. At one end of the excavation, to the right, a muddy brown tarpaulin was held in place by a dozen huge tractor tyres. The top of a wooden stepladder emerged from the trench, and the glow of what looked like a paraffin lamp illuminated the tarpaulin.

This, evidently, was the 'site' – or, as Nancy and Wicketts would have it, the hole in the ground.

He made his careful way down the slight incline towards the excavation.

He stopped by the stepladder, dropped to his haunches and peered into the trench beneath the tarpaulin. He heard a sound from within, the scraping of some tool against the earth and an occasional mutter.

'Hello down there!'

The muttering abruptly ceased, along with the scraping. A muffled imprecation was followed by a stertorous demand. 'Who the hell are you?'

'Langham,' he called out. 'Donald Langham. I understand you wanted to see me at eleven, and here I am.'

'Eleven, by Christ! Surely it's not eleven yet?'

Langham consulted his watch. 'Five past, actually.'

The professor grunted. 'Well, in that case you'd better come on down. What're you wearing?'

'An overcoat. Gieves and Hawkes of Savile Row, if you're interested.'

'I mean on your ruddy feet!'

'Gumboots,' Langham said, smiling to himself.

'That's fine and dandy, then. It's like the Somme down here. Well, what're you waiting for?'

Langham eased himself down the stepladder, squelched along the bottom of the trench and ducked under the lip of the tarpaulin.

The trench opened out and he found himself in a small, square chamber with scaffolding boards underfoot and a single board spanning the excavation at head height, from which hung a paraffin lamp. Langham was indeed reminded of a dugout in the trenches of the Great War.

Professor Robertshaw was hunkering down on a folding stool, a trowel gripped in his right hand. A trestle table stood to the left of the entrance, scattered with oddments that Langham assumed had been recently excavated. Also on the table was a scale model of a stone circle, constructed from what looked like matchboxes.

Robertshaw stood and shook Langham's hand. He was stockier than Langham had imagined he might be, and less intimidating. In fact, with the flaps of his deerstalker tied under his chin, he resembled an overgrown baby in a bonnet.

He regarded Langham with bright blue eyes sunk between a big Roman nose and bushy brows. 'Ever seen an archaeological site before, Langham?'

'Can't say I have,' he admitted. 'What are these?' He indicated the oddments on the trestle table.

'You could say it's a physical calendar of long-gone epochs,
ranged in chronological order. Oldest on the left, newest to the
right.' He picked up a tiny flint arrowhead and passed it to
Langham. 'Neolithic, up to ten thousand years old. Amazing
to think that the last person to handle that, before me and thee,
was a stone-age tribesman.'

Langham turned over the silvery-grey arrowhead, amazed
that its point was still sharp after so many centuries.

Robertshaw pointed a stubby finger at the items arrayed on
the tabletop. 'Then we have the remains of a necklace, potsherds,
an axe-head and bone tools. Right up to stuff from the last
century – remnants of clay pipes, bits of cups, even an old
penny.'

'Excuse my ignorance, but what exactly are you looking for?'

'Aha!' the professor declared, staring down at the model of
the stone circle. 'That!'

He pointed at the model and squinted at Langham as if to
gauge his reaction.

'Ah . . . Other standing stones?'

'Precisely. I have a theory. Want to hear it?'

'I'd be delighted to,' Langham said.

'Good man,' Robertshaw said. He tapped the model of the
stone constructed from a pair of England's Glory matchboxes
standing in the centre of the circle. 'That's the henge you passed
behind the house. Widespread belief is that it's a singleton, not
part of a circle at all. Y'see, there are no other stone circles in
Suffolk. They're relatively common in the West Country, from
Wiltshire onwards, and up in Yorkshire and Scotland. All to do
with the availability of stone, you see. But there's no similar
stone in this area. So the idea is that a local tribe had it brought
all the way from Wiltshire or beyond, even from as far afield
as South Wales. Which would fit in with the singleton theory.'

'However?' Langham said.

'However, I made a discovery in the village before I bought
the manor ten years ago, and when the house came on the
market, I snapped it up.'

'A discovery?'

'In the churchyard, or rather in the wall of the churchyard. The wall's foundation and first two courses are constructed from a stone quite unlike the upper courses, which are of sandstone. The lower ones are of igneous bluestone – the same as the henge out there.'

'I see. So you think . . .'

'It's not uncommon, at other places around the country, for the stones to have been removed, or "borrowed", over the centuries and used in the construction of walls, buildings, et cetera. My theory is that there were originally a number of other stones which over the years have been removed – vandalized, if you will – and repurposed, leaving just the one you see out there. Others might simply have toppled over and become buried over time.'

'I see, and you're attempting to locate these other stones?'

'That's it in one,' the professor said. 'Either locate them or find evidence of their erstwhile existence – over the centuries, with the weight of the stones, the earth would become compacted, you see, before they were removed.'

'And have you located any?'

'Early days yet, Langham. Early days. I've only been seriously excavating for two years.'

Langham gazed down at the model of the stone circle. 'Does anyone really know the reason our ancestors erected these things? Something to do with an early, primitive religion?'

'The jury's still out on that one, old boy. I subscribe to the theory that the various circles up and down the land are vast ceremonial calendars, aligned to the sun and the moon at times of equinox and solstice. Farming was of prime importance to our ancestors, and they were more in tune with the land and the turning of the seasons.'

He tapped the central stone. 'This is a scale model. I've worked out that if this stone were to have been aligned with others at the summer solstice, then a stone of the same height would have been positioned thirty yards from the central stone.' He gestured about him. 'In this approximate area, in fact. And, of course, there would have been others, ranged in a great circle.'

Langham nodded, trying to appear impressed.

'But Rome wasn't built in a day, Langham. I might be digging around here for another decade before I come up with anything. It'll see me well into my seventies, at any rate!'

'Well, it's important to have an abiding preoccupation,' Langham said.

Robertshaw unhooked a rag from the scaffolding board above his head and wiped his hands. 'I'll call it a morning. I presume I've bored you for long enough. How about a hot drink?'

'I wouldn't say no,' Langham said.

The professor extinguished the paraffin lamp, plunging the pit into gloom, and gestured Langham to lead the way along the trench.

As they climbed the stepladder and crossed the snow towards the standing stone, Langham said, 'In your note, you mentioned Charles Elder.'

'That's right. He's a fellow Mason.'

'He is?' Langham said, surprised. He'd known Charles for more than twenty years without learning of this fact.

'He's a regular at the Bury St Edmunds Lodge,' Robertshaw went on. 'We often put the world to rights over a snifter or two. Old Charles advises me on matters literary, y'see, and I give him the benefit of my knowledge of the Greeks. That was my specialism, Langham – ancient Greece, with especial interest in the Hellenistic period.'

'Is that so? I was under the impression that you specialized in British history.'

The professor laughed. 'Not a bit of it. This' – he approached the standing stone and slapped its flank – 'is merely a hobby in which I indulge myself in my old age.'

As they walked on, the professor said, 'You were asking about Charles. As I said, he's fascinated with the Greeks.' He shot Langham a glance. 'Everything about them, in fact.'

Langham steered the conversation towards the reason for his presence that morning. 'The note you sent yesterday . . .'

'Ah, yes. That. Well, rum business all round, Langham. Thing is, the village is full of all sorts of folk you wouldn't trust with the silver.'

'Is that so?'

'Oh, all very civilized on the surface, but underneath . . .'

'Still-waters kind of thing?'

'You have it in one, sir. In one!'

Langham glanced at the professor. 'Do you have anyone in particular in mind?'

'Where to start! The Wellbournes are odd sorts, especially the chap. Mad as a coot. Plays classical music to his cows. His wife, Harriet – she claims to be clairvoyant. More like a ruddy witch, if you ask me. Away with the fairies but harmless enough. Then there's the publican at the Green Man, Newton – wouldn't trust him with my grandmother. He dabbled in the black market during the war and these days deals in stolen goods, so be warned.'

'Indeed.'

'Then there's young Roy Vickers – the chap's a scoundrel.'

'The fellow who lives in the caravan on Wellbourne's land?'

'That's him. Thieving hound, and a poacher to boot. I caught him on my land just last summer.'

'Poaching?'

'That or eyeing the place up for a midnight raid, I'll be bound.'

'What happened?'

'Confronted him and threw the blighter out neck and crop. Sent him away with his tail between his legs and told him that if he showed his face in the place again, I'd take my twelve-bore to him and perforate his giblets.'

'I take it he hasn't been back?'

'No fear! But I heard on the grapevine that he's been sniffing around young Nancy – that's my niece – so I read her the riot act and told her that if she so much as looks at the chap I'd not let her out of the house for a whole year.'

Langham smiled to himself. 'A veritable gallery of rogues,' he said.

'You said it, Langham; how right you are!'

They squeaked on through the snow. He waited for the professor to continue. When he didn't, Langham said, 'So, the fishy business?'

'Ah, that . . .'

They stopped outside the French windows and the professor

kicked his boots clean of snow. Langham did the same and followed the old man into a room full of antiquated furniture, calf-bound books, framed photographs of standing stones, and three monumental settees positioned before a blazing fire.

'Leave your boots on, Langham. I'd offer you a whisky, but that filly of yours said you don't drink.'

Langham stared at the old man. 'She said what?'

'Told me you're teetotal, Langham.'

'But I'm nothing of the kind,' he exclaimed. 'I wonder why she told you that?'

The professor shook his head. 'Strange beasts, women. Don't know where the hell you are with 'em. A whisky, then?'

'Actually, at the moment I'd prefer a hot drink, if it's all the same. Tea, black, no sugar.'

'Bit too early for you, eh?' Professor Robertshaw stomped over to the door, snatched it open and bellowed, 'Nancy! Nance! We have a guest!'

He unfastened his deerstalker and placed it atop a phrenologist's pottery head, then returned to the fireside and warmed his buttocks.

'I think Nancy will still be at our place,' Langham said, and explained her visit. 'She said she'd be back at noon.'

Robertshaw grunted and squinted at his fob watch. 'Just after half past eleven,' he said. 'A man can't be expected to make his own ruddy tea. Are you sure you won't join me in a snifter?'

'A small one, then,' Langham said, 'with soda.'

Robertshaw poured the drinks and resumed his place before the roaring fire.

Langham subsided into one of the settees and only then saw the dog curled up on the rug. He reached down and scratched it behind the ears.

'Ruddy animal,' the professor grumbled. 'I wouldn't mind, but Nancy can't be bothered to train the blessed thing.'

The dog opened one lazy eye and regarded the professor with languorous disdain.

Langham took a mouthful of diluted Scotch. 'Now, this fishy business?'

Robertshaw crossed to a small walnut bureau, opened it and withdrew a sheet of light-blue notepaper. He returned to the fire and passed Langham the sheet. 'What d'you make of that, hmm?'

Langham read the typewritten note. *I know all about you and your affair. If you don't pay up, Nancy will find out. I'll be in touch.*

The letter y had a broken tail.

'When did you receive this?'

'Three days ago – Tuesday morning, first post.'

'Can I see the envelope?'

Robertshaw frowned. 'Fact is I burned the thing. Didn't think. I collected the mail from the doormat, brought them in here and went through 'em one by one. Tossed the envelopes in the fire.'

Langham read the note again. He lowered the sheet and looked at the professor.

'"I know all about you and your affair,"' he murmured. 'I take it you know what the writer is referring to?'

He watched Robertshaw as he shook his head. 'That's just the thing, Langham. I haven't a clue. I'm no saint, I'll tell you that – I've done some things in my time I'm not proud of, but nothing that I could be blackmailed about. I am not having an affair. The idea is preposterous.'

Langham recalled what Vickers had said about seeing the professor with another woman in the Midland Hotel at Bury St Edmunds.

He tapped the sheet. 'And this – "If you don't pay up, Nancy will find out." What on earth does that mean?'

Robertshaw shrugged his powerful shoulders. 'Search me, Langham. I've been racking my brains for the past couple of days. I was on the blower to old Charles yesterday, and he happened to mention that you'd just moved into the village. I recalled that he'd said, just a couple of weeks back, that you were a writer chappy who dabbled in private detection, so I thought I'd pick your brains.'

Langham waved the note. 'Do you mind if I hang on to this, Professor?'

'Be my guest. Any thoughts?'

Langham folded the note and slipped it into an inside pocket.

'When you picked up the envelope, I take it you read your name on the front?'

Robertshaw pursed his lips in a frown. 'To be perfectly honest, I don't think I did. The mail is usually addressed to me, you see. So I assumed . . .'

'In that case, there's always the possibility, as you say you don't know what the note refers to, that you were not meant to be the recipient.'

'Well, blow me down.'

'I understand that just you, your wife and Nancy are resident here?'

'And our son, Randall – though he's away on business for a few days. Back tomorrow, I believe. He's been staying here for the past couple of months following a messy divorce.' He shook his head sadly. 'The chap's not yet twenty, and already divorced . . .'

'I suppose the note might have been intended for him or – forgive me for suggesting this – your wife.'

'My wife? I don't see how it could be, Langham. She's bedridden most of the ruddy time.'

'Then what about your son?'

The professor pulled a face. 'Well, it's possible, I suppose. He's a bit of a dark horse – keeps himself to himself.' He knocked back his whisky. 'Anyway, what do you advise?'

Langham thought about it. 'Sit tight. Don't do anything for the time being. As the writer states, he or she will be in touch, no doubt with a demand. As soon as you hear from them, inform me.'

'Will do, Langham.'

'When your son returns, I'd like a discreet word with him, if that's all right?'

'Certainly. Should I tell him about the note?'

'Perhaps it'd be best not to,' he said. 'If I could meet your wife at some point, that might be helpful, too, though I'd understand if she's too ill—'

'She has her better days, Langham. Tell you what, I'll see how she is over the weekend. If she's chipper, I'll have you and your better half round for tea at some point, what?'

'That sounds perfect,' Langham said.

Deciding that he was sufficiently roasted, Robertshaw stepped over the dog and slumped on to a sofa, his legs outstretched and his whisky glass lodged on the rise of his stomach.

Langham noticed a framed photograph on the mantelpiece showing Professor Robertshaw in uniform. 'Where did you serve?' he asked.

The professor regarded the photograph. 'That's when I commanded a unit of the Home Guard in Oxford. During the Great War, I served with the Norfolk Regiment. Yourself?'

'Field Security,' Langham said. 'Mainly in India.'

'Field Security, eh? Good show. I knew a few security bods over at Oxford during the last shindig. Decent coves. In my opinion, Field Security was vastly undervalued.'

The professor recounted a few stories about his time in the Home Guard, and Langham reciprocated with stories of his time in India. He found himself warming to the man.

A little later, after a short silence, the professor said, 'Heard that you've only recently married, Langham?'

'A little over six months now.'

'Going well?'

'Swimmingly.'

'Delighted to hear that.' The professor stared into space, wistful. 'Nothing better when it's going well. Nothing like it. Makes the world seem a fine place, doesn't it?'

'I'll say.'

'It's later, when things turn sour . . . That's when you've got to steel yourself. The dashed world seems a dark, hopeless place, then.'

Langham sipped his drink, sensing that the professor wanted to talk.

'My first wife, Deirdre, walked out on me after ten years. It came as something of a shock, I must admit. Out of the blue. She bearded me one day and said, "Edwin, I've met someone and I'm leaving you." *Fait accompli.* Not a thing I could do to change her mind. She'd fallen out of love with me and in love with some other chap.'

'I'm sorry.'

'What does a man do in those circumstances, Langham? What could I do? Two choices: mope and feel ruddy sorry for myself or chin up and get on with it. Changes you, though. Makes you wary, suspicious. Hardens the heart.'

'I should think it must,' Langham said.

The professor reached out for the decanter, splashed himself a generous measure, and went on, 'Then I met Xandra and despite everything – warnings to self to be ruddy careful – I fall head over heels.' He stared at Langham with watery eyes.

'Don't know if you've heard,' he went on, 'but Xandra's dying. Kidneys are packing up. Only a matter of time now. I did my best in the early days, nursing her.'

'That can't have been easy, along with what happened to your brother and his wife.'

'So you've heard about the blasted Barnes prang?' He shook his head. 'We adopted Nancy, and I took a back seat and left the looking after my wife to the girl.'

Langham said, 'She's a nice kid.'

'But she's a *female*, goddammit, and how the blazes do you communicate with 'em is what I'd like to know. P'raps I'm a trifle hard on the filly . . .'

The silence stretched, and Langham said finally, 'Well, I really should be pushing off. Thank you for the whisky.'

'Don't mention it. I take it you'll be attending the Wellbournes' bash this evening?'

'We are. And you?'

'I'm not sure. Richard's as batty as hell, but I'll give him this: for a mud-grubber, he keeps a fine cellar. I might drop by.'

'Do you know if it'll be a formal do?'

The professor laughed. 'At the Wellbournes'? Far from it. Casual – very casual. Oh, and the food will be excellent. Harriet might be loopy, but she's something of a wizard in the kitchen.'

Langham climbed to his feet. 'I'll see myself out. And just as soon as you receive another note, please get in touch.'

The professor nodded. 'Will do, Langham.'

He left the overheated living room and proceeded down the draughty hall just as the front door opened and Nancy hurried in. 'Mr Langham! I'm late. Unc will have my guts for garters! How was he?'

'I was expecting a dragon and discovered a pussycat,' Langham said.

Nancy rolled her eyes. 'He's as nice as ninepence with men. It's us of the fairer sex he has something against,' she said. 'Tally-ho! Into the breach once more! Isn't that what they say, Mr Langham?'

'They do, or something similar. And it's Donald, all right?'

The girl smiled. 'Excuse me, Donald. I must dash.'

He watched her put her words into action, then pulled open the heavy front door and hurried home through the snow.

Back at the cottage, he found Maria upstairs in the second bedroom, unpacking boxes.

'Be an absolute sweetheart and make me a cup of tea, Donald, would you?'

He made two cups of Earl Grey and carried them upstairs. He lay on the bed while Maria sat on the floor, leaning against the wall, and blew on her tea. 'And how was the horrible man?'

'Do you know, I rather liked him. His bark is certainly worse than his bite.'

'No? You *liked* him? But he was perfectly horrible to Nancy when I met him.'

'And I think perhaps he knows it,' he said, and reported what the professor had told him about his hapless marriages.

'So do you think that's the excuse he makes for acting as he does?'

'Well, perhaps it's a contributory factor to his curmudgeon-liness.'

'You're too generous, my darling.'

He sipped his tea, then recalled something. 'Oh, and why on earth did you tell the professor I was teetotal?'

'I'm not at all sure. Perhaps I said it to take the wind from his sails – make him question his assumptions that all men were like him and liked a drink.'

Langham smiled. 'Anyway,' he said, fishing the note from his inner pocket and passing it to her, 'what do you make of this?'

She read the brief missive, a frown buckling her forehead. 'What Vickers mentioned last night, about the professor having an affair . . .' She waved the paper. 'Could that be behind this?'

'That was my first thought, although I didn't broach it with

Robertshaw, of course. The thing is, he swore blind he didn't know what the note was driving at. He claimed he wasn't having an affair.'

She looked dubious. 'And you believe him?'

'I'm not sure. And, of course, there's always the possibility that the note wasn't meant for him. He told me he'd burned the envelope, assuming it was for him, and he can't recall reading the addressee.'

'So who else might it be for?'

'Obviously not Nancy, because of that "Nancy will find out" line.'

'The professor's wife, then? Xandra?'

'Or his son, Randall. He lives at the manor, though he's away at the moment.'

She passed the note back to him. 'What did you advise?'

'That he waits till he receives the next one, then contacts me pronto.'

'And then?'

'There'll come a point when whoever sent this will make a demand, and that'll be when the blackmailer will be at his most vulnerable.'

Maria leaned her head back against the wallpaper, making a contemplative moue with her full lips.

'You're wearing that "I wonder" look, my darling,' Langham said.

She tried not to smile. 'I wonder . . . What if the professor *is* having an affair, and when Roy Vickers saw them, he decided to turn his hand to blackmail?'

'Do you believe he would?'

She shook her head. 'My instinctive feeling is that Roy Vickers is not that kind of person. Granted, there's no love lost between him and Robertshaw, but I'd like to think Roy wouldn't stoop so low. What do you think?'

'I've no idea if Roy's the kind of person to try it on or not. But I think the professor was telling the truth when he claimed to be blameless. Or else why would he drag me into this in the first place? Surely if he thought he was being blackmailed for having an affair, he'd keep mum about it.'

'Either that or he's bluffing you.'

Langham sighed. 'I tend to think the note is aimed at either Xandra or Robertshaw's son, Randall.'

Maria finished her tea and climbed to her feet. 'And I dreamed of a quiet life when we moved to the country!'

Langham laughed, rolled off the bed and pulled her to him. 'What are you doing now?'

'Trying on something I might wear this evening.'

'According to the professor, it'll be far from formal. What about that off-the-shoulder thing I bought you for Christmas?'

'Far too sophisticated for a farmhouse soirée,' she said. 'But I have one or two outfits that might suit.'

'Can I come and watch?'

'You're incorrigible!'

He followed her to the master bedroom.

FIVE

Snow had started to fall again by eight o'clock, and as they approached the farmhouse, Maria thought that the scene, with the house mantled in snow and its coach-lights glistening in the darkness, resembled something from a Christmas card. It was so quintessentially English that it made her smile.

'Stop,' she said.

They did so.

'What?' he asked.

'Listen.'

Donald cocked his head. 'I can't hear a thing.'

'Exactly. The silence. I don't think I've experienced such silence for . . . oh, for years.'

'Certainly not in London, hmm?'

'I'm so glad we moved!' she said, tugging him onwards.

A tall, well-built, stooping figure dressed in shabby tweeds greeted them at the door, introducing himself as Richard Wellbourne and taking their coats.

'Harry!' he bellowed, and a small woman came scurrying into the stone-floored hallway. 'Harriet, they came! I didn't know if you'd be put off by the weather,' Wellbourne explained. 'This is Harriet.'

Donald made the introductions.

Maria liked the woman at first sight. A greater contrast to her husband could not be imagined. While Richard Wellbourne was a big, shambling, untidy bear of a man, Harriet was tiny, neat and impeccably attired in a grey two-piece – almost mouse-like. She had silver-grey hair cut very short and a fey, fairy-like face. Maria judged the couple to be in their late fifties.

'I told you they'd come, Richard,' she said, shaking their hands. 'My husband has this thing about city dwellers. He thinks they can't hack life in the country.'

'Tosh, Harry. The woman spouts complete baloney! That said, the Grahams only lasted three months. They bought the old Compton place on the hill,' he went on, 'but soon missed the amenities of London.'

Harriet kept hold of Maria's hand and smiled up at her. 'I know you'll *love* the village,' she said. 'I can feel it in my blood.'

'Harry feels everything in her blood,' Wellbourne said. 'In a previous century, she'd have been burned at the stake.'

'Really, Richard!' Harriet trilled happily.

They were one of those rare couples, Maria thought, so secure in their relationship that affectionate persiflage came as naturally as endearments. She noticed they were forever seeking each other's hand and gripping with a kind of intimate reassurance when they exchanged their banter.

'We love the village already,' Maria said, 'and the cottage is a delight.'

'The folk of the parish aren't a bad bunch, either,' Wellbourne said. 'Come and meet some of them. And let me get you a drink.'

He led the way along a stone-flagged passage towards a room from which came a hubbub of conversation. 'What'll it be?'

A dozen people filled the long, low room, which was hung with oil lamps and illuminated at the far end by a blazing log fire in a huge hearth. Maria recognized Flo Waters from the post office, and Newton, the publican from the Green Man. The young vicar, so toweringly tall and thin in his clerical garb that he resembled a cormorant, was in animated conversation with a shrivelled gnome of an old man. People turned and smiled as they entered.

Wellbourne fixed them up with a gin and tonic and a whisky and soda, and Harriet escorted them around the room, introducing them to the locals. Maria watched Donald as he fell easily into conversation; he had the enviable ability of being able to talk to anyone, and the even rarer gift of listening with interest.

They found themselves in a group consisting of Reverend Evans, Newton the publican, and the shrunken gnome whom Harriet introduced as Wicketts Blacker, the local odd-job man.

Before setting off, Donald had told her of Professor

Robertshaw's assertion that Newton dealt in stolen goods, but the big, balding, genial man didn't strike Maria as belonging to the criminal fraternity. The publican described how he'd taken over the Green Man thirty years ago, when it was no more than a derelict blacksmith's hovel, and rebuilt the place almost single-handedly. Beside him, Wicketts Blacker nodded his wrinkled head from time to time, commenting, 'That 'e did, bor. That 'e did. And durin' the war, bor – those locks-ins! Remember the pig roast, Christmas o' forty-two?'

'I remember no pig roast, Wicketts,' Newton said, winking broadly at Maria. 'You'll get me arrested, you will.'

At one point Wellbourne cleared his throat and tapped an iron poker on the metal rim of an oil lamp hanging from a beam. As the hubbub died down, he said, 'I'd like everyone to raise their glasses to Donald and Maria, our honoured guests tonight. It's always a happy occasion to welcome fresh faces to the village. To Donald and Maria!'

Glasses were raised, their health toasted, and the Reverend Evans said to Maria, 'Do I detect a trace of an accent? French, perhaps?'

She scowled in good part. 'And I thought I'd managed to eradicate every last trace of the Gallic vowel!'

'Not quite, but your English is excellent, I must say.'

'Well, I have lived here for almost twenty years,' she countered, trying not to smile as Donald rolled his eyes.

Wellbourne joined them. 'I understand you've made the acquaintance of Professor Robertshaw, Donald. What did you make of him?'

'News travels fast,' Donald said.

Beside the vicar, Wicketts raised his hand like a guilty schoolboy, acknowledging himself as the source of the intelligence.

Donald said, 'Fascinating chap. Gave me a little talk on the history of the standing stone.'

'Did he mention his crackpot theory?' Wellbourne asked.

'About the possibility of there being a stone circle at some point? Yes, he did.'

Wellbourne cocked an eye at him. 'Buy it?'

Donald shrugged. 'I'm really in no position to say one way

or another – knowing next to nothing about the Neolithic era. Robertshaw seemed to know what he was talking about.'

'Poppycock,' Wellbourne said. 'Excuse me, but the professor's an amateur when it comes to British history.'

Reverend Evans said, 'But I understood Robertshaw was a professor of archaeology?'

'Chap's a Greek specialist,' Wellbourne said. 'He's merely dabbling with the stone. Also, the man's a liar. Can't believe a word he says.'

Maria exchanged a glance with Donald.

Harriet gripped her husband's hand and piped up, 'Richard's like a bear with a sore head when it comes to the professor! And all because of the dispute.'

Donald looked from Harriet to Richard. 'The dispute?'

Wellbourne waved this away, clearly not wanting to speak of it, but his wife, gripping his big hand and almost swinging from it, said, 'It's all because the professor is digging on Richard's land, and the big angry bear doesn't like it.'

'You do exaggerate, Harry,' Richard grunted. 'Fact is I own the land over the river, abutting the edge of the land where the stone stands. The area where he's started his tomfool trenches is actually mine.'

Maria sipped her gin and asked, 'Did he ask your permission before he started digging?'

Harriet rolled her eyes and wrinkled her nose conspiratorially at Maria.

'Not a word,' Wellbourne said. 'First I knew of it, I saw a ruddy great pit in the ground one spring a couple of years back. I moseyed on over and pointed out that he was digging up my land.'

'What did he say?' Reverend Evans asked.

'Said he'd give me twenty guineas a year as rent for the next ten years.'

Harriet tugged his hand. 'And you jumped at it! Go on, tell the truth.'

'Balderdash, Harry. I accepted his offer, but I wasn't best pleased. It was the principle of the thing. He should have had the courtesy and good manners to come and see me about it *before* turning a sod.'

'But you must admit, Richard,' Harriet went on, poking him in the ribs, 'that, as farmland, the paddock is almost useless.'

Wellbourne sighed. 'That's not the point, woman. It's the principle of the thing, as I said. And I had plans for the place.' He grunted and looked around the group. 'Anyway, he's castigating a deceased mule—'

'He's *what?*' Maria asked.

Harriet said, 'One of Richard's pet sayings, my dear. He means "flogging a dead horse" – pursuing a hopeless cause, in other words.'

'Ah, I see,' Maria said. 'And why is that?'

'Because the standing stone is a singleton,' Wellbourne said, 'and anyway, it isn't as old as the professor believes. Isn't that right, Wicketts?'

The little gnome winked sagely. 'You're right, bor,' he said.

As old as Wicketts might have been, Maria doubted that his knowledge extended back to Neolithic times.

'Tell 'em,' Wellbourne said, with evident satisfaction.

Wicketts grinned. 'I knows 'cos me gran'father tells me, and his gran'father told 'im, and his gran'father afore 'im. Stone were raised just afore the village here were founded, and that ain't be four thousand year ago, no way.'

'When was the village founded?' Maria asked.

'It's mentioned in the Domesday book,' Wellbourne said. 'Historians reckon there was a settlement here around 950.'

Donald asked, 'And what does Professor Robertshaw think of this? He's been told, presumably?'

'Oh, he's been told, all right, but he won't hear a word of it. Calls it ignorant gossip and sticks to his theory that not only is the stone Neolithic but that he'll unearth more of the things.'

Newton guffawed. 'Had a right shindy in the taproom a few months back, he did. The professor popped in for a quick one and ends up in a blazing row with Piggy Pawson and his crowd.'

'Piggy?' Maria said.

'On account of his resembling a hairy old boar,' Wellbourne explained.

Harriet caught Maria's eye and made an expressive face, as if to say *boys will be boys*.

She clapped her hands. 'But enough of the chatter, ladies

and gentlemen. Richard, if you could announce that dinner will
be served in five minutes.'

'No sooner said than done,' Wellbourne said, and in lieu of
a dinner gong he employed his poker on the oil lamp. 'I'm
given to understand that the good lady is about to serve dinner,'
he called out. 'This way, ladies and gentlemen, please!' To
Harriet, he said, 'I'd better fetch Roy – I said I'd tell him when
grub was up.'

Wellbourne slipped away and Harriet led the guests into the
kitchen with a leaded Victorian range at one end and a long,
scrubbed pine table taking centre stage.

The guests took their seats and Harriet, assisted by another
woman, dished up a huge steak and kidney pudding and roast
vegetables; the wine flowed. Roy Vickers arrived – evidently
having been instructed to dress for dinner, as he was wearing
a tired-looking blue suit – and slipped into the seat beside
Donald with an acknowledging nod. Maria noticed that he'd
gone to the trouble of shaving, though his lean chin was blue
with fresh stubble.

Wellbourne sat to Vickers's right and chatted amiably with
the young man as dinner progressed. At one point, Maria
mentioned that she worked as a literary agent; evidently, they
were thin on the ground in Ingoldby-over-Water, and she had
to explain what the job entailed.

Harriet asked Donald what he was currently writing, and he
told her he was taking a break while they knocked the cottage
into shape.

Maria couldn't help noticing that Roy Vickers wolfed his
food as if he hadn't eaten for days. She wondered at the kind
of life he led in his gypsy caravan, and why he didn't lodge
with the Wellbournes in the house itself: it was, she thought,
more than large enough to accommodate three people.

She overheard the vicar asking the young man how long he'd
been in the village.

'A couple of years now,' Vickers answered with marked
reluctance, not looking up from his plate.

'And I understand you work on Richard's farm.'

'I do bits here and there,' came the grudging admission.

Richard beamed at Reverend Evans. 'The lad earns his keep.'

'Oh, more than that,' Harriet said, smiling across at Vickers. 'You're a godsend, aren't you?'

'Wouldn't say that,' Vickers muttered, clearly uneasy at the attention.

Maria smiled to herself when Donald sensed the young man's discomfort and changed the subject. 'What's the size of your herd, Richard?' he asked.

For the next ten minutes, Wellbourne treated his guests to a lecture on the finer points of maintaining a herd of a hundred Jersey cows.

Dinner ended with coffee and cognac, and afterwards the guests split into two groups; one remained in the kitchen, drinking coffee around the table, while the other repaired to the living room and gathered before the banked fire with Scotch and port. Maria found herself in the latter group, with Donald, the Wellbournes, Roy Vickers and the Reverend Evans.

The vicar reminisced about his Oxford days for a while, then Richard Wellbourne told the guests about his education at an agricultural college in Malvern. 'Best years of my life,' he said, 'and do you know why?'

Maria noticed that Harriet was blushing as she fiddled with the hem of her blouse.

'I met Harriet there,' he continued. 'She worked in the cheese shop, a Saturday girl. Tiny slip of a thing. Nothing much changes—'

'You silly old duffer, Richard! I wasn't much smaller than you at the time.' Harriet looked around the group. 'I didn't know how big he was going to get, or I might have had second thoughts!'

Maria asked Wellbourne, 'Was it love at first sight?'

'Do you know something,' he allowed, 'I rather think it was. Our eyes met above a round of Stilton, and nothing was ever the same again.'

'And you?' Donald asked Harriet. 'What did you make of Young Farmer Wellbourne?'

She laughed. 'I thought him a galumphing oaf of a chap, and still do! He had the gall to ask me out there and then, in the shop, with a dozen customers looking on!'

'But you accepted,' he said.

'And you wined and dined me with only one thing on your mind.'

'My sweet,' Wellbourne said, his eyes twinkling.

Maria noticed, across the room, a sideboard arrayed with a collection of black-and-white photographs. They showed a young man wearing an RAF uniform. In one of them, he stood beside the fuselage of a Hurricane.

She turned to Harriet, intending to ask about the young man, but Roy Vickers was saying, 'I don't know if anyone noticed, but Randall Robertshaw is back in town.'

'Didn't know the chap'd been away,' Wellbourne said.

'I saw his Morgan speeding past the green at five,' Vickers went on. 'He'd been away on business, according to Newton. Left owing a bar bill the length of his arm, by all accounts.'

'He likes the sauce?' Donald asked.

'Just like his father,' Wellbourne said.

Vickers muttered something, and Wellbourne said, 'What was that, Roy?'

'I said, he's even worse than his old man.'

'What is it that you have against young Randall?' Harriet asked Vickers, concern creasing her features.

Roy Vickers's hatchet face turned to the dancing flames, embittered. 'He's a conceited oaf,' he said. 'As you'd know if you had any dealings with him.'

'And you have?' asked the vicar.

'Bumped into him in the Green Man a few times,' Vickers said, nursing a glass of port in his bony right hand. 'He's the kind of toff who looks down on people for no good reason. He's not liked in the village, I can tell you.'

The vicar said, 'I heard on the grapevine that you and he once came to blows.'

The young man looked uncomfortable. 'That's an exaggeration.'

'But I heard that he hit you . . .'

The young man reddened. 'What if he did?'

'Roy!' Harriet said, shocked. 'You never told me!'

Vickers shrugged. 'You didn't need to know.'

Wellbourne asked, 'What happened? What was it all about, Roy?'

Vickers swigged his port in one gulp. 'He just said something that he shouldn't about someone, and I put him right.'

'So he hit you – and you hit him in return, I hope?'

Vickers looked anywhere but at the farmer. 'He wasn't worth the effort,' he muttered, 'and anyway I don't believe in violence.'

'Good for you!' said the vicar.

Wellbourne asked, 'Who was he talking about?'

The young man shook his head. 'Doesn't matter who,' he muttered.

Changing the subject, Donald asked, 'What line of business is Randall in?'

'I understand he has something to do with a bank in Norwich,' Wellbourne replied, 'though I heard he's in hot water with them.'

'Fingers in the till?' Donald asked.

'Not quite that serious,' Wellbourne said. 'According to Newton – the fount of all gossip hereabouts – his wife caught him *in flagrante* with his secretary. The wife did the right thing, gave the hussy a piece of her mind and chucked hubby out on his ear. The bank found out and gave him the old heave-ho, and Randall scurried back to the manor with his tail between his legs.'

'That wasn't the first time, according to Newton,' Vickers went on. 'You should see him in the Green Man, trying it on with all the single girls in the village, and some not so single.'

'The professor must've taken a dim view of his infidelity,' Wellbourne said.

'Robertshaw doesn't know,' Vickers said. 'Randall told his father that his wife'd met someone else. As well as being a cad, the chap's a barefaced liar.'

'You paint a delightful picture of the Robertshaw scion,' Donald said. 'I can't wait to meet him.'

In the kitchen, the back door opened and Maria heard a chorus of greetings. Nancy appeared in the doorway to the living room, her face rosy with exertion. She waved a mittened hand. 'There you all are.'

Harriet patted the cushion beside her. 'Nancy! Come and get warm, and do help yourself to a drink.'

The girl strode into the room, removed her coat and pulled

off her mittens. 'Well, perhaps a tiny little glass of port,' she
said. 'I've just put Xandra to bed, and I remembered your
invitation, Richard. Sorry I couldn't make it in time for dinner.'

She poured herself an inch of ruby port and squeezed on
to the sofa beside Harriet, wrinkling her nose in greeting to the
others like a naughty schoolgirl.

She looked across at Roy Vickers and smiled. 'Hello, you.'

He flushed and smiled at the girl, murmuring, 'Hello, Nancy.'

'I noticed you all fall silent when I arrived.' She laughed.
'What were you talking about?'

Maria noticed that Vickers was grimacing at the flames.

Wellbourne said, 'We were observing what an all-round good
fellow your cousin is, Nancy.'

The girl rolled her eyes. 'What's he done now?'

'Merely arrived back in the village,' Harriet said.

'Yes, I heard the car earlier,' Nancy said, 'and managed to
avoid him.'

'So there's no love lost between you two?' Donald asked.

'I'll say not! He treats me as if I were a schoolgirl, and
leeches off his father something frightful. And the worst of it
is that the silly old man falls for it every time.' She clapped a
hand over her mouth. 'Listen to me, blabbing! And I haven't
even had one sip of port yet!' She proceeded to put that right.

Maria laughed. 'Thank you for helping me unpack earlier.
There's plenty more to do if you find yourself at a loose end.'

'I jolly well enjoyed it,' Nancy said. 'It was a relief to get
out of the house.' She turned to Roy Vickers and asked, 'How's
life in the gypsy wagon, Roy?'

'Not as cold as it was, thanks to the stove Richard kindly
gave me last week.'

Their heads came together and they chatted in lowered tones.
The vicar turned to Donald and asked him about his novels.
Wellbourne, seeing that two or three glasses were perilously
close to empty, picked up the decanter and played the perfect
host.

Harriet, having noticed Maria's earlier glance at the photographs on the sideboard, took her hand and said, 'Come, I'll
show you.' She led Maria across the room.

There were perhaps a dozen photos, some showing a little

boy behind the wheel of a tractor and others depicting the same young man in uniform. Maria picked up the photograph which showed him standing before a fighter plane.

'My son, Jeremy,' Harriet said.

'He's very handsome,' Maria murmured, replacing the picture.

'Just like his father.'

'I can see the resemblance.'

Harriet said, 'It was the last photograph ever taken . . .'

Maria felt her throat constrict. 'Oh, I'm sorry.'

'It's hard to believe that it happened way back in '41,' Harriet said. 'He would be almost thirty-seven, now.'

Maria nodded.

'He was flying over Holland, escorting a bombing raid back to Kent. They were attacked, and Jeremy went down in the Channel. I still recall the feeling when I read the telegram. "Missing in action." I knew, of course. A mother feels these things, you see.'

'I'm sorry,' Maria said again, aware that the response was wholly inadequate.

Harriet smiled and patted her arm. 'Oh, don't be. You shouldn't be sorry. Jeremy isn't dead.'

Maria blinked. 'Oh, I thought . . .' She imagined the young man terribly injured, laid up in some hospital.

But Harriet went on, 'Well, I suppose he is dead, in that he's let go of his *physical* persona – but he really and truly still exists. He's over there, standing in the corner, leaning nonchalantly against the wall and smiling at me.'

Maria felt a cold shiver travel down her spine. 'He is?'

Harriet gripped her hand and whispered, 'Don't let people believe that this life is all there is, my dear. Death is not the end. Life goes on, but life very different from that which we're accustomed to. But listen to me! I'm giving you the heebie-jeebies!'

'Harriet!' Wellbourne called from beside the fire, concern etched on his craggy features. 'Fetch another bottle of port, would you, old girl?'

'Of course,' Harriet said, smiling at Maria and taking a bottle from a cabinet and moving back to the fire.

The back door opened again, and the murmur of conversation

in the kitchen fell suddenly silent. Then Maria realized why. A figure appeared in the doorway of the living room, short and squat and bristling with ill-contained anger. He glared across at the group before the fire.

Nancy stopped talking to Roy Vickers and looked up, her expression stricken.

'You didn't ask my permission, young lady,' Professor Robertshaw growled.

The girl looked shocked. 'I . . . But Xandra was in bed. She was fast asleep, and you were in the study with Randall. I . . . I didn't want to disturb you.'

'And what if Xandra had awoken and needed attention?'

'Edwin,' Wellbourne said in his best man-to-man tone, 'cut the girl a bit of slack. There's a good fellow. It isn't as if she's keeping bad company.'

Professor Robertshaw glared from Wellbourne to Roy Vickers and said, 'That's your opinion, Richard. Nancy, it's time we were leaving.'

Before the girl could acquiesce, Roy Vickers jumped to his feet and strode the length of the room. He confronted the professor, a head higher than the old man, and spoke to him in lowered tones. The professor went red and spat something in reply. The others looked on, their expressions frozen. Nancy appeared on the verge of tears. Harriet squeezed the girl's hand consolingly.

Professor Robertshaw prodded Vickers in the chest with a stubby forefinger, leaned forward and said something too low to catch.

The effect was instant. Maria half expected Vickers to respond with violence; instead, he just stared at the old man for a second, murder in his eyes, then pushed past him and stormed through to the kitchen. The back door slammed on his exit.

The professor cleared his throat, strode up to the hearth and took his niece by her upper arm. He almost dragged her from the room, pausing only briefly so that the tearful girl could collect her coat, beret and mittens.

As they disappeared into the kitchen, Maria stepped forward. She felt a hand clutch her arm. 'There's nothing you can do,' Donald murmured.

'I know, but . . .' She shook her head, impotent. 'But I feel I should have done *something*.'

He smiled. 'I know what we can do,' he said, 'but not tonight.'

'What?'

He told her; she laughed, then hugged him. 'Let's,' she said. 'Let's do that, Donald!'

Beside the fire, Richard Wellbourne hoisted the decanter of Scotch.

'I think that,' he said, 'calls for another drink.'

SIX

Langham yawned and stretched, basking in the luxurious lethargy that comes from occupying a warm bed on a cold Saturday morning, having slept in way past the time he usually rose.

Maria was watching him, her head propped on a hand. 'It's so quiet,' she said.

'No growl of double-decker buses or rattling milk floats.'

'Just birdsong.' She ran a hand through his hair. 'How's your head?'

'Do you know,' he said, 'surprisingly clear.'

'Mine, too. I'm glad you made a pot of tea before we turned in.'

'Ralph Ryland's patent hangover prevention,' he said. 'Did you enjoy last night?'

'Yes, I did. Until the professor's treatment of poor Nancy, that is. You?'

'I like the Wellbournes; they seem genuinely nice people.'

It was well past midnight when they had finally taken leave of their hosts, the last hour spent before the fire, quietly drinking with Richard and Harriet. Richard had told them all about the village and its inhabitants, an account far more charitable than Professor Robertshaw's assessment of the villagers. He had also told them about the farm, which they had bought almost thirty years ago when he'd inherited a considerable sum on the death of his father.

Now Maria said, 'What do you think Roy Vickers said to Professor Robertshaw when he confronted him last night?'

'I don't know, but I was more intrigued by what Robertshaw said to him. Roy shot off pretty damn quick, didn't he?'

Maria stared through the window. 'Poor Nancy. I do feel sorry for the girl,' she said. 'It's a good idea of yours, anyway. I feel as though we'll be getting back at Robertshaw.'

'Of course, the old devil might not be amenable.'

'I'll charm him into agreeing,' she said.

Langham sat up. 'Now, how about I cook some scrambled eggs on toast, then after a leisurely breakfast we can go for a long walk and explore the place?'

Maria squinted at the bedside clock. 'My word, it's after ten.'

'Brunch,' he said, swinging out of bed.

The telephone rang downstairs.

'I'll get it, Donald.' Pulling on her dressing gown, she hurried downstairs.

He dressed, and a minute later Maria appeared in the doorway and leaned against the frame. 'Who do you think that might have been?'

'Surprise me.'

'The professor—'

'Apologizing for last night?'

'Hardly. He wanted to know if we'd like to pop round for tea at two thirty today. Xandra is having one of her good days, and he said that we could meet his son, Randall, at the same time.'

'Did you accept?'

'I had half a mind to say we were busy, but then I thought we could ask him if Nancy can come to dinner tonight. Also, I'm more than a little intrigued at the prospect of meeting his wife and son.'

'The ne'er-do-well scion,' he said. 'Wellbourne and Roy didn't paint a very complimentary picture of the chap last night, did they?'

'Like father, like son,' she said. 'I'm surprised you took to the professor, Donald.'

'I think he must have been presenting his best side when I met him.'

They went downstairs, and while Langham scrambled half a dozen eggs and toasted the bread, Maria made a pot of coffee. Before he met Maria, he'd made do with Camp Coffee and professed himself satisfied. Maria had introduced him to the real thing, made in a big silver Italian coffee pot that sat directly on the stove, and now he was addicted to his daily dose of caffeine.

He heard the letterbox rattle in the hall and Maria said, 'I'll get it.'

She returned with a postcard showing an unprepossessing view of Portsmouth docks.

'Anything interesting?'

'It's from Ralph,' she said. She read out loud: "Dear Don and Maria, wish I wasn't here! Portsmouth is a right dump – at least the bit where I am is. But the good news is my brother's on the mend and he'll be home in a few days. Hope the move is going well. See you soon. Regards, Ralph."'

Langham laughed. 'Sounds as if he's really enjoying himself. Poor Ralph.'

They breakfasted in the kitchen, warmed by the Rayburn that Langham had remembered to bank with coal when they'd returned from the Wellbournes'. The room was on the eastern side of the house and received the full glare of the winter sunlight.

Maria recounted what Harriet had said about her son, Jeremy, and her belief that he was still with them, in spirit if not in body. 'She is a little odd,' she said. 'But I do like her.'

Langham chewed his toast. 'I think that might explain why they have a soft spot for young Roy.'

She thought about it. 'I still don't understand why he makes do with that caravan when he could live in the house.'

'Perhaps he wants his independence – doesn't want to impose.'

She sat back, cupping her coffee in both hands, and closed her eyes with the contentment of a satisfied cat.

Langham fetched a map of the area he'd bought from a stationer's in Bury St Edmunds, showing the village and others in the area, and the various walks through common land and woods. He spread it across the table.

'If we set off just after midday, leave the village to the west and walk up and around Cock Hill, we could swing round and arrive at the manor at two thirty, just in time for refreshments.'

'Let's do that,' Maria said.

'I wonder if the professor will be at all contrite today, after his little performance last night?'

'That kind of man, my darling, is never contrite.'

They spent the rest of the morning unpacking crockery in

the kitchen, and just after twelve wrapped up well against the cold wind and set off.

They turned along the lane and walked around the village green, blanketed with untrodden snow. Few people were abroad. Newton, the publican, was sweeping the new fall of snow from the path before the Green Man and waved cheerily as they passed. The postman acknowledged them with a nod and stepped carefully across the icy road.

They left the village along West Lane, then cut through an area of forest known as Culkin's Wood. Only a limited scattering of snow had settled beneath the cover of elm and ash, and the going was much easier. Ahead, orange sunlight splintered through trees as bare and stark as witches' brooms. Far off, rooks cawed raucously and wood pigeons gave throaty, muffled coos.

The land rose, climbing the hillside; halfway up, Langham realized how out of condition he was after his sedentary life in London.

Maria laughed as he puffed his way along. 'You need a dog, Donald – that would be one way of ensuring you got out of the house. You did suggest we get one.'

'Maybe once we're settled in,' he said. 'They are something of an expense and a tie.'

She gripped his hand. 'We can afford it, you cheapskate!'

'Touché.'

They came to the crest of the hill and the trees petered out. They stood, panting, and gazed down on the village in the vale. What was striking from this elevation was the near-total lack of movement, the frozen stillness of the place. Smoke drifted from a dozen chimneys; sunlight dazzled from windows. The postman hurried on his rounds, and Langham pointed out Reverend Evans crossing from the rectory to the church. They were the only figures moving in the silent winter landscape. The stream twisted, a braided silver thread, along the southern margin of the village.

'No cars,' Maria said. 'No vehicles at all.'

Beyond Ingoldby, the land rose and fell into the misty distance; other villages showed as collections of tiny cottages, church spires, and drifting pennants of smoke.

'Look,' Maria said, pointing.

Beyond Crooked Lane and the stream, the manor house stood in isolated splendour. A figure moved on the front lawn, reduced to the size of a tiny doll. Bill the dog danced in attendance.

'Isn't that Nancy?' Langham said. 'I wonder what she's doing?'

She was bent over, rolling something that looked like a big white barrel, her breath pluming in the freezing air.

Maria laughed. 'I know! She's building a snowman.'

'We might arrive just in time to help her finish it off.'

A path wound down the hillside, and the going was more difficult now that they were no longer under the cover of the trees. They held hands for support, before realizing that this was not the safest ploy: if one went down, so did the other. They finished the descent in single file, by some miracle remaining on their feet all the way.

They came into the village from the east and passed a row of tiny, thatched cottages which, long ago, had been the abode of farmworkers. By the time they reached the green, more villagers were venturing out, hurrying back and forth between their houses and the shops. They stopped to exchange pleasantries with a neighbour, then struck off along Crooked Lane and crossed the bridge to the manor house.

Langham checked his watch. 'We're early – it's just after two.'

'Then we'll have to do as you said, Donald, and play out here in the snow.'

They walked down the drive, passing the Morgan Coupé Langham assumed belonged to Randall Robertshaw. Nancy was still labouring away on the lawn, so absorbed in the task of rolling snow to make the upper section of the snowman that she didn't see their approach. Bill romped back and forth, a white tennis ball clutched in his teeth.

The lawn was criss-crossed with bare tracks where Nancy had rolled up the snow.

The girl looked up. 'Oh, hello there,' she panted, rosy-cheeked and exhausted.

'You look the very picture of rude health, my girl,' Langham said.

/led at them. 'I'm angry!'

.ted up to them and dropped the ball at Maria's feet.

.ii, about last night,' Maria said. 'I'm sorry. I wanted to do something – or at least *say* something.'

'But I stopped her,' Langham said. 'I had a better idea to help you get back at your uncle.'

Nancy lodged her mittened hands akimbo on her hips, panting still. 'You have?'

'Do you think the professor would let you come to dinner tonight, if we asked him nicely?' Maria said.

Nancy compressed her lips, looking dubious. 'I'm not so sure.'

'Leave it to me,' Maria said. 'I'll have a quiet word with him.' She glanced at her wristwatch. 'Your uncle invited us to afternoon tea, but we're early.'

'Then you can help me with this.' The girl indicated the vast snowball she'd created. 'I need to lift it on to the base. It's taken me ages because every five minutes I have to stop and play ball with Bill. You can be a pain, boy!'

Between them, they lifted the packed snow – more like a fat section of Swiss roll than a snowball – on to the base, then scraped up loose snow to fill in the join and create a seamless torso.

'Now for the head,' Nancy said, and rolled a much smaller ball.

While Nancy worked on the head, Langham fashioned an arm at either side and Maria scraped a line with a stick from the snowman's crotch to its base to denote a pair of legs.

The tip of her tongue poking between her lips, Nancy concentrated on moulding a face. She made it squarish, slab-like, adding two nubbins of coal for eyes and, above them, bushy brows fashioned from moss. She made a big nose from the thick end of a carrot, and a downturned grumpy mouth, then stood back and admired her handiwork.

'My word,' Langham said, 'I do believe it's the professor!'

Nancy grinned at them. 'I was reading all about voodoo the other day. Did you know, in some countries they believe that if you mould a likeness of your enemy and stick pins in it or burn it, then that person will be stricken with bad luck?'

Maria put a gloved hand to her mouth to stifle her laugh.

'As I don't have any pins, and I can't burn a snowman,' Nancy said, delving into her coat pocket, 'do you think these will do instead?'

She proceeded to stick a dozen short twigs into the snowman's torso with malicious relish, then stood back and laughed. 'There! That should show him!'

Langham looked up to see the front door of the manor swing open and Professor Robertshaw peer out. 'Ah,' he called, 'there you are. Well, come on in, all of you. What are you waiting for? Nance, run along to the kitchen and prepare the tea things, would you? There's a good girl.'

Bill nosed the ball closer to Maria's feet, and she picked it up and threw it through the open door. Bill bounded inside after it.

Laughing, Nancy took Maria's hand and hurried into the house. Langham followed them inside.

As Nancy disappeared along a corridor to the kitchen, Professor Robertshaw said, 'This way, this way. Xandra will be down presently. She's just preparing herself.' He looked at Langham. 'You know what women are like, Langham,' he went on, as if Maria were invisible. 'Here we are.'

He opened the door to the living room and they entered, Bill squirming through their legs to claim his place before the fire.

The three large settees had been pushed back from the fire to make room for an oval teak coffee table. Standing before the fire was a tall young man in a blazer and white flannels, who looked as if he'd just stepped from the deck of a yacht. All that was missing was a cravat and a nautical cap.

He was slim and good looking; he had a thin face, a high forehead and black hair brilliantined in place, with comb furrows as pronounced as corduroy. He appeared much older than his nineteen years.

'Randall, my son and heir,' the professor said. 'Randall, this is Donald Langham and his charming wife, Maria.'

Randall shook Langham's hand. 'Delighted.' He turned and smiled at Maria, his lifted lip making him appear almost vulpine.

'Enchanted, as they say across the water. I understand you're French?'

'That's right,' Maria replied coolly, 'but I'm feeling more English every day. I've lived here for almost twenty years.'

'I was going to ask you what you made of the place, but that would be something of a *faux pas*, wouldn't it?'

'I think it would, all things considered.'

'Won't you take a seat, Donald, Maria?' the professor said. 'Xandra will be here lickety-split, and then Nance will be along with the tea things.'

They sat side by side on the sofa, Maria shooting Langham a glance which he intuited as indicating her surprise at Robertshaw's blasé attitude: the professor was acting as if the little contretemps last night at the Wellbournes' had never occurred. The convenient amnesia of the tyrant, Langham thought.

Randall sat back in a commodious armchair, crossed his legs and eyed Maria up and down. 'My father mentioned you'd moved here from London,' he said. 'Which rather begs the question: what on earth possessed you?'

Langham was about to reply but Maria beat him to it. 'We'd come to dislike the hustle and bustle of the capital,' she said, smiling at the young man without warmth, 'and we both like this area of Suffolk.'

'Where in the Smoke did you live?' Randall asked with a superciliousness Langham found annoying. 'Shoreditch?'

'Kensington, actually,' Maria replied, taking Langham's hand and squeezing. 'We still have a nice apartment across from the park, which we'll use from time to time when we're in London on business.'

The professor said, 'Always nice to have a base in the city. I use my club, the Explorers.'

'And I understand you scribble?' Randall said to Langham.

'I write novels.'

'Thrillers, my father told me. Don't read the things myself.' He turned to Maria. 'And you?'

She was saved from replying when the door opened.

Langham had expected Xandra Robertshaw to be approximately her husband's age – in her sixties – but she appeared to be in her mid-forties, a tall, thin woman with piercing grey eyes, who might once have been beautiful. Now her face was haggard, and she moved circumspectly, wincing with every step she took. She wore a canary-yellow silk dressing gown which hung from her bony shoulders.

Langham stood up as she slowly crossed the room, and the professor made the introductions. Randall moved to his mother's side, took her elbow and assisted her to an armchair. She thanked him with a murmur and a pained smile.

The woman looked from Langham to Maria, grimacing as she arranged herself more comfortably in the chair. Her breath rasped in her chest.

'It *is* nice to have guests,' she said in a husky voice, and Langham wondered if this was an affliction of her illness. 'We're so sequestered out here. I did prefer it when we had a little place in Oxford. It was closer to London and, *you know*, in the swim.'

For the next five minutes, Professor Robertshaw took over the conversation and held forth on life in Oxford and the archaeological excavations he'd overseen in Greece and beyond. Langham glanced across at Randall. The young man was looking supremely bored and did nothing to hide the fact from his father.

Professor Robertshaw said, 'Xandra's read one of your books, Langham.'

Langham winced inwardly and wished Nancy would hurry up with the tea.

Xandra leaned forward and placed a claw-like hand on his knee, her fingernails as yellowed as old ivory. 'I very much enjoyed it,' she wheezed. 'So exciting. I do appreciate a good story, well told.'

Maria saved him from having to reply, and said to Xandra, 'I hope you don't mind my asking, but haven't I seen you somewhere before?'

The question surprised Langham; he looked at Maria who was frowning as if trying to recollect exactly where she might have met the woman.

The professor looked surprised. 'Your fame precedes you,' he muttered.

'Why, it's so nice to be recognized,' Xandra said. 'Long ago, in another life, I was on the stage, and I even appeared in two or three films.'

'Of course,' Maria said. '*A Quiet Wedding.*'

'My word, your memory! Yes, my very best role, even if it was a minor part.' She went on to regale the company with stories of the film's production and scandalous tales of one or two of its cast.

Randall lit a cigarette from a silver lighter, his attention elsewhere.

'I couldn't land film parts in the mid-thirties,' Xandra said, 'so I returned to the stage. Repertory, for my sins. That's where I met Edwin. He was something of a stage-door Johnny in those days.'

'I was nothing of the sort!' the professor objected, scowling at his wife. 'Though I did meet Xandra after some West End production. Wangled myself an invitation backstage.'

'And the rest,' Randall drawled, 'is history.'

Xandra's eyes darkened. 'In the winter of '48 I fell ill with tuberculosis and was treated with . . . what was the name of that awful stuff, Edwin?'

'Strepto-something or other,' he said.

'That was it. Streptomycin, by injection – and my, were they painful!' She smiled bleakly from Langham to Maria. 'It worked, cured the TB – but at a cost. I now have the kidneys of an eighty-year-old.'

'Xandra,' the professor said, 'I'm sure that Donald and Maria don't want all the gory details.'

'I was merely saying, dear . . .'

The professor drummed his fingers on the settee arm. 'Where is the girl? Is she *baking* the blessed cakes?'

'Go easy on her,' said Xandra. 'She really does do her best.'

The professor muttered something under his breath.

Randall said, 'Don't know if you've met my little cousin, Langham? She really is a pain. Physically twenty but mentally ten – and truly nauseating when she puts on her jolly-hockey-sticks act.'

Langham was about to say that they had not only met but had got along very well when Xandra snapped, 'That's enough,

Randall. As if you've got any room to accuse anyone of acting beneath their age.'

'Keep a civil tongue in your head, would you, old boy?' the professor said ineffectually.

As if in reply, Randall blew an unconcerned plume of smoke into the air.

The door opened and Nancy wheeled in a silver trolley loaded with a teapot, china cups and a trefoil tray of assorted cakes.

'Here we are,' she said. 'Whew! I thought the kettle would never boil!'

Randall said, 'We were wondering if you were baking the cakes from scratch.'

'No,' the girl replied with an equable smile. 'I'm afraid they're shop-bought – but they're very good,' she went on.

She transferred the cakes to the coffee table and poured the tea, then smiled around the gathering. 'There, I'll leave you to it. If you need anything, just ring.'

Maria said, 'Nancy – you must join us. I insist!' She patted the sofa beside her. 'Come.'

Nancy looked unsure. 'Uncle?'

The professor harrumphed and muttered, 'Very well, then. Don't see why not.'

'I'll run and fetch another cup!' she said, and hurried from the room.

'"I'll run and fetch another cup",' Randall mimicked in a high-pitched voice as she left the room. 'See what I mean about her playing the schoolchild, Langham?'

Maria said something under her breath, and Langham was relieved that it was in French.

Nancy returned with a cup and poured herself a tea.

The professor passed around the tray of cakes. 'Go on, help yourself,' he said. 'Dig in. I rate the Bakewells, myself. The local confectioner's is rather good.'

Langham took a date slice, Maria a Bakewell. They ate in strained silence for a while, Langham racking his brain to come up with a topic of conversation.

Nancy said, 'I helped Maria unpack yesterday. I've never seen so many books!'

'They're mostly Donald's,' Maria said. 'He collects obsessively, don't you, darling?'

'I find it impossible to go out without going into a bookshop, and even more impossible to leave a bookshop without purchasing at least one book.'

'And he's obsessive, too, about shelving his collection,' Maria said. 'They must be in alphabetical *and* chronological order.'

'I understand that,' Nancy said. 'I'm neat and tidy, too.'

'In complete contrast to me,' Xandra said. 'I'm the untidiest person in the world. Isn't that so, Edwin?'

'I'll say. She's sometimes hard to find amidst the piles of debris and cast-off clothing that litter her damned bedroom.'

Randall sat back in his chair, smoking his cigarette and staring at the ceiling with a studied air of boredom.

At the next lull in conversation, the young man said, 'I heard all about the fracas at the Wellbournes' last night, Nancy.'

The girl turned bright red.

The professor said, 'I'd hardly call it a fracas, Randall. But I'm not having a charge of mine hobnobbing with the likes of—'

Nancy glared at her uncle. 'Roy is a perfectly decent young man!' she declared.

The professor sighed. 'Nance, you're young. Too young, in fact, to be able to assess the character of a chap like Vickers.'

'If you'd only heard some of the stories I've heard,' Randall drawled, staring across at his cousin. 'Fair turn your stomach, some of them.'

'You're beastly!' Nancy cried.

'Oh, poor, naive, innocent youth,' Randall simpered. 'Fact is the man's an inveterate liar and a thief.'

'He's not a thief, nor a liar!'

'He's a poacher,' her uncle said. 'That damns him in my eyes, my girl.'

'And I've told you about some of his lies,' Randall said.

Nancy stared down at her half-eaten jam tart and murmured, 'I don't believe you.'

Randall climbed to his feet, tutted as if pitying her and grabbed a cake from the tray. 'I'll take one of these and push off. Excuse me, but I'm expecting a phone call. Been nice meeting you.'

He left the room and the atmosphere seemed to lighten.

Maria said into the ensuing silence, 'Professor, I'm cooking Nancy's favourite French dish tonight, and I'd very much like her to join us.'

'Her favourite *French* dish?' The professor looked mystified. 'And what might that be?'

Quick as a flash, Nancy said, '*Coq au vin*, Uncle,' and smiled at Maria with almost pathetic gratitude.

'I'd like to have her over for dinner to thank her for helping me unpack, you see.'

'Well,' the professor muttered. 'Don't know about that. There's Xandra to see to.'

'Phooey!' Xandra said. 'I can put myself to bed for once. I'm not a child, Edwin.'

'But if you need anything—'

'Then I can get it myself,' she said. She turned to Nancy. 'You go and enjoy yourself, my pet.'

Nancy looked relieved. 'Oh, thank you!'

The professor said, 'Anyone else attending this dinner, Langham?'

'Just the three of us.'

'Then I don't see why not. But I want you back by eleven, my girl. Understood?'

'Of course, Uncle. Thank you.'

She turned to Maria, almost tearful, and thanked her, too.

The gathering broke up a little later, Maria making the excuse that she had to get back and begin the meal. Xandra pronounced that it had been a delight to meet them and that they *must* come to dinner soon.

The professor saw them to the front door. 'And if I get another one of those letters,' he murmured in Langham's ear as they were leaving, 'I'll be in touch.'

They thanked him again and hurried from the manor.

Maria gripped Langham's arm and hung on, shivering. 'Wasn't that perfectly *horrendous*!'

'I'll say.'

'What a beastly man!'

'Who, the professor or his son?'

'Randall, though only marginally more than his father,' Maria said. 'I really don't like the way they treat Nancy.'

'I must say, though, I thought Xandra a decent sort,' Langham allowed.

'At least she seemed to appreciate the girl.'

They made their careful way over the bridge and turned left along Crooked Lane.

Maria grinned and squeezed his hand. 'Are we terribly naughty, Donald?'

He laughed. 'Not at all,' he said, then went on, 'I just hope the professor doesn't get wind of it.'

They passed the Wellbournes' farm, then the meadow.

Maria said, 'You pop in to see Roy, and I'll start dinner.'

He kissed her. 'See you soon. Put the kettle on, will you?'

She hurried off, and Langham pushed open the farm gate and tramped through the snow to the caravan.

He climbed the three wooden steps and knocked on the door. 'Hello? Anyone home?'

'That you, Donald?' Vickers called. 'Come in; it's not locked.'

Langham pushed open the door and ducked inside. He found Roy Vickers sitting hunched up in a blanket before a wood-burning stove, a book on his lap.

'Anything good?' Langham asked.

Vickers hoisted the volume. 'Dickens. *Hard Times*. Seems appropriate.'

Langham laughed. 'Thing is, how would you like to come over for dinner with us this evening?'

The young man narrowed his ink-black eyes. He appeared unsure. 'Well . . .'

'I know it'd mean you dining out two nights running – living the high life. But, you see, we've invited Nancy along, too.'

Vickers blinked. 'You have?'

'You two seemed to be getting along pretty well last night, before the interruption.'

'Yes, we *were*.'

'So why not resume things, and Professor Robertshaw be beggared?'

Vickers grinned. 'She is a pippin, isn't she?'

'I'll say she is,' Langham said. 'So you'll come?'

'Try keeping me away.'

'Excellent. We dine at eight. Come over a little earlier.'

Smiling, Langham left the caravan and made his way home.

Maria was in the kitchen and turned as he stepped through the back door. 'Well?' she asked nervously.

'He'd be more than delighted.'

She opened her arms. 'Come here, Donald, you wonderful matchmaker!'

SEVEN

angham was putting more coal on the living-room fire when a knock sounded at the front door. It was seven thirty.

'Get that, would you, Donald?' Maria called from the kitchen.

He opened the door to find Nancy kicking her boots against the doorstep. Behind her, huge snowflakes drifted down through the inky night. She wore her duffel coat and was hugging herself.

'It's got even colder, Donald!'

'Come in and get warm. Here, I'll take your coat.'

He hung it on the coat stand as she prised off her boots. 'I brought these along,' she said, pulling on a pair of old-fashioned slippers. 'They're Uncle's old ones. I couldn't find mine.' She stared down at her feet. 'They look ridiculous, don't they!'

He smiled. 'Well, they do look a bit funny,' he admitted. Not only were the slippers more suited to the feet of an old man, but they were too big for her and contrasted oddly with her stockinged legs and red dress.

'I like your dress.'

'A hand-me-down from Xandra. I took it in myself.'

'Can I get you a drink?'

'A gin and tonic would be lovely,' she said, following him into the living room. 'I'm not too early, am I?'

'Of course not – just in time for a drink before dinner.'

Maria joined them from the kitchen, and Langham poured two gin and tonics.

'I say, it's awfully nice of you to invite me,' Nancy said, taking her drink and sitting in a big armchair beside the fire. 'It's wonderful to get away from things from time to time. There are days when I think being cooped up in the manor will drive me mad.'

Maria admired the girl's dress, and Nancy repeated that it was one of her aunt's cast-offs which she'd altered to fit her.

'I have a small allowance, but it doesn't stretch to many new clothes.'

'You seem to get on well with Xandra,' Maria said.

Nancy sipped her drink, making wide eyes at its strength. 'Oh, that's lovely!' she exclaimed. 'Yes, Xandra's like a mother to me. She took me in and made me feel at home. Unc's all right, *sometimes*, but he does like to rule the roost rather. I'm surprised he let me out tonight.'

'Having met your uncle now on a couple of occasions,' Langham said, choosing his words with care, 'I hope I'm not speaking out of turn, but he seems somewhat preoccupied.'

'So you've noticed?' Nancy said, nodding. 'He has been acting a bit oddly for a while now.'

'How long is a while?'

'Oh, I'd say a month or so,' she said.

Langham considered his drink. According to the professor, he'd received the threatening letter just a few days ago.

'Any idea what might be troubling him?' he asked.

'Not the foggiest. Unc isn't one to reveal his feelings. He's always rushing off up to town at the drop of a hat, and seems flustered each time before setting off.'

Langham exchanged a glance with Maria. 'How often does he shoot off like this?'

'Oh, perhaps once a week. He just tells me he's popping out and won't be back for dinner, or lunch or whatever.'

'He doesn't tell you where he's going or who he's seeing?'

She shook her head. 'No, not a word. Just that he's going into town.'

Maria said, 'Doesn't Xandra know where he's going?'

'She doesn't take much notice of his comings and goings.' She hesitated. 'Between you and me, things don't seem to be going too well. I mean . . . Well, they hardly have anything to do with each other these days. They rarely dine together, and when they do meet, they're forever bickering. Perhaps it's just as well that they lead separate lives.'

'I'm sorry,' Maria said. 'It must be difficult for you.'

Nancy smiled brightly. 'Oh, not really. I just keep out of the way when Unc's on the warpath.'

'It can't be easy having Randall back under the same roof, either,' Langham observed.

'So you noticed he hates me?' Nancy said.

'It did seem blatantly obvious,' he said. 'What on earth have you done to offend him?'

'Have the temerity to exist? Have the gall to get myself invited to live at the manor?' She shook her head. 'I think he'd dislike me anyway, but the real reason is that I was friendly with his ex-wife, and I know what Randall is *really* like.'

'Ouch,' said Maria. 'That could be awkward.'

'I'll say. Randall likes to play the part of the badly done-to husband whose wife met another fellow and ran off, but the fact is that Randall was unfaithful on more than one occasion, and on the last one, Olivia had had enough. She left him, and only later met her new fellow. Randall is one of those self-centred chaps who don't like getting what they dish out themselves, and it suited him to play the aggrieved party to his father.'

'How long ago was this?' Langham asked.

'Olivia finally walked out six months ago.'

'Do you still see her?' Maria asked.

'I've sneaked off once or twice and met her in town,' Nancy admitted, 'but it's all very cloak and dagger. Unc thinks Olivia is evil personified – well, it wouldn't take much to persuade him of that – and if Randall got to know I was still in contact with her . . .' She grinned to herself.

'What?' Maria asked.

'It's just struck me,' Nancy said. 'I think Randall looks like a young twit from a Wodehouse novel, don't you?'

Maria laughed. 'I suppose he does,' she agreed. 'Though he doesn't much act like one.'

'No,' Nancy said. 'He's more like' – she thought about it – 'like Flashman from *Tom Brown's School Days* – nasty and sadistic!'

'And which literary character would you say you most resemble, Nancy?' Maria asked.

Grinning, Langham said, 'How about Heidi?'

Nancy poked her tongue at him. 'No! I'd like to think of myself as more like a heroine in a Brontë novel.'

He saw Maria's indulgent smile as she regarded the girl.

Nancy hiccupped, then stared down at her drink and exclaimed, 'I say, where did that go all of a sudden?'

Maria laughed. 'I'll get you another.'

She was pouring more drinks when a knock sounded at the back door. 'I'll get it,' she said, passing Langham and Nancy their gins.

'That must be our second dinner guest,' Langham said.

Voices drifted in from the hall. Nancy's eyes widened. 'Oh,' she said, standing suddenly and looking like a child on Christmas morning.

'It's the least we could do, after last night.'

Roy Vickers halted suddenly in the doorway, then grinned across at the smiling girl. 'Hello there.'

Nancy blushed. 'Hello again.'

Entering the room behind the young man, Maria said, 'Perhaps, tonight, the professor won't storm in and drag you off.'

'He would if he knew *I* was here,' Vickers said, crossing the room and taking Nancy's hand. 'He seems to have it in for me. Has me down as a poacher and who knows what else.'

Vickers wore the same frayed suit as he had the previous night, a white shirt and a blue RAF tie.

'Can I get you a drink?' Langham asked. 'Gin, Scotch or beer?'

'A beer would be nice, thank you.'

Langham moved to the kitchen and poured a bottle of Fuller's bitter into a pint glass. When he returned, the three were sitting around the fire discussing the weather. Apparently, the snow was so bad that the twice-daily bus service into Bury St Edmunds had been cancelled. 'More snow's forecast for the next few days,' Vickers said. 'That east wind is murderous, all the way from Siberia.'

Nancy said, 'I don't know how you can live in that little caravan, Roy.'

'Do you know, it's not half bad. The stove heats it up a treat, and I have a constant supply of coal and logs, thanks to Richard. It's very pleasant in the summer.'

'Where did you buy the caravan?' Maria asked.

'I didn't. It was in the meadow when I came to the farm looking for work, two years ago. As luck would have it, Richard wanted someone to give him a hand around the place, and he said I could lodge in the caravan over the summer.'

'And in winter?' Langham asked.

Vickers shrugged uncomfortably. 'Well, he did say there was a small room in the house, but to tell the truth, I was comfortable enough where I was. I didn't want to be a burden.'

'What were you doing before you moved here?' Maria asked.

'I worked in a drapery in Norwich. I hated it. I wasn't cut out for shop work, having to be nice to customers all day long.'

Maria slipped into the kitchen, then returned to announce that dinner was almost ready.

Langham opened a bottle of French Merlot and they ate in the dining room next to the kitchen. It was obvious to Langham that Nancy was smitten with the young man; she could hardly keep her eyes off him and chattered to him about her previous life at the boarding school in Cambridge.

At one point, Vickers stopped eating and stared down at his plate. 'My word, this is excellent.'

'French cooking at its best,' Langham said, and Maria murmured her thanks.

Vickers looked across the table at Langham and Maria. 'Thank you very much for inviting me. It's much appreciated.'

Langham raised his glass. 'It's nice to have friendly faces around the table.'

A little later, Maria asked if Roy had any brothers or sisters.

'I was an only child,' he replied, 'and my parents died just after the war.'

'So we're both orphans,' Nancy said.

Vickers smiled at her. He indicated the photographs on a side table which Maria had unpacked just that morning. Two of them were of Langham in uniform, one in Madagascar, off duty in a bar in Antananarivo with a couple of friends, and the other in India, sitting on a wicker chair on the veranda of a bungalow.

'Where did you serve?' the young man asked.

'Madagascar and India, for the most part. Field Security, so I never really saw front-line action, other than initially in Madagascar. In '42 we were sent to India, and I supervised an area almost the size of Britain, mainly tracking down spies and monitoring Nationalist activity. I must admit, it was something of a cushy number.'

Nancy listened, wide-eyed. 'Gosh. I can hardly remember the war. I was just eight when it ended. You make me feel so young.'

Langham laughed. 'And you make me feel dashed old, my girl.'

Maria turned to Vickers. 'Tell me what you did, Roy.'

His reluctance to do so was obvious. He regarded his almost empty plate and murmured, 'Did my best to shoot down Messerschmitt 109s.'

Nancy shook her head. 'That must have been . . .' she began.

'It's not something I think about much, these days. Or talk about, either, if I can help it.'

Langham was about to change the subject, but Nancy said, 'I'll tell Randall what you did, next time he pipes up.'

Vickers sighed. 'Randall's a fool. Just ignore what he says.'

'Anyone for more drinks?' Langham said.

He moved to the kitchen and opened a second bottle of wine. When he returned to the dining room, Nancy was saying, 'He's so arrogant! The way he goes on. I think it's because he was too young to be in the war, and he's always resented the fact. Do you know what he told me, Roy?'

Forbearing, Vickers said, 'No, what was that?'

'He tried to tell me that you were just a quartermaster in the RAF,' she said, 'and that you never flew. I told him he was being beastly, and jealous of a war hero.'

Vickers winced. 'Well, he was partly right, Nancy. After a year in hospital, I did work in stores at a base near Lincoln.'

'Yes, but the point is that you flew, and were shot down and injured, and Randall just can't accept that. Sometimes I just want to stab him to death!' she finished melodramatically.

She stopped and stared around the table, then hiccupped. 'I say, am I a little tipsy?'

'Just a tad,' Vickers said, smiling. 'Thank you for wanting to defend my honour, but don't go stabbing anyone, all right?'

She smiled. 'I promise.'

Maria made coffee, and they returned to the living room and

sat around the fire, chatting until Nancy sat up straight, pointing to the carriage clock on the mantelshelf. 'Crikey! It's almost eleven. Unc said I had to be back for eleven!'

'Or you'll turn into a frog?' Vickers said.

'Or he'll be on the warpath and I'll be grounded for a whole month. I'd better dash.'

'Hold on,' Vickers said, climbing to his feet. 'I'll see you home. We could cut along the back lane to save time.'

'It's beastly treacherous, and there's no lighting,' she said, 'but we could hold hands to support each other. I just hope Unc doesn't see you!'

Vickers exchanged a smile with Langham, and Maria fetched their coats.

'Thank you for a super meal,' Nancy said, hugging Maria and shaking Langham by the hand.

Vickers said, 'That was grand. Pity I can't invite you round to the caravan. It'd be a bit of a squash, and all I cook on the stove is eggs and beans.'

'Then let's have a session at the Green Man at some point,' Langham said as Vickers and Nancy ducked from the cottage and made their way carefully down the back garden, hand in hand.

'A success, I think,' Langham said as they returned to the living room and sat before the fire. 'Another little drink before bed?'

EIGHT

Maria spent all Sunday unpacking crates in the bedroom and helping Donald to arrange books in his study.

After a late breakfast on Monday morning, just as she was about to go upstairs to finish unpacking, the telephone rang.

'Hello?' she said.

'Maria,' Nancy said, 'are you terribly busy at the moment?'

'Just about to do a little unpacking. How can I help?'

The girl sounded tentative. 'Well, you see, I was hoping to go into town later this morning to pick up something I'd ordered. But the buses are still not running, and I don't want to ask Randall, and Unc's in a foul mood and told me he didn't want to be bothered.'

Maria smiled. 'Would you like a lift, Nancy?'

The girl sounded relieved. 'Oh, that would be heavenly of you. I know you drive – I saw you in the car the other day – and when Flo at the post office said the buses were still off, I thought of you.'

'It will give me an excuse to go out, and anyway I could do with getting one or two things from town. What time were you thinking of leaving?'

'Would half past eleven be all right?'

'Lovely, Nancy. I'll pick you up from the manor.'

'No, it isn't on the way. I'll be outside the post office. And I'll buy you lunch as thanks.'

'There's really no need,' Maria said. 'See you at eleven thirty.'

'I'm ever so grateful, Maria. See you then.'

Donald called out, 'Who was that?'

Maria moved to the study and recounted her conversation with Nancy. Donald was crouching beside a bookcase, meticulously reordering a row of crime hardbacks.

He peered up at her. 'You look bemused.'

'It's just that . . . I offered to pick her up from the manor, which would make sense, but she said that she'd meet me outside the post office.'

'She probably doesn't want the professor to see her leaving,' he said.

'Yes, that's probably the reason.'

He frowned. 'You're not convinced?'

'I don't know. There was something in her tone. She sounded nervous.' She smiled at him. 'But as you say, it's probably to do with her uncle and the short leash he keeps her on, poor girl.' She pushed herself from the doorpost. 'I'll do a little unpacking, then get off.'

'And while you're away, I might wander down to the Green Man.'

Later that morning, having completed the last of the unpacking in the spare bedroom, Maria changed into her favourite navy-blue trouser suit, made up her face, then kissed Donald goodbye and eased the Rover from the driveway.

As she turned on to the lane that ran alongside the village green, she saw Professor Robertshaw's silver-grey Daimler emerge from the lane to the manor, accelerate past the row of shops and motor away from the village. At the same time, Nancy's duffel-coated figure ducked back into the entrance of the post office.

Maria smiled to herself: so the poor girl *was* venturing out contrary to her uncle's wishes.

She made her way around the green and pulled up in front of the post office.

Nancy opened the passenger door and jumped in. Maria set off, saying nothing about having seen Nancy's uncle or the girl's evasive action.

'I had a wonderful time on Saturday evening,' the girl said. 'Thanks ever so.'

'It was lovely to have you around,' Maria said. 'Do you think Roy enjoyed himself?'

'Rather. He told me so on the way home.' She hesitated. 'What do you think of him, Maria?'

'Roy?' She smiled to herself as she drove north from the village along the narrow lane. 'I think he's a thoroughly decent young man who seems to have been dealt an unfair hand.'

'Yes, he does rather, doesn't he?' She fell silent for a while, then said, 'And what Randall said, about Roy's lying, and never really having flown . . .'

Maria glanced at the girl. 'I think you're probably right in what you said last night. Randall is jealous. You've no reason not to believe Roy, have you?'

'Oh, no,' Nancy said. 'But he is reluctant to talk about the war.'

'That's not uncommon, and entirely understandable. Look at Donald. He might have said the other night that he had a cushy war, but he was in a nasty battle at Diego Suarez. He hates talking about it. It's entirely natural that Roy should think the same. He was badly injured, after all.'

Nancy nodded and fell silent.

The main road was icy in patches, and in one or two places the snow had drifted across the open fields and piled in the lee of hedges, blocking the way. Maria had to slow to walking pace and edge carefully past the drifts. It was little wonder that the bus service had been cancelled.

'Oh, we had drama at the manor this morning, Maria.'

'Do tell.'

'Richard Wellbourne came across at nine,' Nancy said. 'When I answered the door, he asked to see my uncle and strode in before I could reply. I took him along to the study and showed him in.' She looked across at Maria and hunched her shoulders conspiratorially. 'Then I hovered outside the door to see what he wanted.'

'And?'

'It wasn't long before they were at it hammer and tongs. Something about the land Unc is digging up. It belongs to Richard, and apparently my uncle rents it at peppercorn rates. I got the impression that Richard wants the land back.'

'What happened this morning? Did they come to any agreement?'

'I don't think so. I heard the French windows opening, and then they walked outside. So I went next door to the living room and peered through the window. They were still arguing, way beyond the standing stone. I saw them waving and gesticu-lating, and then they came back about ten minutes later. My uncle had a face like thunder, and Richard didn't look much happier. He let himself out, and Unc was in a foul mood for the rest of the morning.'

Maria thought about it. 'But if by any chance your uncle does locate any further standing stones, or evidence that they existed, wouldn't that be to Richard's benefit? The field would become a site of archaeological interest – and surely then he'd be handsomely compensated.'

'I'm not sure about that,' Nancy said, 'but what I do know is that there's no love lost between them.'

'Your uncle does come across as a somewhat prickly customer.'

'It doesn't take much to rub him up the wrong way.'

The streets of Bury St Edmunds had been largely cleared of snow; what had covered the roads was now piled in the gutters, turning sooty-grey with exhaust fumes. There were few pedestrians abroad, and a fierce wind whipped the trees that stood along the main road. Nancy suggested they park in the market square, not far from the milliner's where she had ordered a new hat.

'Xandra gave me some money for Christmas, and I thought I'd splash out on a hat. My beret is fine, but I've had it for years.'

'Do you know a nice place for lunch?' Maria asked. 'I suppose we could always go to the Midland.'

'No,' Nancy said. 'No, I . . . I've heard the food isn't that good. We could go for a quick drink, though, after I've picked up my hat, and then go to a little café I know along Abbeygate Street.'

'Let's do that,' Maria said.

She pulled into the square, climbed out into the teeth of a fierce easterly wind and turned up her collar. They leaned into the wind and hurried along the street to the milliner's.

'I came here last week for a fitting,' Nancy said as they entered the plush establishment. 'I had it especially made, and it cost a fortune!'

The hat was waiting for her, and a helpful assistant showed the girl to a mirror. Nancy pulled on the hat – a stylish tweed affair that reminded Maria of something that Robin Hood might have worn, but which suited the girl. She examined her reflection and declared herself delighted. She handed the cashier a five-pound note, from which she received scant change, and waited while the hat was expertly wrapped and inserted into a bespoke brown-paper bag bearing the establishment's name.

They left the shop and made their way to the Midland Hotel. Nancy said, 'I'll buy you a drink – I insist.'

Maria said, 'In that case, I'll have a small dry sherry as an aperitif.'

As they were just about to enter, Maria glanced to her left and saw a familiar car parked beside the hotel. It was Professor Robertshaw's Daimler.

Frowning, she followed Nancy into the public bar.

Nancy ordered a sherry and for herself a pink gin, and they sat at a circular glass-topped table in the corner, the only customers in the room.

Maria considered the fact that the professor's car was parked beside the hotel, and the significance of Nancy's insisting that they should take a drink at the Midland rather than dine here. This, along with the girl's reluctance that morning to be picked up from the manor, made Maria more than a little suspicious.

She was about to voice these suspicions when Nancy said, 'Excuse me one moment, Maria. I must go and powder my nose.'

As a parting line to excuse her leaving, Maria thought, it was rather lame.

Nancy slipped from her seat and disappeared through the swing door.

Maria sipped her sherry and considered the most likely scenario. Nancy was following her uncle, of course: that much was blatantly obvious. Not so apparent was how Nancy had come to learn of her uncle's affair, if indeed Roy Vickers was correct in his assertion that the professor *was* seeing someone. She wondered if Roy Vickers had mentioned it on their walk home on Saturday night.

She was considering how to broach the subject when the girl returned, and she saw that it might not be that awkward to ask Nancy, after all: the girl was white-faced and seemed to be in shock.

Maria leaned forward and took her hand across the table. 'Your uncle is here and is seeing someone, *oui*?'

The girl nodded, ashen-faced. She squeezed Maria's hand and seemed on the verge of tears. 'Don't hate me, Maria. I'm sorry I lied to you. I should have told you this morning, but I thought . . .' She shook her head. 'I didn't think that my uncle could be . . . be so—'

'Nancy?'

'He's in the dining room with *her*. Go and look. He won't see you – he has his back to the door. It's just across the hallway.'

Curious, Maria stood and left the bar. She crossed the plush carpeted hall and paused beside the double door of the dining room. Its upper panel was of bevelled glass, and peering through she made out, quite clearly, the distinctive shape of the professor's bald head. Across the table from him sat an elegant blonde-haired woman in her mid-fifties.

Maria moved from the door and walked along the hall to the bathroom, where she took out her compact and reapplied her lipstick. She recalled the threatening missive the professor had received the week before – and what Nancy had said on Saturday night about the parlous state of her uncle and Xandra's relationship.

She closed her compact, snapped her handbag shut and stepped back into the hallway.

Robertshaw and the woman were leaving the dining room, and for a heart-stopping second Maria thought the professor had seen her.

His attention, however, was firmly focused on his escort. He was leaning towards her, an arm around her waist, and murmuring endearments as they left the hotel.

Maria rejoined Nancy in the public bar.

The girl was in the process of wiping her eyes when Maria returned, and she quickly slipped her handkerchief into her handbag.

She looked up, her eyes red. 'Did you see her?'

Maria nodded.

'Oh, how *could* he? I don't know which is the more shocking, Maria – that he should be having an affair or that he's having it with *her*.'

'You know her?'

'Well, I've seen photographs of her in my uncle's study.'

Maria stared at her. 'He keeps photos of his *mistress* in his study?' she said incredulously.

'In a drawer,' Nancy said, smiling through her tears. 'You see, the woman is Deirdre, his ex-wife.'

NINE

Langham unpacked the last of the books just before lunch-time and stood back to admire his handiwork.

His desk and writing chair were positioned before the window at the far end of the room, overlooking the back garden. Shelves and bookcases lined the other three walls, all filled with books. The threadbare two-seater sofa, which he'd managed to convince Maria not to throw out, stood somewhat incongruously in the middle of the room, with his standard lamp beside it. He could see himself being very happy and productive here.

He made himself a cheese sandwich and a pot of Earl Grey tea for lunch and ate in the study, leafing through the previous day's *Sunday Times*. The sports page announced a win on Saturday for Arsenal, who had beaten Sheffield Wednesday at home 6–3. By contrast, Millwall had lost 3–2 away at Brighton. Ralph would be most unhappy with the result.

He'd been only half serious when he'd mentioned the pub to Maria earlier, but the thought of a pint before the blazing fire in the snug of the Green Man was inviting. Better still, he thought, a game of darts. He wondered if Roy Vickers would be around.

He finished his sandwich, fetched his overcoat, gumboots and hat, and left by the back door. Instinctively, he locked the door, even though Nancy had mentioned the other day that there hadn't been a burglary in the village for over twenty years, and all the locals left their doors unlocked when they went out. More than ten years of living in London since the war had instilled no such trust in his fellow man.

The blizzard blew huge flakes of snow in a ceaseless, horizontal barrage. He fought against the wind and made his way down the lane, dodging an obstacle course of frozen puddles. Vickers's caravan wore a foot-thick mantle of snow, and smoke chuffed from a stove pipe on the roof.

Langham knocked and the door was opened immediately,

though not by Roy Vickers. The ursine form of Richard
Wellbourne filled the doorway. 'Come in, Langham. Take a
pew,' the farmer said, backing into the confined space and sitting
down carefully on a tiny footstool. Vickers crouched at the far
end of the caravan, next to the stove. *Hard Times* lay open,
spine uppermost, on a shelf to his left.

'Just filling Roy in on the latest,' Wellbourne said.

Langham sat down on a narrow bunk. 'The latest?'

Wellbourne ran a big hand through his unruly grey thatch.
'Had a call this morning – I'd just got in from milking and I
was about to sit down to breakfast. It was the professor, and
he wanted to see me.'

'About?'

Wellbourne shook his head. 'Wouldn't say, other than that it
was important. So I told him he could wait till I'd finished my
breakfast, put the phone down and tucked in. Fellow had
quite spoiled the meal, though. In the event, I didn't get over
to the manor until nine – the wind had blown a tarpaulin off
the silage, so I had to fix that.'

'What did he want?' Langham asked.

Beside the stove, Vickers swore pithily.

'Robertshaw questioned me about the deeds to the farm,
asked if I had copies of them covering the specific field we
were squabbling over – the West Field, as it's known.'

'Have you?'

The farmer spread his hands. 'God knows. I have a vague
memory of my solicitor handing them over when I bought the
place back in '27, but I'll be damned if I can put my hands
on 'em.'

'Why was Robertshaw asking?'

'That's what I wanted to know, and when I asked' – he shook
his head grimly – 'he said he'd been going through some legal
papers and came across a document relating to the West Field
– a deed of ownership, according to him.'

'Did he say how he came by the document?' Langham asked.

Wellbourne shook his head. 'No, he just said he came across
it in a bunch of paperwork in his office.'

Langham looked from Vickers to the farmer. 'Did he show
you the deeds?'

'That's the thing. He didn't have the document. He'd taken it across to his solicitors in Bury the other day and left it for them to have a look-see and ratify that it was what he hoped it was – proof of ownership of the field.'

'And if it is,' Vickers said, 'Richard hasn't a leg to stand on.'

Langham thought about it. 'Did Robertshaw say how old this document was?'

'He mentioned that it dated from the late eighteen hundreds.'

'There's always the possibility that it's been superseded by a later deed,' Langham said. 'You need to ransack the farm and see if you can locate the deeds, and if you can't find them, get on to your solicitors. There's a chance they might be holding the records, and anyway, they'd be able to give you some sound advice.'

Wellbourne nodded. 'I'll certainly be doing that.'

'Typical kind of dirty trick a chap like Robertshaw would pull,' Vickers muttered.

'But if the land isn't that valuable,' Langham said, 'and isn't particularly good farmland . . .'

'It's the principle of the thing,' Vickers said.

'That's it,' Wellbourne said. 'The principle. Also, what if Robertshaw does unearth something of value in those trenches? Legally, it'd belong to him. And don't think I'm being greedy, Langham; I'm not bothered about losing out in that respect. It's the thought of the gloating Robertshaw would indulge in that rankles.'

'I can imagine,' Langham said. 'I should think, knowing the professor, he'd certainly remind you about it at every opportunity. Still, what are the chances of him uncovering buried treasure? And anyway, you haven't seen these deeds yet. You never know, he might be bluffing.'

'I'll drive up to Bury right away and see what old Cockshott has to say about it all.' He turned to Vickers. 'See to the herd at four, would you, Roy? I'll give you all the gen when I know a bit more, Langham.'

He slipped from the caravan and banged the door shut after him.

'Ruddy Robertshaw,' Vickers said. 'For two pins, I'd tell the chap what I thought of him.'

Langham grunted. 'You'd only have his son on your back then, Roy, and I don't know who's the pricklier customer. Anyway,' he went on, 'I take it you're free till four. Fancy a game of darts?'

'Bit strapped at the moment.'

'We'll only have a pint, and this one's on me.'

'Well, only if you're sure.'

Vickers pulled on his RAF greatcoat and led the way out into the blizzard. Langham noticed that he didn't bother to lock the caravan door. Not, he supposed, that there would be much of value to steal in there, anyway.

They took the back lane to the village green and crossed to the Green Man.

A couple of regulars were propping up the bar, and old Wicketts Blacker was enjoying a pint of stout beside the fire in the snug. He raised his glass when he caught sight of the pair and mumbled an incomprehensible greeting.

Langham ordered two pints of Fuller's and they moved to the taproom. 'Best of three,' he said. 'Three hundred and one up, start and finish on a double.'

'Beats an afternoon in the van with Dickens.'

The young man proved to be a proficient player, with a good eye and a steady hand. The first game was close, with Vickers needing a double ten to win, Langham a double twenty. Vickers fluffed the shot and Langham won with a successful last throw.

'I had a grand time on Saturday night, Don,' Vickers said as they began the second game.

'I think Nancy enjoyed it, too. I know we did.'

Vickers paused before taking his second throw. 'I think I put my foot in it on the way home, though.'

Langham winced. 'You didn't invite her back to the caravan?'

The young man went bright red, launched a dart at the double twenty and missed. 'Nancy mentioned she was upset about her uncle, said he was acting oddly – making secretive phone calls, shooting off unannounced.'

'I wonder if it has anything to do with the deeds?' Langham surmised, aiming for a double ten and hitting the wire.

Vickers shook his head, licked his lips as he concentrated on getting a double eighteen and threw a perfect shot. 'That's when

I put my foot in it,' he said. 'I mentioned that it was probably all about the woman Robertshaw was seeing in Bury.' Vickers grimaced at Langham. 'I know, I know. I should have kept my trap shut. But I was a little tight by then and I wasn't thinking straight.'

'What did she say?'

'Just looked upset, clammed up and hardly said anything until we reached the manor.'

'I'm sure she'll be fine.'

'It's just that I care for the girl,' Vickers said, 'and I don't like to think that something I said might have hurt her.'

Langham smiled. 'She probably suspected her uncle was up to something, anyway. She's a smart kid, for all her apparent naivety. I'm sure she doesn't think her uncle's a paragon of virtue.'

They finished the second game, which Vickers won comfortably.

'The third decides it,' Langham said.

They were halfway through the final game, with Vickers well ahead, when a familiar voice sounded from the main bar. 'Scotch and soda, and whatever you're having, Newton,' Randall Robertshaw said.

'Christ,' Vickers swore. 'I really don't want to . . .' He trailed off as Randall's louche frame appeared in the doorway.

His drink in his right hand, Randall reached up with his left and gripped the lintel, affecting a pose that was somehow at once casual and yet confrontational. Langham was reminded of Nancy's likening him to Flashman, the school bully.

'Enjoying a quiet afternoon game, gentlemen?' Randall slurred, and Langham judged that the Scotch was not his first drink of the day.

'We *were*,' Vickers murmured, thankfully too softly to be heard.

Langham concentrated on his next shot, hoping Randall would get the message and go away.

'Two things, gentlemen,' Randall went on.

Langham lowered his dart. 'Yes?'

'The first, a message for your boss, Vickers. Tell Wellbourne that we've just been on the blower to my father's solicitor-johnny in town. Good news. Well, good news for Pater, that is. Not so good for Old Farmer Wellbourne.'

'What about it?' Vickers said, taking a mouthful of ale.

Randall swung from the lintel, a little unsteadily. 'Enright said he has a copy of the deed concerning the West Field, and apparently it was signed over to the owner of the manor in . . . let me get this right . . . in 1895, for the princely sum of five guineas. So it would appear that the field belongs to my pater. If you would be so good as to inform Wellbourne of this, Vickers.'

Vickers lodged his pint on a table and faced Randall. 'Does the professor always get his lapdog to do his dirty work, Randall? You can tell your ruddy "pater" to tell Wellbourne himself.'

Randall grinned. 'I'm sure he'll be delighted to convey the information.'

Langham gestured to the board and murmured, 'Ignore him.'

They resumed their game, uneasy under Randall's supercilious gaze.

Vickers lowered his dart and looked at Randall. 'Right, you've delivered your message, so you can sling your hook.'

'I said I had a couple of things to say.'

'Then get on with it.'

Randall released his grip on the lintel and stepped into the taproom. He stared at Vickers with a venomous expression. 'I saw you last night, Vickers. With Nancy.'

The young man affected nonchalance and launched a dart. He missed his intended target. 'So what?'

'So I advise you to keep your filthy little paws off my cousin, is what.'

To his credit, Vickers refused to be drawn. He watched Langham hit a treble eight, congratulated him, then stepped up to the line and aimed for a double ten to win the game. He missed.

'Oh, bad luck, Vickers,' Randall said.

Vickers turned to the young man. He was shaking visibly. 'Why don't you just sod off?'

'As I was saying, keep away from Nancy. She's too good for a lying little criminal like you. And if you don't heed my advice—'

'What?' Vickers snapped, staring at Randall. 'What'll you do?'

Randall took a mouthful of Scotch, savoured it, then said, 'Then I'll tell Wellbourne all about your lies.'

With that, he turned on his heel and strode from the taproom. Vickers watched him go, fuming impotently.

'Come on,' Langham said, 'let's finish the game. As I said back at the caravan, Richard might have later deeds. And as for Randall's warning you off Nancy . . .' He shrugged. 'So much hot air.'

Even as he said this, he was aware that Randall's threat to inform Wellbourne of Vickers's 'lies' had hit home, and he wasn't going to add to the young man's distress by asking what Randall might have meant.

They completed the third game, which Vickers won narrowly. Langham suggested a second pint, but Vickers shook his head. 'I wouldn't mind, but I really must be getting back. One or two things to sort out. Another time, OK?'

There was no sign of Randall Robertshaw as they left the pub and made their way along Crooked Lane. Vickers nodded a terse goodbye when they reached Wellspring Farm, then hurried across the snow-covered cobbles to the cow byre.

Back at the cottage, Langham stoked up the Rayburn, lit the fire in the living room and for the rest of the afternoon unpacked boxes of clothing in the spare bedroom.

He heard the Rover roll into the drive just after four and descended to meet Maria. She came in carrying a string bag containing a brown-paper parcel of cheese and six bottles of beer.

'For you,' she said, handing them over and pulling off her snow-spangled hat. 'Oh, you lovely man: you've lit the fire. I'm frozen. How was your day?'

As she sat before the blazing fire and warmed her stockinged feet, Langham recounted Richard Wellbourne's news concerning the deeds and his and Roy's encounter with Randall Robertshaw in the Green Man.

'What a nasty piece of work he is,' she said. 'What do you think he meant about Roy's "lies"?'

'I have a theory,' he said.

'Go on.'

'Not that this lessens Roy Vickers in my eyes one iota – I think he's a decent chap. But I also think that the closest he ever came to a Wellington bomber was when he worked all the war in the quartermaster's store.'

She considered this. 'Of course, there's always the possibility that Roy's alleged shady past has nothing to do with the war. He might simply be hiding the fact that he got into trouble at some point. He might have a criminal record, for all we know.'

'That's possible,' he allowed.

'Whatever it is,' Maria said, 'I just hope that Nancy doesn't think ill of Roy, if or when she finds out.' She patted his thigh. 'And speaking of Nancy . . .'

He looked at her. 'What? Is something wrong?'

'Well, the scheming little monkey had ulterior motives for going into town today. This morning, she overheard the professor on the phone arranging to meet someone in the Midland for lunch.'

'Ah, so he *is* having an affair?'

Maria quirked her lips. 'That's right – but you'll never guess with whom.'

'Some pretty young film star, perchance?'

She leaned forward and said, 'No, he's seeing his ex-wife, a woman called Deirdre.'

Langham sat back and absorbed the information. 'The sly old dog,' he said. 'Poor Xandra. How did Nancy take it?'

'I think she was in shock.'

'Poor kid. We should arrange to take Nancy and Roy out for a meal at some point.'

Maria smiled. 'That would be nice.'

'Right, I'll put the kettle on. Earl Grey?'

'You're a darling. And tonight, after all the adventures of the day, I want a quiet evening listening to the wireless and drinking wine.'

He hugged her. 'You're a creature of simple pleasures, my sweet.'

TEN

L angham was dozing the following morning when the telephone rang downstairs.

'I'll get it,' Maria said, rolling out of bed.

'You wonderful woman,' he murmured, watching her pull on her red silk dressing gown and hurry from the room.

He was sinking back into slumber when she returned. 'For you, Donald. The professor. He said it was urgent.'

'Damn!' He sat on the edge of the bed and rubbed his face. 'What time is it?'

'Just after seven.'

'Is nothing sacred?'

He dug his feet into his slippers, pulled on his dressing gown and made his way downstairs. The air was freezing. 'Hello?'

'Langham. Another missive . . . and something else.'

Langham tried to gather his thoughts. 'Something else?'

'Get yourself over here quick sharp,' the professor said, and cut the connection.

He stared at the receiver, dropped it back on to its cradle and returned to the bedroom.

'What did he want?' Maria had climbed back into bed and pulled the sheets up to cover the lower half of her face; only her eyes peeped out.

Langham relayed the professor's communique verbatim.

'"Something else"? Whatever can he mean?'

'Search me.'

'What are you going to do?'

He smiled. 'Climb back into bed and snuggle down with you.' He sighed. 'No, I'd better get myself across to the manor.'

'And I'll have breakfast waiting for when you get back. Porridge?'

'Wonderful.' He kissed her. 'See you soon.'

He dressed and went downstairs, pulled on his overcoat and found his hat.

After Monday's blizzard, the morning was calm: the sky was clear and blue, and the land beneath it lay sealed in an undulating mantle of snow. He took the back lane to the bridge and slithered over the ice on the far side. A set of footprints marred the perfection of the snow: evidently those of the postman. He followed them to the front door of the manor and knocked.

The professor opened it himself, his face like thunder. 'You'd better come in,' he muttered without a word of apology for getting Langham out of bed so early or the slightest suggestion of gratitude.

Langham followed him to the living room where a welcome fire blazed. The professor pointed to the coffee table: a light-blue envelope sat next to a big brown-paper parcel tied with twine.

'I didn't burn anything this time, as per instructions.'

Langham picked up the envelope. It was addressed to Professor E.A. Robertshaw and bore a London postmark. He pulled out the single sheet of notepaper and read the typed missive.

> Place one hundred pounds in used five-pound notes in the accompanying valise. Drive to Pleasance Park in Market Hemshall. At three o'clock today, the 28th, place the valise on the ground against the leg of the first park bench on the left of the path from the eastern entrance. Then walk away from the bench and do not look back. If you inform the police, or anyone else, you will pay the price.

The note was typed on the same machine as the first one, as the downstroke of the letter y was broken.

Langham opened the brown-paper parcel. Inside was an ancient, battered leather valise with a leather strap handle on brass rings. The material of the handle was curiously scuffed and ripped.

'What I don't understand, Langham, is why the blazes they want the money placed in the valise?'

Langham shook his head. 'I can't begin to guess.'

He read the note again.

The professor said, 'What do you suggest?'

'If I were you, I'd go to the police.'

'No!' Robertshaw growled. 'The last people I want involved – bunch of incompetents, in my opinion. I'll handle this in my own way.'

Langham sat back in the armchair and regarded the professor.

'The other day, you said you had no idea what the blackmailer wanted – if, indeed, the letter was meant for you. Now that we know it is, are you any the wiser?'

He watched the old man as he wrestled with whether or not to come clean. At last, he shook his head, his jowls wobbling. 'Dashed mystery, old boy.'

'Then perhaps I can help you on that score, Professor.'

'What?' Robertshaw sounded shocked.

'Let me hazard a guess at what the blackmailer knows.'

The professor muttered, 'I think this calls for a drink.' He poured himself a slug of Scotch. 'You?'

'Far too early for me, Professor. I haven't had my porridge yet.'

Robertshaw took a swig, swilled it around his gums as if it were mouthwash, then said, 'Go on, then, dammit!'

'Whoever sent you the missives, whoever is attempting to extort a hundred pounds from you – for starters, is my guess – knows that you're having an affair with Deirdre, your ex-wife.'

The professor's lined face crumpled. He stared at the rug, blinking, then looked up at Langham like a kicked dog. 'How the blazes do you know?' he muttered.

'I'm a private detective. You asked for my help. I investigated the case.'

They sat in silence for a time, the fire crackling away.

'What do I do?' the professor asked.

'As I said, if I were you, I'd go to the police. But you don't want to do that, for your own reasons.' Langham shrugged. 'I take it you don't want your secret to be made public?'

'Too damned right I don't.'

'Can you afford to part with a hundred pounds?'

'Just about.'

'Then follow the instructions to the letter. Do you have the cash to hand?'

'No, and certainly not in used fivers. I'll have to make a detour to the bank in town.'

'Do that, and then leave the money in the valise by the park bench.'

'Then sit twiddling my thumbs, waiting for the greedy blighter to ask for more?'

Langham shook his head. 'I'll be in the park, concealed. I can't promise anything, but I'll do my best to apprehend who-ever's behind this. They're committing a criminal act, and the police will come down on them like a ton of bricks.'

'But wouldn't that mean my secret—?'

'Adultery isn't a criminal offence. There's a fair chance we could keep it from getting out.'

The old man had the good grace to look contrite. 'Look at it from my point of view, Langham. Xandra is dying, and then, out of the blue, I bump into Deirdre. I . . . I never really stopped loving her, you know? I hated her, of course, for a while after she walked out on me. But a part of me always loved the damned woman.'

The professor hesitated, then went on, 'She left me for someone else, twenty years ago, but the chap died a while back. They were living abroad at the time, and she returned to England. We met quite by chance last year and . . . well, one thing led to another.' He stopped and looked directly at Langham. 'I wrestled with what I desired, Langham. I tried to talk myself out of it.' He smiled sadly. 'But the flesh is weak. I no longer loved Xandra – and I couldn't resist what Deirdre was offering. And, God help me, for the past few months I've been a very happy man.' He finished his whisky. 'Until now, that is. Now I'm being made to pay, aren't I?'

Langham sighed. 'Let's see how this pans out,' he said, 'and take it from there.'

'Thank you, Langham. You know, I feel a little bit better for getting that off my chest.'

Langham considered the initial blackmail letter. 'There's one thing that puzzles me,' he said, watching the professor closely. 'In that first letter, the blackmailer wrote: "If you don't pay up, Nancy will find out." But why does the blackmailer think that Nancy would be overly concerned – or, rather, why does he or she think that *you* wouldn't want Nancy to know about your affair? Surely the person you wouldn't want knowing is Xandra?'

The professor pursed his lips as he contemplated the question. He appeared to be genuinely puzzled. At last, shaking his head, he said, 'I honestly don't know, Langham. Unless, of course, they meant to write Xandra, not Nancy.'

'There is that possibility,' Langham said, but didn't believe it for one second.

'So what now?' the professor asked.

'As I said, obey the instructions. Go to your bank, withdraw a hundred pounds in used five-pound notes, then leave it at the designated park bench and walk away. Leave the rest to me. We'll meet up at four o'clock in the public bar of the Old Swan on the High Street in Hemshall. If I'm not there by four thirty, come back here and I'll contact you later. Understood?'

The professor nodded. 'Thank you again,' he said.

Langham said he'd show himself out, then left the manor and made his way home.

Over breakfast, he recounted his conversation with Professor Robertshaw. Maria listened in silence, then said, 'Be careful, Donald. If this person realizes that you're—' She stopped. 'I've just had a flash of déjà vu. That time, two years ago, when you delivered the cash to the blackmailer and received a cosh over the head for your pains . . .'

'Don't worry, I'll be more careful this time.'

He assisted her with the unpacking until midday, had a leisurely sandwich and a cup of tea, then set off for Market Hemshall, a small town five miles east of Ingoldby, at one o'clock.

Langham parked the Rover outside a tea room across the road from the park, facing away from the town centre. He reasoned that if the blackmailer arrived by car, then he or she would desire a quick getaway into the country rather than risk a delay going through the busy town. If need be, he could follow at a moment's notice.

The snow had held off and the sun shone, bright but without heat. He left the car and made a casual circuit around the periphery of the park, a journey of perhaps a mile and a half which took him thirty minutes. The park was accessed by three entrances, one to the east, another to the west, and the third from the north. Stone lions guarded each entrance atop high stone pillars.

He returned to the east entrance and strode into the park, his pace brisk as if he were simply a pedestrian taking the shortest route between two points. A wide tarmacked pathway linked the three entrances, bordered by clumps of hydrangea and rhododendron and empty flower beds. Park benches lined the path on both sides, positioned every twenty yards. He passed the first bench to his left; it was backed by a stand of elm which would provide inadequate cover. However, thirty yards away across snow-covered grass was a desolate-looking bandstand. He wondered if it was too obvious a place for him to lie in wait.

He could see why the blackmailer had selected this place as the drop-off point. Other than himself, it was deserted. Pigeons vied with crows for scant pickings in the snow, their flurries of activity providing the only sign of movement in the park.

He emerged from the northern entrance and followed the railings of the periphery around to the east. He consulted his watch. It was just after two o'clock. He would warm himself with a hot drink in the tea room and make his move at two thirty, employ the bandstand as an observation post and await developments.

He ordered a cup of black tea and sat at a window table, wiping a porthole in the condensation with the cuff of his coat. From here he had a clear view of the road and the eastern entrance to the park, should the blackmailer show himself early. He sipped his tea and kept a lookout.

Fifteen minutes later, a maroon Vauxhall pulled up behind his Rover and a smartly dressed, middle-aged couple climbed out and hurried back into town. He dismissed them immediately as not having the demeanour of citizens bent on blackmail.

He kept an eye on the entrance, but not a soul entered the park or emerged from it. Few people passed the tea room, and those that did so hurried with the express intention of getting out of the freezing east wind as soon as possible.

He glanced at his watch. It was almost half past two. He finished his tea, left the premises and, rather than enter the park by the eastern entrance in case the blackmailer was observing, he walked clockwise around the park and used the northern entrance.

Ensuring that there was no one about to witness his curious behaviour, he stepped off the path behind a growth of rhododendron and made his way under cover of shrubbery around the inner periphery of the park towards the bandstand. The soil was wet, and he wished he'd thought to wear his gumboots. By the time he came to the margin of the shrubbery and halted, his brogues were caked in mud.

He had intended to conceal himself behind the bandstand, but better still was an evergreen bush beside it. He slipped from the shrubbery and quickly crossed the snow to the bush, crouched and duck-walked into the boscage. He manoeuvred himself into a comfortable position, lowered a spray of leaves and peered out. He had an unimpeded view of the path and the designated park bench, and was confident that he was perfectly concealed from suspicious eyes. He looked at his watch. It was five to three.

At one minute to three, he saw movement at the eastern entrance. The shambling figure of Professor Robertshaw, dressed in a Crombie coat and deerstalker, the battered leather valise tucked under his right arm, strode into the park and approached the first bench on the left of the path. The old man looked around, his attitude suspicious, as if he expected the blackmailer to be lurking in plain sight.

The professor came to the bench, paused, looked ahead and then behind him to ensure that he was unobserved – for all the world like a ham actor playing the part of a spy in a bad B-movie – then placed the valise next to the bench's iron leg. His duty done, he walked on without looking back and disappeared from sight around the bend of the pathway.

Watching, Langham was aware of his increased heartbeat as he prepared himself to emerge and follow the blackmailer. He estimated he could cover the distance between his present position and the bench in ten seconds, the snow notwithstanding.

A minute later, a black Ford Popular passed beyond the park entrance, pulled into the side of the road and parked just out of sight. He heard the car engine cut out and waited, counting the seconds.

After a minute, the expected figure failed to appear. He inhaled the cold air and steadied his breathing.

Something moved to his left, entering the park, and Langham tensed. He relaxed immediately when he saw that the newcomer was merely a dog – a medium-sized brown and white foxhound that trotted perkily along the path. He glanced left and right, but there was no sign of human activity. He settled down to resume his vigil, wondering how long it might be before the blackmailer chose to show himself.

The park was silent and deathly still; even the pigeons and crows had departed. A wind started up, freezing him. He rubbed his hands and willed the blackmailer to hurry up.

He returned his attention to the dog, which had increased its pace along the path. As he watched, incredulous, it dashed to the bench, grabbed the handle of the valise in its teeth, then turned and sprinted back along the path to the entrance.

Thus the scuff marks on the handle were explained . . .

The dog shot through the entrance and disappeared from sight.

Langham dashed from his hiding place. He had intended to set off like a sprinter from the blocks, but the reality was somewhat different. Encumbered by shoes clogged with soil, and impeded by lashing fronds, he fought his way free of the bush and staggered across the snow-covered grass, slipping and slithering as he went. He would admit, later, that he must have presented a comical sight as he chased the canine accomplice to blackmail, but at the time he was both frustrated that in all likelihood the dog had made its escape and annoyed with himself for not foreseeing such an ingenious pick-up.

He heard a car door slam and an engine gun into life before he reached the stone pillars of the entrance. By the time he swung on to the pavement, the Ford Popular was at the end of the road and turning left, heading out of town.

Langham sprinted across the road, slipped in behind the wheel of his Rover and started the engine. He pulled out into the road and accelerated, turned left and scanned the road ahead for the

Ford. He caught a glimpse of it disappearing around a right turn between rows of houses. He increased his speed, thankful that the road was quiet. He came to the street and swung right. There was no sign of the car on the short road, which terminated in a T-junction. He came to the end of the street, pulled out a couple of yards, peered right and left, and swore heartily. The car had vanished.

He had two options. The road to the right headed back into town; the road left meandered south into the countryside. He chose to turn south, reasoning that the Ford would be easier to spot in the snow-covered country than in the built-up town – though at this stage he was grasping at straws and trusting in blind luck.

He accelerated through the outskirts of the town, and presently the semi-detached villas on either side of the road fell away to be replaced by rolling, snow-blanketed farmland. Ahead, he made out the grey ribbon of the road, undulating up and down hill and vale. There was no sign of the Ford Popular. He imagined the wily foxhound standing up on the back seat and peering through the rear window, its tail wagging in glee as its owner made good his escape.

He swore to himself again, and then had to laugh as he imagined Maria's reaction when he regaled her with his sorry tale.

He drove for another two miles and came to the crest of a low rise. He cut the engine and slowed to a halt, then climbed out and scanned the land ahead. Under any other circumstances, he would have admired the beauty of the panorama, with the open land, scintillating under the low afternoon sun, stretching away for miles to the hazed horizon. All he felt at the sight, however, was frustration at the fact that there were no black cars to be seen on any of the narrow lanes that threaded their way through the countryside.

Reluctantly, he made a three-point turn in the opening to a farmer's field and headed back into Market Hemshall.

He would have a consolatory pint at the Old Swan, explain his abject failure to the professor, then make his way home in the hope that Maria had cooked something heart-warming for dinner.

*   *   *

He parked outside the public house, found an oily rag in the boot and did his best to make his mud-covered brogues half-respectable. It was after four o'clock when he entered the public bar and found Professor Robertshaw ensconced at a corner table with a small glass of sherry and smoking a cherrywood pipe. He ordered a pint of Fuller's and joined the professor, rehearsing his opening gambit.

His demeanour obviously forewarned the old man, as the professor said, 'No luck, Langham?'

'I'm sorry.' He took a long drink of bitter.

The professor sank back against the banquette. 'I take it you caught sight of the blighter, though?'

'I'm sorry,' he said again. 'Not even that.'

'But how the blazes—?'

Langham sighed and placed his pint glass exactly on the centre of a beer mat. 'Do you know anyone who owns a foxhound?' he asked.

The professor regarded him as if he'd taken leave of his senses. 'Come again?'

Langham repeated the question.

'A foxhound? What the blazes?'

'Recall those scuff marks on the handle of the valise?'

Robertshaw lowered his bushy eyebrows. 'What about 'em?'

'They were made by the teeth of a dog, a foxhound, trained to pick up the valise.'

'You mean to say we were outfoxed by a foxhound!'

Langham smiled. 'That's one way of putting it,' he admitted. 'The dog trotted into the park, as happy as you like, snatched up the valise and jumped into a waiting car. I gave chase, but the driver lost me.'

'You didn't get its registration?'

'Too far away.'

'Well,' the professor muttered, 'I suppose you did your best.'

Langham took another mouthful of ale. 'I suspect that the driver saw me in his rear-view mirror, so I shouldn't think they'd use that pick-up ruse again. I'm sorry.'

The old man scowled. 'What did the note say? That if I

inform the police or anyone else, I'll pay the price? You think they'll spill the beans?'

'Hard to tell. That might just have been an idle threat. If they do reveal your secret, then they're killing the goose that lays the golden eggs – and my guess is that the blackmailer is motivated by greed. I think they'll lie low for a while, then demand another pay-out.'

The professor swore and knocked back his sherry.

'So,' Langham said, 'I take it you know no one who owns a foxhound?'

'No, not a soul.'

'What about anyone who drives a black Ford Popular – though I suspect the blackmailer was taking no chances and probably stole the car.'

Robertshaw shook his head. 'No one springs to mind, Langham. So, what do we do now?'

'There's not a lot we can do,' he admitted, 'other than sit tight and wait.'

'Not to worry, old boy.' The professor laughed. 'Who would have foreseen they'd use a bloody dog, hmm?'

Langham smiled at that and drained his pint.

He asked the professor if he could stand him another sherry, but Robertshaw said he'd better be making tracks, gathered his deerstalker and left the pub.

Langham considered a second pint, then thought better of it and drove home.

Maria was in the kitchen, peeling potatoes at the sink. She turned, smiling, when he entered the room, but her smile faltered when she saw his expression.

'What? The blackmailer got away?'

'I'll say they did. I was well and truly stymied.'

She looked alarmed. 'You're not hurt?'

'The only thing that's hurt is my pride,' he admitted.

'What happened?'

He sat down on a dining chair, braced his hands on his thighs and laughed.

'Donald?' she said, laughing also, but a little uncertainly.

'The valise . . .' he began, '. . . the valise . . . was picked up by a ruddy dog!' And he explained the farrago in the park.

'Oh!' she said, wide-eyed. 'Oh, you poor man!' Then her concerned expression collapsed and she laughed. 'A *dog*?'

It was almost worth the abject failure to witness Maria's tearful mirth.

ELEVEN

'What I really like about moving house,' Maria said the following morning, 'is meeting new people. There they were, existing before you knew them, with their own lives, cares and concerns, and then you move in and meet them. And it's almost as if you've known them for years and can't believe that you *didn't* know them before.' She paused. 'Am I making sense, Donald?'

They were in the master bedroom, unpacking boxes. Donald was prying open the hardboard lid of a packing crate to reveal folded bed linen. He looked up and smiled. 'Perfect sense, my sweet. I was thinking just that the other day in the pub with Roy – I felt as if I'd known him for a long time.'

'Take Nancy – I feel so close to her, despite the age difference and everything else.'

'Everything else? You mean despite your worldly sophistication and her gauche naivety? Despite your intellectual superiority?'

She threw a duster at him. 'I don't feel intellectually superior at all. Despite our differences, we're still close.'

'Maybe she reminds you, on some level, of your chums at boarding school in Gloucestershire. Where do you want these?'

'In the chest of drawers.' She laid her head on one side, considering. 'There is something schoolgirlish about her, isn't there?'

Donald slipped the folded sheets into the drawer. 'She's led a sheltered existence. Straight from boarding school to looking after her aunt.' He hesitated. 'I hope she and Roy hit it off.'

'They're certainly attracted to each other,' she said. 'I just hope the combined forces of Professor Robertshaw and Randall don't conspire to nip their romance in the bud.'

'The prof's just a reactionary old duffer,' he said.

'And Randall?'

'A privileged, arrogant, self-centred . . .'

She looked at him. 'Go on – a self-centred what?'

'I was going to say "egotist", but that would be tautological, wouldn't it?'

She helped him unpack the crate and put the bed linen away in the drawers, considering the other people she'd met, and liked, in the village since the move.

'What do you think of the Wellbournes?' she asked.

'I like Richard. He seems a solid, dependable, open sort of chap. I can't say I've spoken to Harriet that much. She seems a little . . . what's the word? Odd?'

'But in a nice way?'

'Oh, she's harmless enough.' He laughed.

'It's interesting how they seem to have unconsciously replaced their son with Roy Vickers, isn't it?'

He looked at her. 'What makes you think it's unconscious?'

She pressed a top sheet flat and pushed the drawer shut. 'I don't know. I just assumed it was. Do you think it was intentional, their offering him the caravan? I mean, of course they knew they were offering it, but that they were conscious of replacing their son in doing so?'

He frowned. 'I honestly don't know—'

They were startled by a sudden hammering on the back door. Maria, closest to the landing, rushed downstairs, along the hall and into the kitchen. A shape moved beyond the pebbled glass, swollen out of all recognition. It raised a hand and hammered again.

She crossed to the door and pulled it open, Donald behind her.

Roy Vickers stood on the threshold. The first thing she noticed was his expression of wild-eyed shock; the second, the pair of binoculars that hung around the turned-up collar of his greatcoat.

'Roy?'

He turned and pointed down the garden towards the manor house. 'There! I noticed it earlier,' he said, hardly making sense. 'I ran to get Richard, but he's out somewhere in the top field. So I grabbed these.' He lifted the binoculars. 'Look!'

He passed her the binoculars and she raised them to her eyes. 'Where am I looking?'

'Straight ahead. Through the trees, beyond the stream.'

'All I can see is trees. Oh, there we are . . . But what's going on?' The image was out of focus. All she could make out was blurred images of people, a big blue van and a few cars parked behind the manor.

She adjusted the focus and the scene sprang into life. Half a dozen uniformed police officers and several plainclothes men were congregated around the standing stone and seemed to be examining something at its base.

'The thing is,' Vickers was saying, 'I can't make out Nancy among the crowd, and when I saw what was going on . . . I rang the manor from the farmhouse. Nancy usually answers, but there was no reply. I'm worried.'

'Can I see?' Donald said.

Maria passed him the binoculars and he pressed them to his eyes, adjusting the focus. 'A few forensic fellows . . . and that's Montgomery.' He lowered the binoculars and looked at Roy Vickers. 'Montgomery's a detective inspector from Bury – I've worked with him a couple of times in the past. If he's been called in, it's serious.'

Vickers swore. Maria reached out and took Donald's hand. 'We'd better go round.' She turned to the young man. 'Come in while we get our coats.'

She ran off to fetch their coats and boots. They dressed quickly in the kitchen and followed Vickers from the house, not bothering to lock the back door.

They hurried along Crooked Lane, slipping and sliding in the snow. A fresh fall had come down during the night and lay across the land to the depth of a foot or more.

'I'm sure it's nothing to do with Nancy,' Maria said. 'And there'll be a good reason she hasn't answered the phone. It's probably being used by the police.'

'But it wasn't engaged!' Vickers shouted against the wind.

'Even so, there'll be a perfectly good reason, you'll see.'

Vickers looked from Maria to Donald. 'You said a forensic team . . . But they're only used in the event of murders, right?'

Maria looked at Donald; he was grim-faced. 'Not exclusively.'

'Christ!' Vickers said, increasing his pace.

Maria found Donald's hand as they hurried after the distraught young man.

They crossed the bridge and made their way down the lane, then turned right into the drive of Standing Stone Manor.

Two squad cars were drawn up before the house, and a uniformed constable stood like a sentry before the manor's open front door.

Nancy's dog bounded from the house, its tail lashing in delight at seeing them. He dropped his tennis ball at Maria's feet and looked up at her pleadingly.

'Not now, boy,' she said. She picked up the ball, meaning to lob it back into the house. Instead, it hit an ornamental flower urn beside the door and bounced off under Randall's Morgan parked to the right of the house. She bent down and retrieved the ball from the gravel beneath the car. This time she succeeded in throwing it through the door and into the hall. Bill bounded into the house and the constable obligingly pulled the door shut.

She rejoined the others and they hurried on, Donald leading the way around the house. A hundred yards across the snow, the grey standing stone loomed tall against the blue winter sky. A police photographer stood beyond the stone, taking pictures of something at its foot.

'Wait!' Donald said, halting Maria and Vickers. 'We'd better not trample those prints.'

He pointed to a track of footprints in the snow, leading from the French windows at the back of the house across to the standing stone. Another, fresh set of footprints formed a long curve from the side of the house to the stone. He led the way along this second path, evidently made by the investigating officers.

Maria felt suddenly sick. Three or four men in boilersuits were minutely examining the snowy ground, incongruously down on all fours.

Whatever was on the other side of the stone was hidden from view.

Detective Inspector Montgomery stood to one side, a small, bald-headed man smoking a cigarette with an air of studied detachment.

Roy Vickers stopped dead in his tracks. He turned to Maria,

his expression one of fraught apprehension. 'It's Nancy, I know it is!'

'What makes you think—?'

'Because I love her! I've found her, and now this . . .'

'Wait here,' Donald said.

Montgomery looked up as Donald approached. 'Langham? What the blazes are you doing here?'

The two men spoke in lowered tones while Maria and Vickers looked on.

Montgomery pointed to something on the other side of the stone, as if inviting Donald to take a look. Maria watched him hesitate, then step forward. He raised a shocked hand to his brow, then turned and hurried back to them.

'Donald?' Maria said, her voice catching.

Beside her, Roy Vickers was trembling.

Donald walked back to them, his face ashen. 'It's not Nancy,' he said. 'She's fine. She's in the house.'

Vickers swore with relief.

Maria said, 'Then who . . .?'

Vickers turned and ran back to the manor.

Half a dozen scaffolding boards had been arranged to protect the crime scene. Maria stepped on to a board, rounded the stone and stared down at the body.

Professor Robertshaw sat with his back against the stone. Lying in the snow a little way from his upturned right hand was a grey service revolver. A bullet hole the size of a half-crown coin had shattered the bone of his temple. His jaw hung open and his eyes stared across the snow to the trenches a hundred yards away. A rubber-encased torch, still switched on, lay in the snow to the professor's left.

She looked from the corpse to Donald. He was staring down at the professor, and she saw something calculating in her husband's eyes.

'Donald,' she murmured, 'do you think what happened yesterday—?'

He shook his head. 'He was left-handed,' he said.

'What?'

'The professor was left-handed. I noticed that yesterday when he poured himself a Scotch.'

She swallowed and looked at the revolver lying next to the right hand.

'He didn't kill himself, Maria. He didn't take his own life in reaction to being blackmailed.'

Montgomery joined them and Donald began to explain. The detective inspector stopped him with an officiously raised hand. 'We know that, Langham. It was pretty obvious from the outset. This is murder, plain and simple, clumsily made to look like suicide.'

'The size of the wound?'

Montgomery nodded. 'Forensics reckon the revolver was fired from a distance of at least three feet, and the chap's arm isn't that long, is it? And as you say, he was left-handed, which his son Randall verified when I questioned him.' He pointed at the weapon lying in the snow. 'It's the professor's own service revolver, according to his son.'

'Did Randall discover the body?' Donald asked.

'We received a call from him at a little after six this morning.'

'He heard the shot?'

'Apparently not. Professor Robertshaw's been dead for approximately twelve hours. Forensics put the time of his killing between eight and midnight. Randall stated that he couldn't sleep and went out for a walk at five thirty. As he was passing along the lane' – Montgomery pointed across the stream to Crooked Lane – 'he happened to look across and see a body slumped against the stone. He hurried back and made the discovery.'

'Oh, the poor man,' Maria said.

'The fellow's pretty shaken up, and no mistake,' Montgomery said.

Donald gestured to the trodden snow around the body. 'Any decent prints?'

'Due to last night's snowfall, not many good ones. We've taken snaps of a dozen partials and might make something of them. We'll be attempting to match the prints with the foot-wear of locals later today.' Montgomery finished his cigarette, was about to flick it to the ground, then thought better of it. He nipped out the burning end and slipped the butt into the breast pocket of his overcoat.

Maria heard a sound coming from the house. She turned and looked up. A window in the upper storey, just under the eaves, was wide open and a figure was leaning out and waving.

'Maria!' Nancy cried. Even at this distance, the girl appeared distraught.

Maria said to Donald, 'I'd better go to her.'

'Of course.'

She turned and hurried across to the manor.

TWELVE

The constable previously stationed at the door of the house was now leaning into the squad car, speaking into the radio handset. Maria hurried past him and slipped into the manor.

As she moved towards the stairs, she passed the open door to what she assumed was the library. Randall Robertshaw sat at the far end of a long table with a bottle of brandy before him, his chin lodged on his fist in a desolate recapitulation of Rodin's *The Thinker*.

She hurried past the door and up the sweeping staircase. At the top, she found a door behind which was a narrow flight of stairs leading to what had been the servants' quarters.

She was about to reach out for the handle when the door opened and Roy Vickers appeared.

'You found her—?' Maria began.

He nodded. 'I'm going to get her a stiff drink.'

He moved past her, and she ran up the staircase.

She found Nancy in the third bedroom along a narrow landing. The girl sat on the edge of her bed in an untidy room strewn with piles of books, scattered clothing and shoes. A dressing table stood against the wall at the foot of the bed, littered with bottled perfumes, lipsticks and compacts. An old teddy bear lay on the bed beside the girl, face down, as if she had quickly discarded it on hearing Maria's approach.

Nancy looked up when Maria appeared and halted in the doorway. Her eyes were red, contrasting with her pale face. Her golden curls were an uncombed tangle.

Maria sat on the bed and pulled the girl to her.

'He's dead,' Nancy said. 'I heard all the cars at six and came down. Randall told me. He said my uncle had shot himself.' She shook her head as if in shock. 'But he wouldn't do that, would he, Maria? Why would he shoot himself?'

Maria stroked the girl's hair, then kissed her head. She tried hard to find words that would not sound trite or crass. 'I'm sorry. It's terrible, but you have friends, and Roy. We'll be here – all right?'

The girl nodded, and something in Maria's words, or simply her presence, caused Nancy to break down and sob on to Maria's shoulder. She held the girl tight, unable to prevent her own tears.

'Xandra had a restless night,' Nancy said a little later, sniffing. 'I was with her after dinner, and she asked me to sleep in her room. She often does. I have a small camp bed made up, so I can be on hand. Xandra slept fitfully, but I could hardly sleep. Randall . . . when I saw Randall this morning, he said that my uncle had taken his service revolver and gone out there . . . Randall said the police thought he died about ten last night.' She opened her hands, palms upwards, in a curiously helpless gesture. 'I must have been asleep by then, and I didn't hear a thing.' She looked at Maria, appealing. 'But why would he have done that? Why would he have killed himself like that, Maria? What about everyone he loved? Didn't he think about what he was doing?'

Maria pressed her lips to the girl's head again, not so much to comfort her as to hide her own conflicted expression.

'Perhaps . . . I don't know,' Nancy went on, 'but perhaps it was something Richard said to him?'

'Richard Wellbourne?'

'He came to see my uncle last night. I answered the door. I could tell he was angry about something. He wanted to see my uncle, so I took him through to the study.'

'Did he want to see the professor about the disputed land?'

'I don't know. He didn't say.' She shrugged. 'But I suspect it was something to do with that.'

'Do you know what time Richard left?'

'I let him in about eight, and not long after that Xandra called me. I heard raised voices shortly after I showed Richard into the study, and then I heard the French windows open and they went outside.'

'Are you *sure* they went outside?'

'I saw them, a little later, from the window on the staircase when I went up to see to Xandra. They were striding around the standing stone, gesturing to the land beyond. Maybe it was something Richard said that made my uncle . . .'

Her voice had risen, and Maria calmed her. 'I don't think so. I'm pretty sure that the professor had come across some deeds which stated the land belonged to him . . .' She trailed off. 'Do you know what time Richard left?'

The girl shook her head. 'I'm sorry, no. I went back upstairs to Xandra.'

'Did Richard come by car – did you by any chance hear it when he drove off?'

'No, he walked. There was no sign of his car when I answered the door.' She hesitated. 'Do you think it important, Maria – about Richard?'

'Perhaps he could tell the police what kind of mood your uncle was in when he left him,' she said, her mind racing. 'It might be of some help.'

She looked through the window. All she could make out, from this angle, was an expanse of blue sky, the tops of distant trees and the knuckled summit of the standing stone. The thought of what sat beneath it made her shiver.

She asked, 'Does Xandra . . .?'

'Randall told her, and then I gave her a sleeping draught and left her. That was about seven. What time is it now?'

Maria looked at her wristwatch. 'Just after eleven.'

The girl exclaimed. 'I'd better go and see if she's awake. She'll be in a terrible state. Oh, I don't know how I'll cope, Maria!'

'I'll come with you.'

'Would you? That's kind. She likes you.'

Maria looked at the girl, surprised. 'She does?'

'When you left the other day, Xandra said how much she enjoyed meeting you and Donald. She said you were a lovely person.'

Maria squeezed her hand. 'Come on, let's go and see if she's awake.'

They left the tiny bedroom and made their way single file down the narrow staircase. Nancy led Maria along the carpeted landing to a door at the far end of the corridor, knocked gently, then entered.

Maria had expected to find the woman in bed, if not still sleeping then prostrated by the death of her husband. She was surprised to see Xandra up and dressed in a canary-yellow silk trouser suit redolent of the 1930s. She stood with her back to the door, staring through the window. Even at a distance, the rasp of her breathing was loud.

She failed to acknowledge their arrival, other than to say, as if to herself, 'He didn't kill himself, you know – it wasn't suicide.'

Nancy stopped in her tracks, staring at her aunt. 'What?'

Xandra turned and stared at them. Her eyes appeared sunken, haunted. 'He wasn't the type,' she wheezed. 'Egotists don't take their own lives. Their existence is too precious for that.'

Maria came to Nancy's side and slipped an arm around her thin shoulders. Nancy sagged against her, moaning softly.

'What do you mean?' the girl murmured. 'Randall said—'

'What does Randall know about anything like that?' Xandra said. 'He's a banker, not a psychologist.'

'Can I get you a drink?' Maria asked. 'Perhaps a cup of tea?'

'I'd like a bloody large brandy,' Xandra said. She turned and stared through the window which overlooked the stream and the village beyond.

'Xandra, I don't think that would be a very good idea,' Nancy said tentatively.

'Stop being such a bloody officious little nursemaid and get me a brandy! You'll find a bottle in the escritoire, and a glass.'

Maria murmured, 'I really don't think . . .'

'Then I'll help myself,' Xandra said. She moved to the escritoire, found the half-empty bottle and poured a small measure with a shaking hand.

She knocked back half the glass, pursed her lips bitterly, then looked from Nancy to Maria. That she had once been an actress was apparent: she had lost none of her ability to hold an audience, despite her debilitation. She had presence, poise and timing. She said, 'Everyone hated him, you know.'

She pointed to a chaise longue. 'Sit down, both of you. And please stop staring at me as if I were a ghost.'

They sat down as ordered, and Xandra carried a hoop-backed chair from her dressing table and sat before them.

'You don't know that he was . . . was killed,' Nancy said. 'You've no evidence.'

Maria saw something supercilious in the older woman's eyes. 'I knew my husband, Nancy. We've been together for twenty years; I know what kind of man he was. He was a self-centred bigot who made enemies easily because he considered only himself and didn't give two damns what people thought of him.'

Nancy shook her head. 'I . . . I didn't know you hated him so.'

Xandra sipped her drink. 'I'm not sure that I did hate him. A part of me loved him – certainly in the early years. He could be a pain, but then show me the man who isn't. What I did hate about him was how he never considered the feelings of others. He lacked the ability to *empathize*.'

'But who hated him so much they would have . . .?' Nancy gestured feebly, unable to say *murdered him*.

Maria wondered when Xandra's love for her husband had turned to apathy, and then to the cold dispassion that allowed her to be so analytical so soon after his death.

Was the woman aware that her husband had been having an affair with his ex-wife? That, Maria thought, might explain her behaviour.

'Believe me,' Xandra said, 'people were lining up to have a pot-shot at Edwin. Many would have drawn the line at murder, of course, but it would have taken only one soul whom my husband had pushed so far that they snapped, and perhaps in anger sought their revenge.'

She finished her brandy and looked across the room to the bottle on the table beside the kettle.

'You can go now,' she said.

The girl stood. 'Do you need anything?'

'Not at the moment, thank you, but perhaps a little lunch at noon, as I missed breakfast. Toast will suffice.'

The girl stood and moved to the table in the corner, clearly intending to take the brandy bottle, but Xandra said, 'You can leave that, thank you, Nancy. That will be all.'

The girl bit her lip, then moved to the door. Maria followed her from the room.

'She's not rational,' Nancy said as she pulled the door shut. She stared at Maria. 'I wonder . . . Do you think she found out about my uncle seeing Deirdre? Perhaps that's why she hates him and is saying awful things about him.'

They moved along the landing to the stairs, the girl lost in thought. 'I know my uncle was a difficult man to like,' she murmured, 'but he wasn't all those things she said he was.'

They came to the foot of the stairs. Roy Vickers appeared, clutching a bottle of whisky and two glasses.

Nancy crossed the hall and held him. As Maria watched, she wondered at their sudden intimacy. Before Saturday evening, when they had dined at Yew Tree Cottage, they had apparently met only briefly.

Apparently, she thought, smiling to herself.

She noticed movement to her left and turned to see Randall Robertshaw leaning against the open door of the library. He pushed himself upright with an effort and staggered along the hall, disappearing from sight.

Alarmed, Vickers said, 'Was that . . .?'

Nancy stroked his cheek. 'Ignore him,' she said.

Randall reappeared, weaving his way along the corridor. He stopped at the far end of the hallway, staring at them with an ugly expression on his lean face.

He was carrying a double-barrelled shotgun.

He took a step further into the hall and raised the gun at the couple.

Maria stepped forward, raising her hand. 'Randall . . .'

'Stop right where you are!' he cried, swinging the gun so that it pointed directly at her chest.

She halted, her pulse pounding.

Randall nodded, smiling his satisfaction, and brought the weapon to bear on Vickers and Nancy.

'Now get the hell out of here, Vickers, or you'll end up as dead as my father!'

THIRTEEN

'Let's get this straight,' Detective Inspector Montgomery said. 'You say Professor Robertshaw here was knocking off his ex-wife?'

'That's one way of putting it, yes,' Langham said.

'You have this on good authority?'

'My wife saw the professor and Deirdre dining together in the Midland Hotel on Monday, and Professor Robertshaw admitted it to me yesterday. According to Nancy, the professor's niece, it's been going on for a few months.'

'I understand the professor was married?'

'That's right.' He told Montgomery about Xandra's illness. 'She had tuberculosis a few years ago and was badly affected by the treatment. She's largely bedridden and hardly gets out.'

Montgomery lit another cigarette and stared down at the corpse. 'So the professor sought solace in the arms of his former wife,' he grunted. 'Do you know if this woman, this Deirdre, ever remarried?'

'According to the professor, she left him for someone else twenty years ago—'

'Open-and-shut case, then,' Montgomery interrupted. 'Jealous hubby doesn't like his wife playing fast and loose with a previous husband, and bang.'

'The only flaw in that argument,' Langham said, 'is that Deirdre's second husband died a few years ago.'

'Dammit,' Montgomery said. 'How about this, then – Xandra finds out about the professor and Deirdre, takes exception and shoots him?'

'Or it might be any of another dozen people,' Langham said. 'The professor had a way of annoying people. He was a cantankerous old duffer who assumed he was always in the right.'

'How well did you know him?'

'Not that well at all. He called me in because he wanted my professional help.'

'He was writing a book?'

'No, he was being blackmailed.'

Montgomery stroked his straggling moustache. 'Right. This is getting interesting.'

Langham explained about the first note, then the arrival of the second missive along with the leather valise. 'I advised him to see you chaps, but he wasn't having any of it.'

'No, you'd be surprised how many people on the end of blackmail threats prefer to handle it themselves. Often with dire consequences. What happened?'

'When he elected not to go to the police, I said he should follow the blackmailer's instructions and I'd stake out the drop-off point.'

He went on to describe, not without misgivings, the events of the previous day in the park.

His fears that Montgomery would enjoy his failure were not without grounds. Wide-eyed, the little detective stared at him. 'A dog?' he said. 'A bleeding dog snatched the valise and gave you the slip?'

'That's the long and short of it, yes.'

'Oh, that's ripe! That's precious! I can just picture the scene. Dog with case in its jaw and desperate man in pursuit! You must have looked a rare sight, Langham! Were there witnesses?'

'Not that I noticed. It was a raw day.'

'So you say this mutt jumped into a car, a Ford Pop, and off it shot?'

'I gave chase, but it was too late. They gave me the slip to the south of the town.'

'And you returned home with your tail between your legs? Sorry. It's just the image . . . Wait till I tell the boys back at the station!'

'If you could omit my name from the story, Montgomery, I'd be grateful.'

'That depends on how much I can rely on you in this case. It sounds as if it might be a bit more involved than I first thought.'

'It certainly looks that way,' Langham agreed. 'I'll give you any assistance I can, of course.'

'Good man,' Montgomery said. 'Jesus, but it's perishing.' He moved around the stone so that they were in its lee, though the wind still managed to find them.

'So someone knows the old prof is knocking off his ex and decides to extract the old spondulicks, starting high. A hundred nicker, eh? They meant business. Any ideas?'

Langham shook his head. 'I was hoping the blackmailer would be in touch, so I could have another crack at him.'

'Him *and* his dog?'

'Touché.' Langham smiled. 'But the chances are they wouldn't pull the trick with the dog twice.'

Montgomery drew on his cigarette and regarded its glowing tip. 'So Robertshaw was being blackmailed, then he turns up dead. Bit of a coincidence if they *aren't* connected, but I doubt the blackmailer would stiff his source of income.'

'Agreed,' Langham said.

'Righty-ho,' Montgomery said, 'let's go inside and get the questioning out of the way.'

Montgomery signalled to his detective sergeant, a portly man almost twice the inspector's size, and Langham accompanied them around the side of the house. They crunched across the snow-covered gravel and mounted the steps to the front door. As they entered the manor, Montgomery stopped in his tracks and swore to himself, and Langham saw what had brought him up short.

Randall Robertshaw stood at the far end of the hallway, directing a double-barrelled shotgun at Roy Vickers; Nancy and Maria stood to one side, holding on to each other.

Roy Vickers spread his hands placatingly, smiling at Randall, and took a step forward.

'I said get out or I'll shoot!' Randall exclaimed.

Langham expected Montgomery to show caution and attempt to cajole Randall into relinquishing his weapon, but the little detective had other ideas.

As Langham watched, Montgomery walked straight up to the young man, his hand outstretched. 'Hand it over, sonny. There's a good chap. We'll have no more killings around here, thank you very much.'

Randall blinked, non-plussed by the policeman's far from cowed demeanour. Montgomery gripped the shotgun by its barrel, directed it at the floor, then eased the weapon from Randall's grip.

He turned to the open front door and called out, 'Constable Grant. Here, if you please!'

The uniformed bobby rushed in, and Montgomery said, 'Lock this away somewhere safe, would you? As for you,' he went on, addressing the now contrite Randall, 'a little word or two in your shell-like. Into the library, if you would, laddie.'

Randall slipped meekly into the library, and Langham crossed to Maria, Nancy and Roy Vickers. The trio looked shaken, and Langham advised them to make themselves a hot drink. 'Montgomery will need a statement from you, Nancy, and he might even want to have a word with you, Roy. I'd hang about if I were you.'

'I'll take them to the kitchen,' Maria said, leading Nancy and Vickers along the corridor.

Montgomery joined Langham. 'Randall's had a drink or two – best time to catch 'em out. I spoke to him earlier: now to see if his story tallies when he has a drink inside him.'

'Mind if I sit in?'

'Don't see why I should mind, Langham; you've been helpful so far.'

Langham followed Montgomery and the detective sergeant into the library, and Montgomery closed the door behind them.

Randall Robertshaw was in the process of pouring himself another brandy with an unsteady hand; Montgomery didn't stop him.

The detective pulled up three chairs, placed them before Randall, and they sat down. Montgomery's detective sergeant took out his notebook and pencil, and Langham followed suit.

'So you say you discovered the body around five?' Montgomery began. 'You were walking on the other side of the river, and you looked across and saw your father.'

'Didn't know it was Pater then,' Randall said. He slumped in his seat, the brandy glass clutched in his right hand. 'And it wasn't five. Nearer six.'

'I know this isn't easy, sonny. But bear with me. We're on your side. We want to clear this up as soon as possible.'

The young man blinked. 'Clear it up?'

'Work out exactly what happened out there,' Montgomery
went on.

'What happened?' Randall shook his head. 'My father took
his service revolver from his desk, went out to his beloved
bloody standing stone and blew his brains out. That's what
happened.'

'I'm sorry,' Montgomery said, exhibiting a solicitude Langham had assumed was beyond the usually blunt detective. 'I'm
truly sorry, but I must inform you that your father didn't take
his own life. He was murdered.'

Randall blinked again, then said, '*Murdered?*'

Montgomery allowed time for Randall to process the fact,
then went on, 'Were you aware that your father was having an
affair?'

Randall was silent for a time, staring down at his drink and
blinking. At last, he said, 'Yes. Yes, I was. I . . . I overheard
him on the phone a while ago, arranging to meet someone.'

'Do you know who the woman was?'

He shook his head. 'No, and I didn't want to know. It was
sickening enough that I knew he was . . . he was doing this to
Mother. I certainly wasn't interested in learning the identity of
the blasted woman.'

'Was your father aware that you knew? Did you have it out
with him?'

'Good God, no.' Randall gave a mirthless laugh at the very
thought. 'How could I begin to broach something like that with
him? He wouldn't have countenanced my interference.' He
shook his head and waved a vague hand. 'We didn't discuss
emotions,' he finished.

'How would you describe your relationship with your father?'

'Strained might be the best word to use. We didn't see eye
to eye on many things. And . . . and when my wife left me,
and I came to stay here . . . he seemed to see that as *my* failure.'

Montgomery made a note of this, then asked, 'Now, I understand your mother is seriously ill.'

'That's right.'

'And did your father care for her?'

'No, he left that to my cousin, Nancy. Pater didn't lift a
finger in that regard. Their . . . their marriage wasn't successful,

as you might have surmised. They led what amounted to separate lives.'

'Just to set the record straight, and to allow me to get a picture of what happened here last night, can you account for your whereabouts and movements between the times of eight o'clock and midnight?'

Randall took a sip of brandy, pursed his lips as if considering, then nodded. 'Yes, I can. As a matter of fact, I was up in Bury. I was with my uncle, Doctor Spencer Robertshaw, who, as it happens, is treating my mother.'

'And his address?'

'The Willows, London Road. He has a flat above his surgery.'

Langham made a note of the address for future reference.

'How long did you spend with your uncle?' Montgomery asked.

Randall considered the question. 'I arrived around six. We had dinner, and for the rest of the evening we discussed business. It was close to half past twelve when I left, and almost one by the time I got back here.'

'You discussed business?'

'That's right. My uncle asked if I'd care to run the financial side of things at the Willows. We were discussing what the post would entail.'

'And did you accept the position?'

'I said I'd give it my serious consideration. That's why I couldn't sleep last night – and why I got up early and went for a long walk, to think through the offer.'

'I see,' Montgomery said, making extensive notes. 'And you're absolutely certain of those times, are you? You were at the Willows from six until approximately half past twelve?'

'Absolutely,' Randall said, 'and my uncle will be able to corroborate the fact, if you'd care to ask him.'

Montgomery said, 'Thank you for your time, Mr Robertshaw. Now, would you kindly inform your mother that I'd like a word?'

The young man climbed to his feet, reached out and took the brandy bottle, then made for the door.

'Oh, one more thing before you go,' Montgomery called over his shoulder, smiling to himself, 'don't leave the area before informing me of your intention to do so, if you'd be so kind.

And be very careful about waving firearms around in future. Because the next time I catch you at it, I'll be far from lenient. Understood?'

'Perfectly, Inspector,' Randall said, and slammed the door behind him as he left the room.

Montgomery laughed. 'Uppity little snob,' he said. 'What did you make of that, Langham?'

'Well, his alibi seems watertight – if his uncle can confirm it, of course.'

'So it seems,' Montgomery said. He looked at Langham. 'He mentioned that his wife left him. Do you happen to know why?'

Langham nodded. 'Apparently, she walked out when she found out he'd been unfaithful.'

Montgomery grunted. 'Like father, like son, eh?'

The door opened and Xandra Robertshaw entered the room, striking in a yellow silk trouser suit. She appeared stick-thin, pale and haggard. She had applied make-up, perhaps in a bid to give her face some colour. All the eyeshadow and lipstick succeeded in achieving, however, was to highlight her gaunt cheekbones and sunken eyes.

She seated herself on the chair her son had recently vacated and crossed her legs. 'I would appreciate it if you could confirm whether or not my husband was in fact murdered?'

Montgomery exchanged a glance with his detective sergeant, then said, 'What makes you think—?'

'As I've just told Nancy and your charming wife' – Xandra glanced at Langham – 'my husband was the last person in the world who'd take his own life. He was too much of an egotist for that.'

'Is that your only reason to suspect he was murdered?'

'Inspector, I knew the man intimately. He loved *his* life too much; he loved *his* hobbies and interests too much to relinquish them in such a way. He couldn't give a tinker's damn about anyone else – only himself. He was not the type to put so violent an end to his pleasures.'

Montgomery nodded, taking his time. 'And were you aware that your husband was having an affair, Mrs Robertshaw?'

Her poise faltered briefly. 'I . . . Yes, I suspected as much.'

'But you didn't confront him with your suspicions?'

'No, I did not.'

'And might I ask why not?'

She tipped her head slightly, considering. 'Perhaps because I didn't give a damn what he might have been up to, Inspector.'

'I take it that your relationship with your late husband was far from satisfactory?'

She gave him a venomous smile. 'You take it correctly, Inspector.'

Montgomery made a note of this.

'Now . . . I appreciate that this is a delicate question . . . but I understand that you suffered from TB, and that the treatment, though successful, had unforeseen consequences?'

'That's correct.'

'And the prognosis, if I might ask?'

'Touch and go, I think the saying is. I might die in a matter of months, or I might hang on for ages. But I've been ill now for years; one learns to live with the impending sentence of death.'

'And you're under the care of your husband's brother, Doctor Spencer Robertshaw?'

'Again, correct.'

'Now, finally, before I let you go, can you tell me where you were between eight and midnight last night?'

'Certainly. I was in my room. My niece, Nancy, will be able to confirm that, as she was with me all the time.'

'Did you hear the gunshot?'

'No, I didn't.'

Montgomery jotted this down in his notebook, then asked, 'I take it you employ servants?'

'A woman from the village comes in to cook in the afternoon,' Xandra said, 'and we have someone to come in and clean three times a week in the mornings. My husband is . . . was . . . somewhat thrifty when it came to hired help.'

Montgomery nodded. 'Thank you, Mrs Robertshaw. If you could send Nancy along – I think you might find her in the kitchen.'

Xandra Robertshaw rose without a word to either man and left the room.

'Cool customer,' Montgomery said.

'She has a hell of a lot to put up with – what with her illness and an errant husband.'

The inspector grunted. 'Seemed not at all put out at losing the latter, I must say. Maybe she hired an assassin.'

Langham smiled. 'Ah, now I recall that your humour did tend towards the black.'

The door opened and Nancy briskly entered the room, her bright smile directed at Langham contrasting with her red and swollen eyes.

'Hello, Donald, Inspector. I've never been interviewed by the police before. In fact, I don't even think I've ever spoken to a policeman.' She glanced from Montgomery to his deputy, smiling tremulously. 'Can you believe that?'

'Well, we're not all ogres,' Montgomery said. 'I'm so sorry about your uncle; I can't begin to imagine . . .'

'I have good friends around me,' Nancy said, beaming at Langham. 'Maria's been a brick.'

'I won't keep you long. I just want to ask a few routine questions, dotting the t's and crossing the i's kind of thing.'

'Of course, Inspector,' she said, smiling at his intentionally addled wordplay.

'I'll be brief. I understand you were with your aunt all night yesterday from . . .?'

'From just after eight, when she called me,' Nancy said, 'all through the night until I was awoken by the noise at six. Xandra wasn't feeling well, which is why I was with her.'

'Did you leave the room at all between the hours you mentioned?'

She thought about it. 'Once, around nine, to fetch some fresh tea from the kitchen, as we'd run out. Then at some point in the early hours, I went to the bathroom, which is *en suite*.'

'And did your aunt leave the room at all between eight and midnight?'

'Well, she might have gone to the bathroom, but if so, I didn't hear her. I was fast asleep before ten.'

'So from ten onwards, your aunt *might* have left the room?'

'Well, yes, she *might* have, Inspector. But I'm certain she wouldn't have gone outside. You see, she never goes out these days.'

Montgomery nodded. 'Thank you, miss.' He made a brief note, then asked, 'I wonder if I might ask about how you and your uncle got on? Were you close?'

Nancy hesitated. 'Unc was a funny old stick. He made it difficult for people to get close to him. I suppose it was his upbringing – that's what they say it's all down to these days, don't they?' She smiled. 'He could be prickly, and then at times very kind. Occasionally,' she finished bleakly, 'he'd buy me chocolates.'

The inspector closed his notebook with a flourish and smiled at the girl. 'There, over and done with, short and sweet. Nothing to fear, was there?'

Nancy smiled. 'Can I go now?'

'Off you pop,' Montgomery said.

She stood, then hesitated. 'I hope you don't mind my asking, Inspector, but I was wondering . . . You see, it's something that my aunt said, and she's rarely wrong with her intuitions. But . . . that is . . . well, she seems to think that my uncle was murdered.'

Langham watched as Montgomery's face creased with kindly paternalism. 'I'm sorry, my dear, but I fear that your aunt is right.'

Nancy smiled bleakly, suddenly sober. 'I thought so,' she said, then thanked them and walked from the room.

'Poor kid,' Montgomery commented when the door closed behind her. 'Right, I've just about done here. I think I'll go and see what else the forensic boys have found.'

The inspector stood and crossed to the door, accompanied by his bulky deputy. He turned to Langham and said, 'Do me a favour, would you, and keep your nose to the ground? I'd appreciate it if you slipped me the word if you came across anything interesting.'

'Will do,' Langham said.

He followed Montgomery and the detective sergeant from the library, then made his way to the kitchen. He found Maria sitting alone by the range, hugging a mug of tea.

'No sign of Nancy and Roy?' he asked.

'They've just disappeared upstairs.' She finished her tea. 'I think,' she went on as they left the kitchen and made their way across the hall, 'that Nancy hasn't told us the whole story about her and Roy.'

He turned his collar up against the east wind as they stepped from the manor and gave Maria a look. 'Meaning?'

'Oh, come on,' she said, tugging on his arm. 'They're far more intimate than they're letting on, Donald. My guess is that they've been lovers for weeks, even months.'

'My word. Well I never! What I'd give to have a bit of women's intuition!'

They crossed the bridge and turned along Crooked Lane.

'What are you doing this afternoon?' Maria asked.

'After a thick cheese sandwich before the blazing fire,' he said, 'I'm motoring up to Bury. I want to trace this Deirdre woman, then have a word with the professor's brother – he's the doctor who's treating Xandra. Apparently, Randall was with him all last night. I want to check the young man's alibi.'

'I'll have something nice ready for dinner when you get back,' Maria promised.

FOURTEEN

Langham drove up to Bury St Edmunds and parked beside the Midland Hotel.

He was working on the possibility – little more than a slight hope, he admitted – that the table at the hotel on Monday had been booked in the name of Professor Robertshaw's ex-wife. He was going on a suspicion that the professor would have been reluctant to provide his own details for fear of his deception coming to light. Of course, the couple might have used assumed names, in which case he would be forced to resort to other means in order to locate the professor's ex-wife.

A young woman with horn-rimmed glasses and an elaborate beehive hairstyle was at reception, poring over a ledger. He quickly flashed his accreditation, gave a winning smile and said that he would like to ask one or two questions regarding an ongoing police investigation.

She returned his smile and asked how she might be of assistance.

'I'm looking into the movements of one Professor Robertshaw and a woman by the name of Deirdre. I understand they dined here at lunchtime on Monday. Do you happen to know whether the table was booked by the professor or his lady friend?'

'One moment, sir.' She moved to an adjoining room and returned carrying a ledger. She ran a coral-pink fingernail down a long list of names. 'Here we are. The table was booked for twelve thirty. The professor and Mrs Creighton are regulars.'

'Mrs Creighton? I don't suppose you have her address or telephone number?'

'Mrs Creighton has an account with us.' She hesitated. 'You *are* with the police?'

'That's correct, the Bury St Edmunds constabulary.'

She turned to the wall where the key-rack hung; next to it was a shelf of thick morocco-bound ledgers. She withdrew one, flipped through its pages, then tapped an entry with her lacquered fingernail. 'Here we are. Mrs Deirdre Creighton, The Old Manse, Elm Lane, Renton.'

Langham copied the address into his notebook, thanked the young woman for her assistance and left the hotel.

Renton was a small village three miles north of Bury St Edmunds consisting of a Norman church, a post office and a row of shops clustered around a small village green with a duck pond and a pair of ancient stocks.

Langham stopped to ask a dog-walker for directions to Elm Lane and was directed back along the main street to the first turning on the left.

The Old Manse was a solitary Victorian pile set in grounds surrounded by elm trees. He pulled into the drive and approached the front door, not exactly relishing having to impart the news of the professor's death to his lover.

His knock was answered by a middle-aged woman he took to be a housemaid; she held a brush and pan in one hand and looked flustered. 'We don't buy from door-to-door—' she began.

'Donald Langham,' he said. 'I'm working with the Bury St Edmunds constabulary. Is Mrs Creighton at home?'

The woman blinked. 'The police?' She appeared even more flustered. 'Yes, madam is at home. If you'd care to follow me.'

He wiped his feet and followed the woman to a drawing room; she left him, and he moved to the window and looked out along a length of snow-covered lawn.

He turned a little later when he heard the door open.

Deirdre Creighton was a tall, elegant woman in her mid-fifties, impeccably dressed in a cream two-piece set off with a necklace of lustrous pearls. He thought her handsome rather than good looking; she wore her blonde hair swept back from a high forehead and had the poise and deportment of good breeding.

She advanced the length of the room and shook his hand. 'Mr . . .?'

He gave his name, and she directed him to a settee while she seated herself in a Queen Anne armchair. 'Milly said you were from the police?' She posed the statement as a question and smiled with genteel puzzlement.

'That's correct. I'm here regarding Professor Robertshaw. I understand you were recently . . . ah . . . reacquainted?'

'That's correct, Mr Langham.' She opened her eyes a little wider. 'Is something—?'

'I'm afraid I must inform you that Professor Robertshaw died at some point late yesterday.'

She took a quick indrawn breath, more a sip than a gasp. Her grey eyes were wide, staring at him, her expression frozen.

'I'm very sorry,' he murmured.

She shook her head. 'But how . . .?' She withdrew a crumpled handkerchief from a pocket and pressed it to her left eye, then to her right.

'He succumbed to a single gunshot wound,' he said, aware that he'd employed the euphemism that seemed appropriate to the circumstances.

'But Edwin would never . . .' she began.

'He didn't take his own life,' he said.

She shook her head. 'He was . . . murdered? But who would . . .?' She dabbed at her eyes again and sat back in her chair.

'That's what my colleagues and I are attempting to ascertain. I hope you don't mind if I ask you a few questions?'

'No. No, of course not.'

At the far end of the room, the door was nudged open a fraction and a grey Persian cat strode across the thick pile carpet with the same regal bearing as its owner. It pressed itself back and forth across his shins and he reached down and knuckled its head.

'Hermione,' Mrs Creighton called. 'Here!'

The cat obediently crossed the carpet and jumped on to the woman's lap; she stroked it absently while gazing out through the window.

'I understand that you were married to Professor Robertshaw a number of years ago?'

'For a little over ten years, yes. We married in 1925 and separated in '36.'

'Amicably?'

She gave a brittle smile. In the ensuing silence, he heard the throb of the cat's contented purring.

'Far from it, Mr Langham. Edwin was unfaithful.'

Langham opened his notebook and made a note. According to what the professor had told him the other day, it was Deirdre who had left him for another man.

'Unfaithful,' he repeated. 'Is that singly or . . .?'

'Is this really germane to the issue, Mr Langham?'

'In my experience, that might only become obvious when I've had time to assess every fact in hindsight.'

She sighed. 'I had been aware for a year or two that Edwin indulged himself in . . . flings, shall we say? On one occasion, I confronted him about one of them, and he was quite contrite. He insisted that it meant nothing and promised to mend his ways.' She shook her head, smiling in reflection. 'I loved him at the time, Mr Langham, so I believed him. Perhaps that was a mistake on my part. Perhaps I should have left him then, but it's so easy for one to be wise after the event, isn't it?'

'But the next time, you did leave him?'

'Six months later, he was at it again, and this time I had had enough. This time, his unfaithfulness devastated me.'

'Because he'd promised that it wouldn't happen again? Or,' he ventured, 'because of whom he had met? Was it serious, this time?'

'Oh, he was never serious, Mr Langham. That is, he had no intention of leaving me for these women. They were mere dalliances. He tried to make light of this one, too, but as far as I was concerned, enough was enough.'

'You left him?'

'I threw him out.'

Langham made a note of this. 'What kind of man was your ex-husband, Mrs Creighton?'

She stroked the cat's long, shining coat, her gaze absent. She said at last, 'He had a sharp mind and an overweening ego, which is always a fatal combination. He had an overwhelming self-regard and a complete lack of interest in other people. Because he was quick, he could argue that black was white and leave you feeling that it was you who were always in the wrong.'

He wrote all this down, aware that it corroborated much that Xandra had said about the professor earlier that day.

'I understand you remarried?'

'I met someone just before the war, an army captain, and we were very happy for the next sixteen years. He passed away in '54 – he was stationed in Gibraltar at the time – and I decided to come back to England – here, to Suffolk.'

Langham looked up from his notebook. 'Then, a few months ago, you decided to contact Professor Robertshaw?'

She smiled at him, quite without warmth. 'I did nothing of the kind, Mr Langham. We met quite by chance three months ago. I was dining alone in the Midland and Edwin entered the room. He saw me and offered to buy me a drink, for old times' sake.'

'To meet him again like that, after so many years, must have been' – he shrugged – 'strange, to say the least?'

'Strange does not describe it in the slightest,' she said. 'I was quite taken aback.'

'But you accepted the drink?'

'I was curious. I wanted to see how the years had treated my ex-husband. I wanted to ascertain if he had any regrets about how he behaved towards me all those years ago.'

'And do you think he had?' Langham asked, sure that he knew the answer.

'I should have known that a leopard of Edwin's ilk does not change its spots. Egotists do not regret their actions, merely rationalize them and condemn others. Although he didn't say so in so many words, I really think he blamed me for throwing him out.'

'Did the professor tell you that he'd remarried? Did he mention anything at all about the state of that relationship?'

'He did tell me that he had married again, yes, and that he was terribly unhappy. He told me – and I took this with a pinch of salt – that he had married his wife twenty years ago on the rebound from me. He painted a vivid picture of his present wife: she was a vain hypochondriac who cared nothing for him and had a penchant for expensive clothes and perfumes. This, too, I took with a pinch of salt.'

Langham watched the cat as it rolled on to its back on the woman's lap and stretched luxuriously.

He said, 'And yet, knowing the professor as you did, knowing that he was a vain egotist with a cavalier disregard of others, you elected to embark on an affair with him?'

She smiled, again without warmth. 'If you want to know the truth, Mr Langham, I was lonely. My husband had been dead for three years, and it had come to the point where I detested my own company. Edwin provided a welcome distraction from the same old routine. And,' she went on, waving an elegant hand, 'for all that I have painted a far from complimentary picture of the man, he did have his attributes. He was intelligent and humorous, and when he was with one, he gave one his undivided attention . . . and he was generous. As well as being very well remunerated at Oxford, he inherited a small fortune when his father passed away.'

'And you had no qualms about beginning an affair?'

'Qualms?'

He considered his words carefully. 'I would have thought, having at one time been on the receiving end of his unfaithfulness, you might have had some consideration for the feelings of his current wife.'

Did he see the slightest trace of pink high on her cheeks as she took this in?

She said, 'As a matter of fact, yes, Mr Langham, I must admit that I did feel . . . qualms. But I suppose those were allayed by the stories Edwin told of his wife.'

'Even though,' he said, trying not to smile, 'you took these stories with a pinch of salt?'

'I suppose I rationalized my actions with the thought that there is no smoke without fire, Mr Langham.'

'So the affair began three months ago,' he said. 'How often did you meet?'

'Every week, sometimes more often.'

'Always at the Midland?'

This time she flushed more obviously. 'Sometimes Edwin came back here, when he could get away,' she murmured.

'Over this period,' he asked, 'did he ever mention that he had made enemies, people who might have wished him ill?'

She shook her head decisively. 'No, never. Nothing like that.'

'And' – he hesitated – 'did he mention, when you met him last Monday, that he was being blackmailed?'

She leaned forward, staring at him. 'Blackmailed?'

'By someone who obviously knew about the affair and was making him pay.'

'No, he said nothing. He was his usual, affable, joking self.'

He made a note of this. 'There was something that struck me as odd about the first blackmail demand he received. It stated that if he failed to pay up, then Nancy – his niece – would "find out". Now, what struck me as strange is that the black-mailer assumed that the professor should care about his niece knowing he was having an affair.'

She shook her head, her eyes narrowed in mystification. 'Yes, I agree. It does seem strange, doesn't it?'

The cat leapt from her lap and trotted to the door. Pointedly, the woman glanced at a carriage clock on the mantelpiece.

'I'll intrude upon your time no longer, Mrs Creighton,' he said.

He closed his notebook, thanked her for her time and said that he might be in contact in due course.

'And again,' he said as she escorted him to the door, 'I'm sorry about the professor.'

She smiled sadly. 'It seems strange to think that I shall never see Edwin again,' she said. 'Goodbye, Mr Langham.'

In the car, he brushed cat hairs from his trousers, then glanced back at the house. Deirdre Creighton was standing by the window, fingertips placed against her cheek as she stared out at him. He raised his hand in farewell and drove from the village.

FIFTEEN

The Willows was an imposing four-square Victorian building hemmed in on either side by redbrick semi-detached villas dating from the thirties.

There were no cars in the gravelled area outside the house, and the waiting room was empty when Langham entered. It was just after three o'clock and a thriving town practice should have had at least one or two patients on a Wednesday afternoon, he thought, especially in the middle of winter.

A grey-haired receptionist smiled from behind a sliding glass panel. 'Do you have an appointment, sir?' she asked, scanning a ledger doubtfully.

'I'm here to see Doctor Robertshaw on a personal matter.'

She began to say that the doctor was very busy, but Langham ignored her and pointed down a corridor at the end of which was a white door with *Dr Robertshaw* etched on a brass plate. 'This way, I take it?'

'But—' the receptionist began. As he paced down the corridor, he heard her speaking hurriedly into an intercom.

He tapped on the door, waited for a second, then stepped into a spacious consulting room with a high ceiling and mahogany wall panels.

A small man was turning from a sink in the corner, quickly rolling down his shirtsleeves. An adenoid-pinching chemical reek filled the room, along with the tinny sound of the receptionist's voice from the intercom.

Robertshaw leaned over his desk and spoke into the microphone in a high-pitched voice, 'That's quite all right, Mrs Greaves.' He flipped a switch to silence her, then looked up at Langham. 'And you are?'

Dr Spencer Robertshaw was no taller than his brother but much thinner both in face and frame. Whereas the professor's chin and forehead had been pronounced, the doctor's head tapered away from the prominent nose in the fashion of a rather attenuated egg.

Langham showed his accreditation, and the doctor slumped into his chair behind the desk. 'Your colleagues have already informed me—' he began.

'I work as a private investigator,' Langham interrupted. 'In this instance, I'm conducting an investigation on behalf of the Robertshaw family.'

'How can I help you?'

'Just a few routine questions, Doctor. I don't know how much the police told you about the incident.'

'The bare facts, Mr Langham. That my brother Edwin had been murdered – shot with a revolver, I understand, some time yesterday evening.'

'He would have died instantly, if that's any consolation. He would have experienced no pain.'

Robertshaw smiled thinly. 'I am a doctor, Mr Langham. I am fully aware that death from a gunshot to the temple at close range would have been instantaneous and painless.'

Langham withdrew his notebook and wrote, *A prickly customer*, while letting the silence stretch. He looked up.

'How often did you see your brother?'

'Perhaps once a month, when I called to see his wife, Xandra.'

'And other than on these occasions?'

'Very rarely.'

'Would you say you were close to Edwin?'

'Not especially. Not that we were at all antagonistic.'

'What kind of person was he, in your opinion?'

The doctor lifted his thin shoulders in a prolonged shrug. 'On the minus side: stubborn, opinionated, egotistical. On the plus: charismatic, generous, loyal.'

'Was he the kind of person to attract enemies?'

'Not enemies, no. His brusqueness could be said to rub people up the wrong way, and he didn't suffer fools gladly. I am aware that individuals certainly disliked him. But enemies? No; at any rate, he never mentioned any.'

'Did you know that Edwin was conducting an extra-marital affair?'

The doctor held his gaze. 'I didn't know that categorically, but I'm not in the least surprised. He was a persistent and incorrigible womanizer.'

'Were you acquainted with his first wife, Deirdre?'

'Of course. We met quite often in the early years of their marriage.'

'What did you make of her?'

'I thought her insecure, perhaps even neurotic, with pretensions above her station. I tolerated her because she was married to my brother. That said, I did feel somewhat sorry for her.'

'You were aware, even back then, that your brother was unfaithful?'

'My brother was *never* faithful, Mr Langham.'

'Yet you said he was loyal?'

'To his male friends, yes, he was.'

'Did you know that Deirdre had returned to the area?'

'I had no idea—'

'Nor that it was with Deirdre that Edwin was having an affair?'

It was evident, from his surprised expression, that this was news to the doctor. He shook his head. 'No, no idea at all. I find that highly unlikely.'

'Why is that?'

'Well, they parted on such acrimonious terms, Mr Langham. Deirdre threw him out when she discovered he was having an affair. I recall that she was on the verge of a breakdown at the time.'

'So you find it surprising that she would have him back, even after more than twenty years?'

The doctor nodded. 'Yes, I do. Of course, people can and do change over the years.' He stopped. 'You don't think that this might have any bearing on my brother's death, do you?'

Langham shrugged. 'One can never be sure. However . . .'

'Yes?'

'Did Edwin mention the fact that he was being blackmailed?'

The doctor winced. 'Blackmailed?'

'He received the first letter a little over a week ago.'

'I haven't seen Edwin for over three weeks.' He thought about it. 'Blackmailed because of the affair?'

'That's what I assume,' Langham said. 'However, there is one curious aspect of the threat.'

'Go on.'

'The first blackmail note stated that if Edwin didn't pay up, then Nancy would get to know.' He spread his hands. 'But why should the blackmailer assume that this might force Edwin to agree to his demands? Why would Edwin care one way or the other if Nancy knew he was having an affair with his ex-wife?'

The doctor shook his head. 'I'm sorry. I honestly can't begin to guess.'

Langham read through his notes, then looked up. His attention was caught by the doctor's left shirtsleeve, at the crook of the elbow. He looked away quickly, so that Robertshaw would not be aware that he had noticed the specks of blood on the material.

'Now, Xandra . . . Everyone I've spoken to appears to be of the opinion that she's dying.'

'The treatment she received to combat her tuberculosis, six years ago, resulted in severe and permanent kidney damage. The drug, streptomycin, occasionally had deleterious side effects. There is nothing that can be done for her, other than ease her pain and attempt to make her as comfortable as possible.'

'So she *is* dying?'

'Her condition is incurable, though it is impossible to state with any certainty just when she might suffer catastrophic renal failure.'

'Does she take medication for her condition?'

Dr Robertshaw nodded. 'I prescribe her with a mild painkiller every month, along with sleeping pills.'

Langham referred to his notes. 'I understand that Edwin's son, Randall, visited you yesterday evening.'

'He did, yes.'

'For what reason?'

'Until recently, I employed a manager to oversee the financial side of the practice. He left, and Randall, having worked in a bank, seemed to me to be admirably suited to the post. He came over to discuss the possibility of my employing him.'

'I understand he dined with you?'

'In the apartment here, yes.'

'What time did he arrive?'

'That would be . . . let me think . . . perhaps six o'clock, maybe a little later.'

'And he stayed until . . .?'

'We discussed the practice over dinner and afterwards, then the talk turned general over drinks. It would have been well after midnight when he left. Perhaps half past twelve.'

'Not before?'

'Definitely not, as I recall noting that it was well after twelve when I poured what proved to be our final drink.'

'Was Randall driving?'

'Yes, but he curbed his drinking after dinner. I recall that the last drink I fixed was a very weak gin and tonic. He was perfectly capable when he left the premises.'

Langham nodded and closed his notebook.

'I think that rounds everything up, for the time being, Doctor. Thank you for your time and cooperation.' He slipped his notebook into his breast pocket. 'If I need anything further, I'll be in touch.'

'I'll be more than happy to oblige.'

He thanked Dr Robertshaw again and made his way from the surgery. On the threshold, he turned his collar up against the wind and the driving snow, then hurried across to his car.

All things considered, it had been an instructive afternoon.

SIXTEEN

Later that afternoon, as dusk fell over the village of Ingoldby, Maria stood at the sink peeling potatoes and carrots. She looked across the stream at the standing stone rising like a pewter blade in the twilight. The police vans and cars had packed up and moved off. Presumably, the body had been removed. The scene was eerily still.

Maria considered Professor Robertshaw, his affair with his ex-wife and the enmities the old man had fomented over the years. It seemed that there were few people with a good word to say about him; certainly, there were many with a reason to hate the professor.

She was about to place the pan of potatoes on the Rayburn when she saw movement at the far end of the garden.

The gate opened and a lolloping shape bounded through, followed by a slight, hooded figure. Maria moved to the kitchen door and opened it before Nancy had time to knock.

The girl stood forlornly on the threshold, her eyes red and swollen in the light spilling from the kitchen. She stared at Maria, tears tracking down her cheeks. Bill, sensing his owner's distress, stood at her side, his tail tucked timorously between his legs and his head lowered.

Maria took Nancy in her arms and the girl sobbed.

'It's all so awful!' she wailed.

Maria eased her into the kitchen, sat her at the table and put the kettle on. Bill curled at Nancy's feet, looking up at the girl with a doleful expression.

Maria drew up a chair and took Nancy's hands in hers. 'Tell me . . .'

'Randall . . . He's thrown me out! He said . . . he said the last thing he wanted at this time was a tearful little bitch under his . . . under his feet!' Her words came in fits and starts, punctuated by sobbing gulps. 'I . . . I didn't know where to go . . . I don't know many people in the village that

well. I knocked on Roy's caravan, but he wasn't there. So
. . . so I came here. I don't know what to do!'

'The first thing we'll do,' Maria said, 'is get you out of your
coat and make you a nice cup of tea.'

The girl sat there sniffing while Maria unfastened the wooden
toggles down the front of her coat. Nancy shrugged it off, and
Maria took the coat into the hall and hung it on the coat stand.
When she returned, Nancy was stroking Bill's head, saying,
'It'll be OK, boy. Things will work out.'

'Of course they will,' Maria said, pouring two mugs of
strong tea.

Nancy took the drink, smiled her thanks, then broke down
again. It was all she could do to place the mug on the tabletop
as sobs racked her. 'And it's all my fault! It is! If I . . . if I
hadn't done what I did . . . my uncle would still be alive.'

Maria squeezed the girl's cold fingers. 'Nancy, Nancy. What
on earth—?'

'But don't you see! The other day . . . the snowman . . .
those sticks I poked into its tummy! I cursed him, Maria! I
really did. It's all *my* fault!'

'It's nothing of the kind. The world doesn't work like that,
you know? It's a coincidence. Your uncle was unkind to you,
and quite naturally you reacted.' She smiled reassuringly. 'It
was someone else who was responsible for what happened to
him, and it had nothing at all to do with you.'

'But I feel so . . . so terrible. Everything is so awful. Xandra
is ill and unhappy, and she really hated Unc, didn't she?
I thought – I thought when I came to live at the manor . . . I
thought that everything would be fine, just like it'd been at
home, with Mum and Dad loving each other. And then I found
out that it wasn't like that at all, that Unc wasn't the man I
thought he was, and my cousin, Randall . . . He was nice and
friendly when we were little, but he's turned into a self-centred
monster. And now he's thrown me out!'

She wailed again, her mouth pulled into such a mask of
tragedy that it looked almost comical.

Maria felt tearful herself at the girl's pathetic outburst. She
picked up both mugs. 'Come on, into the living room where
it's nice and warm. We'll sit in front of the fire and talk it over.'

She led Nancy into the next room. Bill trotted after them and curled on the rug before the blazing fire. They sat side by side on the sofa, and Nancy sipped her tea between taking giant, calming sniffs.

'After I'd been interviewed,' Nancy said, 'I went upstairs with Roy and . . . and we just lay on the bed and held each other. He was frozen . . . I don't mean cold. He was terrified by what had happened. The violence. He can't take violence, Maria. It does something to him – brings back terrible memories, I think. He just held me and told me everything would be fine . . . and then he said he had to get back to the farm . . .'

She took a deep breath and went on. 'And later, I went downstairs to find Randall. I . . . I wanted to know who might have murdered my uncle. He was in the study, looking for something in the drawers. He was drunk and angry, and . . . and when I asked him who might have hated Unc enough to have killed him, he just exploded. I thought he was going to attack me, I really did. He grabbed me by the shoulders, pushed me across the room and into an armchair, then . . . then he said a load of beastly things about me . . . how he'd always hated me, and thought me shallow and thoughtless, and other nasty things. Then he told me to get out – pack my things and get out.' The girl shook her head, her eyes wide as she relived the incident. 'I said what about Xandra? I need to be around to look after her.' She fell silent, shaking her head.

'What did he say to that?'

'He laughed. He seemed to think that that was funny. Then he leaned very close to me and said that Xandra was fine, that all she needed was to stop feeling sorry for herself, to stop being such a . . . such a hypochondriac, and stand on her own two feet.' Nancy waved a forlorn hand. 'Then he accused me of thinking I was indispensable here – but it's not true, I've never thought of myself like that! – and he said that the only reason my uncle took me in was to look after Xandra, and that my uncle had felt nothing for me at all . . . and lots and lots of hurtful things like that!'

Maria stroked the girl's hand. 'That's not true,' Maria murmured, soothing. 'I'm sure your uncle loved you, in his own way.'

Nancy sniffed, staring into the flames. 'Then I ran from the room and went upstairs. I was too upset to talk to Xandra, tell her what had happened. I should have gone to see her! She'll be expecting me. She'll be so angry!'

'She'll be nothing of the kind,' Maria said. 'I'm sure she can look after herself for a day or two.'

'But her medication. She must take her painkillers.'

'I'm sure she can take them herself,' Maria said.

Nancy nodded to herself, then indicated the bag at her feet. 'So I just packed a few things and left the house. But Roy wasn't in his caravan. I thought of going to the Wellbournes. They're nice people, the way they look after Roy. But I couldn't burden them with me and Bill. Then I thought of you.' She smiled pathetically through her tears. 'Oh, Maria, what am I going to do?'

'You're going to stay here until we've sorted everything out,' Maria said. 'We have a spare bedroom, and you'll be more than welcome.'

'But Donald! He won't want me under his feet!'

'What nonsense! He'll be delighted to have you here. You'll be our very first house guest. He should be back pretty soon, and I have a casserole cooking. We can sit down to a nice meal and talk things over, all right?'

Nancy sniffed and smiled bleakly.

'But . . .' the girl said, 'but I really should go back to the manor. I need a few things. I packed so quickly I forgot my toothbrush, and I need more clothes – and Xandra! I really need to see that Xandra takes her medication. You see, I always gave Xandra her pills at night, until a few months ago. Then her medication changed, and she had to take her painkillers in the morning, and Unc . . . he said he'd see to that as he was up earlier than me – I always slept in, especially if I'd had a bad night with Xandra.' She shook her head. 'So she wouldn't have had her medication this morning.'

'Nancy, surely she would have taken it herself, wouldn't she?'

The girl shook her head. 'No . . . No, you see, my uncle locked the medication away from her. I think he feared that . . . that when my aunt was depressed, that she might . . . Anyway, I really should go!'

She made to stand up, but Maria restrained her.

'You're not going back there tonight with Randall in his cups and acting so dreadfully.' She made a decision. 'I'll go. I'll pop across, pick up your toothbrush and some clothes – tell me what you need – and then I'll make sure Xandra takes her medication.'

'Would you? Would you do that?' The girl looked pathetically grateful.

'The medication: where will I find it and what does she take?'

'She takes two pills every morning, some kind of painkiller, and at night two sleeping pills. I'm sure it'll be all right if she has the painkillers now. All the medication is locked in a cupboard above the basin in the *en suite* bathroom next to her bedroom. The key to the cupboard is hidden on a hook at the back of an airing cupboard next to the bath.'

'The painkillers – are they clearly marked?'

'They're in a small brown bottle,' Nancy said. 'I'm sorry, I can't recall what they're called.'

'And the sleeping pills? Does she always take them?'

'Most nights, yes. They're in a clear glass bottle next to the painkillers.'

Maria wondered what kind of mood Randall might be in, considering his earlier drunken display of bellicosity. She hoped that she could complete what she had to do without coming across the young man.

'Will the front door be open?'

'It should be. But if it isn't, my uncle kept a spare key in the garage to the right of the house. It'll be hanging on a nail to the left of the door.'

Nancy listed the items of clothing she needed and where to find them, and Maria fetched a hessian bag from the pantry.

'And Donald won't be angry when he comes in and sees me?'

Maria laughed and crouched down before the forlorn girl. 'Angry? I don't think I've ever seen Donald get seriously angry about anything. Do you know what he'll say?'

The girl shook her head.

'He'll say, and these will be his exact words: "Delighted you can stay, old girl!" And he'll mix you a stiff gin and tonic and make you feel at home. He has a wonderful way of putting people at their ease.'

Nancy stared down at her mug. 'You obviously love him.'

Maria smiled. 'More than anything. And talking about love . . . You're a dark horse, my girl. How long have you and Roy *really* known each other?'

Nancy blushed. 'It was Roy. He said not to tell anyone, you and Donald or the Wellbournes. He was afraid it would get back to Randall and my uncle, and there'd be hell to pay and they'd stop us seeing each other, and that would be terrible.' She shrugged and smiled. 'It happened so gradually, last summer. I saw him when I went out walking Bill, and once or twice Roy would come with me part of the way, and we got talking . . . And, oh, it was so wonderful to have someone . . .' She faltered, colouring to the roots of her golden curls. 'It was just nice that someone took an interest in me,' she went on in a murmur. 'He told me all about his life before the war in Norfolk, and I told him about boarding school, and what happened to Mum and Dad, and he was so . . . he just seemed to *understand* me. He was so sympathetic. You don't know what it was like to have someone take an interest in me as a person. Life at the manor had been all right, but I didn't have any real friends in the village – only Bill! – and then Roy came along.' She shrugged. 'I love him, and nothing Randall can say or do will stop me from loving him.'

Maria squeezed her hand. 'Good for you, Nancy. Help yourself to more tea while I'm gone. I shan't be long.'

Nancy looked up. 'Thanks ever so. I promise not to be a nuisance while I'm here, and Bill says he'll be on his best behaviour.'

Maria laughed. 'I'm sure he will.'

She moved to the kitchen, pulled on her coat and boots, and let herself out of the back door.

SEVENTEEN

There was no street lighting along Crooked Lane, but the snow-covered track was illuminated by a gibbous moon. Maria picked her way carefully through the snow, crunching through the thick ice of frozen puddles. The night was silent; even the wind had abated. From far off, very occasionally, she heard the hoot of an owl.

She hurried over the bridge and turned up the driveway to the manor, hoping she could give Xandra her medication, gather Nancy's things and leave without bumping into Randall Robertshaw.

There were no lights burning behind any of the windows along the facade of the manor house, and the front door was locked. Rather than knock and have Randall answer, she moved to the garage to the right of the drive and pulled open the door. She found a single key hanging on a nail to the left of the door, as Nancy had described, then returned to the house and let herself in.

As she crept across the darkened hallway, she realized that she was giving a very good impression of a cat burglar. If Randall, still drunk and in possession of his shotgun, was to discover her now . . .

She crossed to the stairs. She heard the distant sound of a voice – Randall, she thought, talking to himself or speaking to someone on the phone – and further along the corridor made out a wedge of orange light spilling from a partially open door.

She climbed the stairs, thankful that they were constructed of solid, aged timber that no longer creaked, then ascended the narrow staircase to Nancy's room. She found her toothbrush and toothpaste on the basin in the corner, then went through the drawers and collected the clothing the girl had asked for. She considered packing the threadbare teddy bear, too, but there was no room in her hessian bag.

She descended to the first floor, moved along the passage

until she came to Xandra's room, then paused, listening. There was no sound from within, but a line of light showed at the foot of the door.

She turned the handle, eased open the door and peered in.

Xandra lay in her bed in a pair of pink pyjamas, the sheet thrown back despite the chill of the room. She lay on her side, her face towards the door, fast asleep. A small, shaded lamp burned on the bedside table.

Maria moved across the room to the adjoining bathroom. She located the light switch, closed the door carefully behind her, then turned on the light.

She found a small silver key at the back of the airing cupboard, then moved to the sink and unlocked the cabinet door to reveal a bottle of aspirin, a buckled tube of antiseptic ointment and a box of corn plasters. There were no sleeping pills or painkillers in evidence.

She looked around the bathroom for another cupboard but, aside from the airing cupboard, this was the only one. Above the bath was a shelf arrayed with various shampoos, emollients, sprays and unopened tablets of soap, but no sleeping pills or other drugs.

She made a meticulous search of the room and found nothing.

The only answer that occurred to her was that Xandra had taken the bottle of painkillers and administered them herself. And the sleeping pills?

Maria returned to the bedroom and crept across to the sleeping woman. On the bedside table was the lamp, an alarm clock and a book of crossword puzzles. She examined the bedspread and the sheets beside the woman, then the floor beside the bed. There was no sign of either sleeping pills or painkillers. She did find, however, tucked down the back of the pillow, an empty brandy bottle and a small glass. Xandra had evidently self-medicated.

She was in the process of drawing the sheets over the woman's shoulders when Xandra opened her eyes blearily and murmured, 'Nancy . . . Good girl . . .'

'Go to sleep,' Maria said in her softest voice.

'You're the only one who . . .' Xandra was half asleep, her eyes closed, and Maria caught the reek of spirits on her breath.

'Shh.'

'. . . the only one who really cares.' She tried to sit up.

'Go to sleep now.'

Maria crept away, and Xandra collapsed back on to the pillow.

She slipped from the room, closed the door behind her and leaned against it, a sudden thought occurring to her. What if Xandra had taken the pills – the sleeping pills and the painkillers – along with the brandy in response to her husband's death?

Despite her earlier desire to avoid Randall Robertshaw, now she thought it best if she found him and communicated her concern. She hurried down the stairs, along the corridor, and came to the open door behind which the orange light glowed. She knocked, waited a second for a summons which never came, then pushed open the door.

Randall sat slumped in an armchair before the fire, legs outstretched, staring dolefully into the glowing embers. Only then did Maria take in the state of the room. She assumed it was the professor's study, with his desk situated before the French windows and shelves laden with calf-bound volumes. She noticed the papers piled on and spilling from the desk, the drawers pulled open and their contents tumbled. Books had been pulled from the shelves and thrown across the floor; several paintings on the walls hung askew, and three or four had been removed entirely.

She stepped uncertainly into the room.

Randall stirred and looked up. 'What are you doing here?' he snapped.

'I'm worried about your mother.'

'I said, what the hell are you doing—?'

'Nancy sent me. She hadn't administered your mother's medication – thanks in no small part to you. So I came to check on her.'

'What the hell are you maundering on about?' Randall shouted. He seemed less drunk than hungover and truculent now.

She crossed the room and stood over him. 'Your mother needs her medication, but it's no longer in the bathroom cabinet.'

The young man blinked at her, as if attempting to assimilate this information.

He waved. 'What's that got to do with me?'

As if addressing an imbecile, she said, 'Your mother's just lost her husband. A jar of sleeping pills and some other medication has vanished. Will you please get it into your addled mind that there's a distinct possibility that she might have taken the pills along with the bottle of brandy she's emptied since this afternoon.'

He heard her out, an infuriating smirk playing on his lips. 'I doubt my mother would do anything so foolish.'

'Your doubt, in this case, might be all it takes to consign your mother to a painful death. If I were you – if you don't want to lose two parents within twenty-four hours – I'd get up there and wake her up.'

He sighed dramatically. 'What on earth makes you so certain she's taken an overdose?'

'I'm not certain, you fool. I'm worried about the possibility that she *might* have – as you should be. If you don't wake her up and ask her, then I will.'

He sighed again and, as if ordered to carry out a Sisyphean task, pushed himself reluctantly upright and strode from the room.

She followed him up the staircase and along the corridor to his mother's bedroom.

He opened the door, turned to Maria and said, 'Wait there,' then slammed the door in her face.

She paced back and forth, occasionally pausing before the door and listening. She heard the sound of Randall's voice, cajoling, followed by Xandra's confused replies. Once, she thought she heard what might have been a slap.

She heard the bathroom door open, followed by the sound of running water. A silence followed. She paced again. As she neared the door, she heard the sound of raised voices, then silence.

She heard another slap, and this time she quickly opened the door and stepped into the room.

Xandra lay on the bed, Randall standing over her. A china washbowl sat on the floor beside the bed.

Randall pointed to it. 'There,' he said. 'I hope you're satisfied. I made her sick – stuck a toothbrush down her throat.

I'm delighted to report that she brought up nothing but brandy, and plenty of that. So . . . false alarm.'

Maria examined the contents of the basin, finding only a thin gruel of regurgitated alcohol with no evidence of pills.

Randall moved to leave the room. Maria reached out and gripped his upper arm, intensely disliking the young man and doing nothing to disguise her contempt as she said, 'And what about the pills?'

'What about them?'

'According to Nancy, they were in the cabinet earlier. Now they're gone.'

'In that case,' he snapped, 'why don't you ask your little friend where the damned things are? She looks after my mother, after all.'

He shrugged himself from her grasp and stepped from the bedroom.

Maria followed, closing the door quietly behind her. 'She can hardly look after Xandra when you've thrown her out, can she?'

At the top of the staircase, he turned and stared at her. 'Xandra can look after herself. We don't need Nancy, thank you.'

He set off down the stairs. Exasperated, Maria followed him.

'And your mother's medication?' she asked.

At the bottom of the staircase, with a hand on the balustrade, he paused with his back to Maria, hanging his head as he considered his response. He turned and looked up at her. 'Look, there's a simple answer. The medication is finished and either my father or mother discarded the empty bottles. I'll ask her in the morning, all right?'

'*Both* bottles were finished at the same time?' Maria asked doubtfully.

He sighed. 'How the hell should I know?'

'When is your uncle due to come and see her again? Perhaps you should ring and inform him of what's happened?'

'Fine, yes. I'll do that in the morning.'

He turned and strode along the corridor to his father's study.

Maria paused, watching him go, then made up her mind to follow him.

By the time she reached the study, he'd returned to his

armchair before the fire. She stopped in the doorway, staring at him.

He looked up. 'Yes?' he said.

'Why did you throw Nancy out, Randall?'

'Because she's nothing but a pain. I can look after my mother without her help, and it'll be one less mouth to feed, won't it?'

'Why do you hate the girl?'

'"Hate" is going it a bit. Dislike intensely would be an adequate descriptor.'

She shook her head, recalling what Nancy had told her about being friendly with Randall's much put-upon ex-wife, but she resisted the urge to bring this up.

Instead, she gestured around the room. 'What happened here?'

His eyes followed the sweep of her hand. 'If you must know, I was looking for something,' he said. 'Some legal papers. You might recall that I lost my father last night, and I need to sort out his affairs.'

'I'm sorry about your father,' she said, facing him across the room. She hesitated, then said, 'I wish you'd think again about Nancy.'

'Thank you for that,' he said in his infuriating fashion, 'and if you'd kindly close the front door on the way out . . .'

Biting back a reply, she left the study and hurried down the corridor. She slammed the front door behind her, replaced the key on the nail in the garage and made her way home.

Donald had returned by the time she opened the back door and took off her hat and coat. She heard the comforting sound of his voice in the living room, followed by Nancy's responsive laughter. She smiled to herself. Trust Donald to have jollied the girl out of her slough of despond.

'What did I say?' she said as she entered the room and saw the girl clutching a glass of gin and tonic.

Donald said, 'Just what she needed after all she's been through, my darling. Nancy's filled me in on the afternoon's travails. A little drink before dinner?'

'A *big* one,' Maria said.

'Coming up.' He mixed her a gin and tonic.

'How was my aunt?' Nancy asked.

Maria bit her lip. She took the glass, sat down on the sofa beside the girl and described what she'd found at the manor.

Donald asked Nancy, 'Are you sure that both sets of pills were in the bathroom cabinet?'

'As I told Maria, my uncle took over responsibility for Xandra's morning medication at the start of the year. Before that, I always kept the pills in the bathroom cabinet.' She shrugged. 'I assumed that's where they'd be now.'

Donald nodded. 'Perhaps the professor had his own preferred place to keep them.'

Maria said, 'I must say, Randall's attitude was rather cavalier. I more or less had to force him to go and check on his mother.'

'At least she hadn't swallowed anything . . . other than the brandy,' Nancy said.

Donald considered his drink. 'Do you know if Xandra can go without her painkillers for a day or so?'

'Last year they ran out for a time,' Nancy said. 'She gritted her teeth and battled through.'

Donald was leafing through his notebook. 'I made a note of Spencer's telephone number. It might be an idea to ring him and see what he says.'

He crossed to the telephone stand in the corner of the room and dialled the number. Maria watched him as he listened impatiently to the dial tone, drumming his fingers on the tabletop.

After a minute he gave up. 'No reply. I'll try again first thing tomorrow. I shouldn't worry if I were you, Nancy. We'll sort it all out in the morning.'

Over dinner, Donald changed the subject entirely and made Maria and Nancy laugh – and wince – with an account of his time in India during the war. Maria had heard many of the stories before but listened with a smile, loving Donald for his ability to take the girl's mind off the tragedy of the day.

After dinner, and another gin and tonic, Nancy let Bill out into the back garden, then thanked them for everything and said she'd better be turning in.

'Where will Bill sleep?' Maria asked.

'Would you mind awfully if he slept on the bed with me?' the girl said, wincing.

'I don't see why not,' Maria said. 'His snores won't keep us awake, will they?'

'His won't,' Nancy said, 'but mine might. Goodnight, and thanks awfully for everything.'

Later, they sat before the fire and discussed the events of the day. Donald sipped his drink and told her all about his afternoon interviewing Deirdre Creighton and Spencer Robertshaw.

'Two things were very . . . curious,' he said. 'One – I found it hard to credit that Deirdre would so willingly take back a man she knew to be a serial philanderer, whom she threw out twenty years ago.'

'Mmm. Some women never learn,' she said. 'And the second?'

'The second is that the professor's brother is addicted to opium, or laudanum or heroin – I'm not very up on the difference, to be honest.'

'Addicted? But that's terrible.'

Donald nodded. 'A case of "Doctor, heal thyself", or some such. There was a distinct chemical smell in the surgery when I entered, and later I noticed specks of blood on the sleeve of his shirt. He was taking the stuff intravenously.'

She tapped his chest. 'The question is, my darling, whether either Deirdre's taking back her ex-husband or Doctor Robertshaw's addiction might have any bearings on the professor's murder?'

'I don't know,' Donald said, 'but I do know I'd love another drink. Would you be an angel and pour me one?'

She obliged, and they sat before the glowing coals and nursed their drinks as midnight approached.

EIGHTEEN

After breakfast the following morning, Langham phoned Dr Robertshaw before the surgery opened for the day. Nancy was still in bed, though her dog had wandered downstairs to be let out; now Bill lay before the embers of the fire. Maria sat beside him, absent-mindedly stroking his head.

Morning sunlight slanted through the living-room window as Langham listened to the dial tone.

'Doctor Robertshaw speaking.'

'Doctor, this is Donald Langham. We spoke yesterday.'

'Of course, yes. What can I do for you?'

Langham told him about the missing pills and went on, 'Randall is aware of the situation, and he said he'd contact you, but I thought it wise to phone myself. I wonder if you could tell me whether both sets of pills, the sleeping tablets and painkillers, were almost finished?'

The doctor hesitated. 'To the best of my knowledge, without referring to my notes, they were. I was due to visit Xandra tomorrow.'

'Isn't it a little odd that the pills seem to have run out at the same time?'

'Not especially, if she was taking more painkillers than usual,' Robertshaw said. 'I'll make out a new prescription. However, I have surgery all day and I won't be free until after six. I could drive down with the prescription then.'

Langham thanked him and rang off.

Nancy wandered into the living room, yawning, and sat on the arm of the sofa, bleary-eyed.

'Breakfast?' Maria asked.

'A slice of toast and a cup of tea would be lovely,' the girl said. 'Then I'll take Bill for a long walk.'

At the sound of the last word, the dog jumped up in eagerness, wagging his tail.

'I said after breakfast, boy. I wonder if Bill could have a

slice of toast, too? I forgot to bring his food. I'll pop into the manor later and pick it up.'

Maria led Nancy and Bill into the kitchen, and Langham was about to sort through some papers in his study when a knock sounded at the front door.

'I'll get it,' he called out.

Harriet Wellbourne stood on the doorstep, looking even smaller than usual. She appeared stunned. 'Harriet?'

'I didn't know who to come to,' she said. 'Roy is working in the bottom field.'

'Harriet, what's happened? Come in.'

He took her arm, walked her into the living room and installed her on the sofa.

'The police came this morning at eight,' she said in a voice so soft it was almost inaudible. 'They wanted to see Richard. He was in the byre, and I had to fetch him. It was a fellow called Montgomery – a nasty, officious little man. He had two constables with him, and Montgomery said they were arresting Richard on suspicion of murdering Professor Robertshaw. Then he said that thing they say on all the police programmes on the wireless . . . you know – "Anything you say will be taken down and may be used in evidence". Oh, Mr Langham, it was awful. Richard was speechless. He just looked at me and shook his head before they led him away. Look,' she went on, holding out a hand, 'I'm still shaking. I don't know what to do.'

Maria appeared in the doorway, and behind her Nancy stood open-mouthed, clutching a slice of toast.

Langham took Harriet's trembling hand; it was as cold as ice.

Maria sat beside the woman on the sofa and slipped an arm around her shoulders.

'I'll get you a cup of tea,' Nancy said, and disappeared back into the kitchen.

Langham said, 'Did Montgomery say anything else?'

Harriet shook her head. 'I really can't recall. It's all such a blur. I think I'm in shock. Montgomery just asked Richard to confirm his name, and then they led him away. Mr Langham, Richard *did* go to see the professor on the night he was shot

– he was angry about the disputed land. But I saw him when he got back. He was fuming – the professor wouldn't see reason – but Richard wouldn't do anything like . . . like that. He's a peaceful man, Mr Langham. I've been married to him for more than thirty years and I've never even heard him raise his voice.'

Nancy returned with a cup of tea, and Harriet took it with a wan smile of thanks.

'I'll drive up to Bury and assess the situation,' Langham said. 'I'll try to see Richard and assure him we're doing our best to sort things out. Do you know if he has a lawyer?'

Harriet shook her head. 'I really don't know; Richard deals with all that kind of thing.'

'Try not to worry. I know Montgomery, and he does tend to be impulsive.'

'I should tell Roy,' Harriet said. 'He'll be wondering where we are.'

'You're going nowhere,' Maria said. 'I'll make the fire and keep you supplied with tea. You can stay here until Donald gets back, and I won't hear another word on the matter.'

'I'll go and tell Roy,' Nancy said.

'Would you, dear?' Harriet said. 'That's ever so kind.'

Nancy jumped up. 'Come on, boy. Walkies!'

Bill leapt to his feet and followed the girl into the kitchen, his tail going like a lash.

Langham assured Harriet once again that he'd do everything he could for Richard, and moved into the hall. Maria came with him.

'I'm sure Richard can't have . . .' she began in lowered tones.

Langham pulled on his coat. 'I'll know a bit more when I've spoken to Montgomery,' he said. 'As I'll be in town, I'll drop in on Robertshaw when he's between patients and pick up Xandra's prescription.'

He kissed her on the cheek and hurried out to the car.

On the drive north over lanes and roads whitened with a fresh sprinkling of snow, he considered the possibility that Richard Wellbourne might have murdered the professor. For Montgomery to have made the arrest and read Wellbourne his rights, he obviously had what he regarded as incriminating evidence: more, Langham thought, than just the circumstantial facts that Wellbourne had visited the professor that night and had been in dispute with him over the field.

He parked outside the police station and found Detective Inspector Montgomery in his office, feet lodged on his desk. A steaming mug of tea and a doorstep of a bacon sandwich sat before him on his blotter. The inspector was looking pleased with himself.

Langham drew up a chair and Montgomery brushed his straggling moustache with thumb and forefinger preparatory to taking a great bite of sandwich.

'Thought I might see you today, Langham,' he said around a mouthful. 'Come to see how I did it?'

'What have you got on him?'

'The works. You name it. Open-and-shut case. Motive, opportunity, hard evidence. All we're lacking is the confession, but it'll come. Stands to reason. Chap's as guilty as sin.'

'He maintains his innocence?'

'Yes. But then they all do, don't they? And in my experience, the ones who maintain it with the greatest vehemence are always the guilty ones.'

'You said *hard* evidence?'

'That's right,' Montgomery said, looking like a poker player who was about to lay down a royal flush. 'Not only were his boot prints in the mud surrounding the standing stone, but his dabs were all over the shooter.'

Langham sat back, deflated, and thought of poor Harriet back at the cottage. How the blazes was he going to break that news to her?

'Has Richard seen a lawyer?'

Montgomery nodded, chewing on a mouthful of sandwich. 'Old Bryant sat in on the interview.'

'What next?'

'I'm letting him stew. I want his confession, then I can charge him. I can keep him another few hours. After lunch I'll go in again with Detective Sergeant Bruce, who's enough to frighten the living daylights out of Al Capone. Mark my words, Wellbourne will be blabbing by mid-afternoon.'

'I'd like to see him.'

Montgomery regarded Langham with his egg-shaped head

tilted to one side. 'I don't see why not – and you can do me a favour while you're in there. Tell him he isn't necessarily for the drop. He can save himself.'

'Go on.'

'All he has to do is admit that he pulled the trigger – but that there was a struggle. The way I see it, they were arguing and then it got heated. The professor pulled the shooter and in the ensuing struggle Wellbourne snatched it from him and it went off – and the professor just happened to buy it. That way, we're all happy. I get my conviction and Wellbourne saves his neck.'

'You don't think it was premeditated?'

Montgomery shook his head. 'It was the professor's revolver. Maybe the prof threatened Wellbourne with it. There must have been a struggle, as I see it. Heat-of-the-moment thing. So, Langham, go in there and make him see reason, for God's sake.'

'I'll see what I can do,' he said.

Montgomery led him from the office, along a green-tiled corridor as ugly as a public urinal, and through a heavy metal door to the cells. A duty sergeant unlocked a navy-blue painted door; Langham slipped inside and the door thudded shut behind him.

Richard Wellbourne looked up, registering his surprise at seeing Langham. The big man's face had lost its natural colour and looked grey, his eyes haunted. Langham sat next to him on the bunk.

'Harriet?' Wellbourne said.

'She's at Yew Tree Cottage with Maria. Try not to worry about her.'

The farmer was still in his overalls and exuded the heady farmyard aroma of fresh manure and old hay.

'This is a nightmare, Donald. I don't know where to turn.'

'I want to hear about it in your own words. Take your time and tell me exactly what happened that evening when you went up to the manor.'

Wellbourne leaned forward, his elbows lodged on his knees and his head hanging. 'I needed to see Robertshaw. I'd been into town that afternoon and seen my solicitor. It wasn't good news. All the deeds they had were dated after 1800 and didn't include the West Field. Legally, I didn't have a leg to stand on.'

'Why did you decide to go and see Robertshaw?'

'I wanted to see if he'd be reasonable. I had planned to increase the herd by another fifty head and erect a byre on the field. It's not great pasture land, but I reckoned I could improve it over time. It'd help make the farm that bit more profitable.'

'What did he say?'

'He was adamant. As far as he was concerned, and as far as the law of the land went, the field belonged to him. The last thing he wanted was a byre and a herd of cows on *his* land, he said. He planned to dig more trenches in his damned search for the missing standing stones, and no mud-grubber – that's what he called me – was going to stop him.'

'You were outside at this time?'

'I saw him in his study to begin with, but he was on his way out, so I followed him.'

'To the standing stone?'

'That's right – which is how the police found my footprints.'

Langham watched the farmer as he said, 'And what about the professor's revolver? According to Montgomery, your fingerprints were all over the weapon.'

Wellbourne turned his leonine head and his grey eyes regarded Langham. 'Of course they were,' he said evenly, 'and that's easily explained. A couple of weeks ago, he invited me in for a drink one afternoon. I'd been working in a field near the manor and we got talking. Edwin asked if I'd care for a whisky, and I took him up on the offer. Christ!' he said bitterly, 'if only I'd known . . .'

'Go on.'

The farmer shrugged his broad shoulders. 'We got talking about the war. He asked me where I'd served, and I told him about the gun emplacements I'd commanded in Dover. He said he'd regretted being too old for what he called "useful work". He served in the Home Guard in Oxford and showed me his old First World War service revolver, a Webley. Of course, I took it, had a look. Then he put it back in the bureau and there it lay, covered with my prints, until the other night.' Wellbourne fell silent, staring at his big hands clenched between his knees.

Langham said, 'And you told Montgomery this?'

The farmer nodded.

'What did he say?'

Wellbourne pursed his lips in bitter recollection. 'The little blighter laughed, Donald. He laughed in my face and said "likely story". But it's the truth, as God's my witness. It's the truth.'

Langham let the silence stretch, then said, 'Montgomery wants you to confess. He sees it as an open-and-shut case, and says if you confess to shooting the professor accidentally in the heat of the moment, during a struggle, you'll save yourself.'

'But I *didn't* kill him, for God's sake!'

'I know,' Langham said. 'I believe you. I was telling you what Montgomery *wants*, and I advise you to stick to your guns. Don't tell the inspector I told you this – but don't make a confession, despite what he and his hard man Bruce might have to say.'

'Right, yes. Thank you, Donald.'

'Meanwhile, I'll be working on the case, trying to get to the bottom of what happened.'

'You don't know how much I appreciate that.' Wellbourne looked around the tiny cell. 'In here, all alone . . . I feel so helpless.' He smiled. 'Will you tell Harriet that I'm bearing up?'

'I'll do that.'

He shook hands with the farmer, tapped on the cell door and waited until the duty sergeant let him out.

'Well?' Montgomery asked when Langham returned to his office.

'He's sticking to his story,' Langham said, 'and as far as I'm concerned, he's telling the truth.'

'What, that tale about handling the revolver one Sunday afternoon over drinks? Come on, Langham! Cock and bull story! Wellbourne did it, or I'll eat my hat.'

Langham leaned against the wall. 'I find it hard to believe that the professor carried the revolver around with him night and day, leading to a tussle during which Wellbourne accidentally shot him. And I find it even harder to believe that Wellbourne, that evening, took the gun from the professor's bureau and used it with malice aforethought.'

'And his footprints around the base of the stone?'

Langham shrugged. 'Wellbourne admits they went out to the stone and talked about the disputed land.'

Montgomery shook his head. 'In my book, Langham, it all points to Wellbourne being the guilty party.'

Langham pushed himself from the wall and moved to the door. 'I intend to speak to a few more people concerning the case,' he said. 'I'll be in touch.'

He left the station and drove across town to Dr Robertshaw's surgery.

NINETEEN

He parked in the street outside the Willows and peered through the falling snow at the surgery, its white stuccoed facade bright against the grey winter sky. Oddly, the bay window of the consulting room was darkened, the curtains drawn. To the left of the front door, the window of the waiting room was similarly dark. Yet according to Dr Robertshaw, he had a busy surgery all day.

Langham ducked from the car, adjusted his hat and hurried up the path to the entrance. He tried the door but found it locked. Stepping off the path, he peered through the waiting-room window; through a chink in the blinds he made out empty chairs in the shadowy room. He moved to the surgery window but could see nothing due to the thick damask curtains.

He stepped back and peered at the upper-storey windows. They too were darkened.

The surgery was closed – so why had the doctor lied to him?

He walked down the gravelled drive to the extensive lawn at the rear. The back door was locked, and no lights showed behind the windows on the ground floor. However, a light was on in an upper window. He considered calling out but thought better of disturbing the neighbours. He looked around, returned to the drive and came back with a handful of gravel which he lobbed at the lighted window. It rattled against the pane – surely loud enough to attract anyone in the room – and he stepped back as it fell to earth.

If Dr Robertshaw was thus alerted, he elected not to show himself.

Langham decided to find a phone box and ring the surgery, though he was pretty sure his call would go unanswered.

He was walking back down the drive when a familiar sports car turned and braked suddenly on the snow-covered gravel before him.

Randall Robertshaw climbed out. 'What the deuce are you doing here, Langham?'

'I suspect the same as you, Randall. I rang your uncle earlier today about your mother's prescription. I thought you might not be up to the trip, considering the condition you were in last night.'

'So your lovely wife told you about our little contretemps, did she?' Randall grinned. 'Some woman you've got yourself there. Feisty? I'll say!'

Langham indicated the house. 'Your uncle seems to have shut up shop for the day.'

Randall peered at the darkened windows. 'That's odd.'

'He might be ill.'

Randall nodded absently. 'He's not a well man, Langham. Suffers periodic blackouts. If he knows what ails him, he's never told me.'

Langham wondered if Randall knew of his uncle's addiction but was covering for him.

'It's odd that he told me he had a busy surgery this morning, and yet the place is closed. There's a light on upstairs, round the back.'

Randall followed Langham down the drive. They rounded the end of the house and peered up at the window. 'That's his apartment,' Randall confirmed. 'I wonder if he's all right?'

'I tried rattling the panes with gravel. No luck.'

The young man looked worried, but he had no qualms about alerting the neighbours. He cupped his hands around his mouth. 'Spencer!' he called. 'Come on, Uncle, open up!'

'If he's passed out . . .' Langham began.

'You've tried all the doors?'

'Of course.'

'Mrs Greaves,' Randall said. 'She opens the waiting room every morning, so she'll have a key.'

'Do you know where she lives?'

'Just a few streets away – I gave her a lift home once.' He hurried down the drive to his car. 'Back in a jiffy,' he called.

Langham watched him reverse from the drive and race away.

He turned his collar up against the fierce wind as the snow assumed blizzard proportions. He paced the drive in a bid to keep warm, wondering if Dr Robertshaw would be in any fit state to prescribe the requisite medication if he was, as Langham suspected, suffering from the effects of his addiction.

A few minutes later, Randall turned into the drive, jumped out and rounded the car to the passenger door. 'Mrs G insisted on coming back with me,' he explained as he assisted the woman from the car.

'I was ever so worried this morning,' Mrs Greaves began, then saw Langham and stopped. 'Oh, it's you.'

Randall said. 'I can vouch for Langham, Mrs G. Give me the keys, would you?'

She passed him a bunch of assorted keys and followed him to the front door.

Langham said, 'I understood that Doctor Robertshaw had a full surgery today?'

'He did,' Mrs Greaves said, 'but he took badly at nine o'clock. One of his funny turns. He said it might be wise to close for the day, which is just what I did, then contacted all the patients who had appointments. They weren't best pleased, I can tell you.'

'Has this happened before?'

'We've never had to close like this, no,' she replied. 'For some reason, Doctor Robertshaw's dizzy spells tend to occur later in the day.'

Which, Langham thought, made admirable business sense.

Randall unlocked the front door and led the way inside. A brown linoleum passageway led to a flight of steps. Randall ascended the stairs two at a time and Langham brought up the rear.

'Spencer!' Randall called out as they emerged on to a carpeted landing. He pushed open a door to reveal a cluttered living room, the stereotypical ill-kempt abode of a bachelor. There was no sign of the inhabitant.

'Spencer!' Randall called again, and Langham detected concern in his voice.

Across the corridor, the bedroom was also vacant. Randall led the way to another room and opened the door to what was obviously the doctor's study.

The young man stepped inside, then quickly backed out.

'Mrs Greaves,' he stammered, 'I . . . I don't think . . .'

'Oh!' the woman said, ignoring Randall's advice and peering into the room. 'Oh, my!' A hand pressed to her mouth, she backed moaning from the room. 'Holy Mary . . .'

Langham took her weight and assisted her to the living room, easing her into an armchair and looking around the room. He found a drinks cabinet, poured her a stiff measure of brandy and pressed it into her shaking hands.

He returned to the study.

Randall was still on the threshold, leaning against the wood-work. Langham placed a solicitous hand on the young man's shoulder and eased past him.

Dr Robertshaw sat at his desk, slumped back in a chair. His left arm, its shirtsleeve rolled up, hung over the arm of the chair and a hypodermic syringe was stuck in the crook of his elbow. The man's face was bloodless, his mouth open and his eyes closed. Langham was unable to tell if the expression on his face was one of ecstasy or agony.

He felt for a pulse and was surprised to find that the doctor was still alive.

'Is he . . .?' Randall said from the doorway.

'Ring for an ambulance!' Langham snapped. 'He's alive – just.'

Randall snatched up the receiver on the desk, dialled 999 and stammered a request for an ambulance. He answered a series of questions, becoming increasingly upset, and he was shaking when he slammed down the phone.

'They're on the way. Is there anything we can do?'

Langham had loosened the man's tie but was loath to move him from the chair and arrange him in the recovery position on the floor.

'It might be best to wait till the experts arrive.'

Randall stared at the syringe hanging macabrely from the sunken vein. 'What . . .?' he said, pointing to the syringe.

Langham looked at the young man. 'You didn't know he was addicted?'

Randall hesitated, then shook his head. 'No . . . No, I didn't. Addicted to . . . to what?'

'I suspect heroin or some such.'

'Good God, no. I knew he wasn't well, but I had no idea
. . .'

The sound of sobbing reached them from the living room.
'Go and see to Mrs Greaves, would you?' Langham ordered.
'I'd better phone the police.'

The young man stumbled from the room. Langham picked
up the phone and got through to the station and Detective
Inspector Montgomery.

'How can I help you, Langham?'

'It's Doctor Robertshaw – Professor Robertshaw's brother.
We've just found him, and he's in a bad way.' He briefly outlined
what he and Randall had discovered at the surgery.

'Right, I'm on my way.'

Langham replaced the receiver and paced the room, then
moved to the window and stared out. The snow was coming
down in great, inflated flakes, obscuring the view of the town's
grey rooftops. He heard Randall's voice from the next room as
the young man did his best to comfort the distraught Mrs
Greaves.

A little later, he heard the sound of engines, then the front
door opening and footsteps on the staircase.

He stepped on to the landing. 'In here,' he said as a balding
man he assumed was a doctor appeared at the top of the stairs,
followed by two ambulance men carrying a stretcher.

Langham ushered them into the study. The doctor took
Robertshaw's pulse, conferred with the ambulancemen who
eased the unconscious man from the chair and on to the stretcher.
The hypodermic needle had been removed, and a thread of
blood trickled down his arm and dripped from his fingers.
Langham stepped out on to the landing.

He heard footsteps on the staircase and Montgomery appeared.
The detective nodded to Langham, saw the activity in the study
and joined the medics.

Langham moved to the end of the landing where a window
overlooked the street. He was in the process of lighting his pipe
when Montgomery stepped from the study and joined him. 'The
medico is hedging his bets: he's not saying whether or not it
was a deliberate overdose, but it was a massive injection.'

'Will he live?'

'Touch and go,' Montgomery said. 'To be on the safe side, I'm treating it as a crime scene. I've called out the team. Forensics are on their way.'

'Randall Robertshaw and the doctor's receptionist are in there,' Langham said, indicating the living room.

The ambulancemen edged from the room with the loaded stretcher and eased it through the door at the top of the staircase.

Randall Robertshaw stepped on to the landing, watching the ambulancemen as they carried the stretcher down the staircase. He saw Montgomery and said, 'I'd like to accompany my uncle, if that's . . .' He gestured toward the departing stretcher.

'Off you go,' Montgomery said.

'A quick word,' Langham said to the young man. 'I advise you to take your mother to a hospital and explain the situation about the painkillers, sooner rather than later.'

'I'll do that,' Randall said. 'Thank you.'

'And I'm sorry about . . .' Langham said, nodding towards the stairs. 'If you need to talk to someone, you know where to find me.'

Randall thanked him again and hurried down the stairs after the ambulancemen.

'What's the situation with Richard Wellbourne?' Langham asked Montgomery.

The detective swore. 'I sent Bruce in to give him the hard word.' He shook his head. 'He's sticking to his story. He admits he was there that night and had an altercation with the professor, but that's it. And he's adamant about the fingerprints on the gun – says the professor showed him the ruddy thing weeks ago.'

'So you're letting him go?'

'I'll let him sweat for a while, and then he can go – for the time being.'

'Would it be all right if I drop by and give him a lift back to Ingoldby?' Langham hesitated. 'You never know, he might say more in the car.'

Montgomery thought about it. 'Good idea. I'll ring Bruce from the telephone downstairs and tell him you're on your way.'

Below, a door opened and heavy footsteps sounded on the

staircase. Montgomery greeted his forensics team and led them into the study.

Langham moved to the living room and found Mrs Greaves crying quietly on the settee.

'Oh, Mr Langham!' she said. 'I saw the syringe, stuck in his arm! Do you think . . .?'

'I honestly don't know what to think, Mrs Greaves,' he said. 'Come on, I'll drive you home.'

'That's very kind of you, Mr Langham. Wait till I tell my hubby about poor Doctor Robertshaw, God bless him.'

He assisted the weeping woman down the stairs and out to the car.

After dropping Mrs Greaves at a small, terraced house half a mile from the surgery, he drove to the police station. He found Richard Wellbourne, incongruous in his farm-soiled overalls, sitting in the waiting room.

The farmer smiled when he saw Langham.

'Am I glad to see you!' Wellbourne said. 'I thought they were planning to keep me locked up all day. That Bruce chappie got all Gestapo earlier, then the desk sergeant was as nice as ninepence when he came in and said I could go.'

'Come on, let's get you out of here.'

'Am I looking forward to seeing Harriet's expression when I walk into the room!' Wellbourne said.

They hurried from the station to Langham's car.

TWENTY

Maria soon discovered that Harriet Wellbourne had a prodigious capacity for imbibing tea. She made a second pot, carried it back into the living room and poured the farmer's wife what she estimated must be her sixth cup, strong and black.

They sat side by side on the sofa and watched the dancing flames of the fire.

'Time seems to slow down in situations like these,' Harriet said. 'Do you have any idea how long they might keep him?'

'I'm not at all sure, but I do know that Donald will be doing his best to talk sense into Inspector Montgomery.'

Harriet was silent for a time. 'I've been thinking, Maria – my thoughts have been swirling round and round. Richard *did* go over to see the professor on Tuesday night, as he wasn't at all happy with what he'd discovered at his solicitors. So I couldn't help thinking . . . what if Richard and Edwin argued, then tussled, and in the heat of the moment the professor drew his gun and . . . and Richard had to defend himself.' She stared at Maria with wide eyes. 'What if my Richard *did* shoot the professor?'

Maria shook her head. 'Harriet, I think if it did happen like that, then Richard would have done the sensible thing. He would have gone to the police and told them exactly what had happened, like the honest man he is. Anyway, it looked to me as if the professor wasn't killed accidentally during a fight – the wound was to the side of his head, aimed precisely by the killer. I know it's difficult, but try not to worry.'

Harriet hugged her cup. 'This is a nightmare . . .' She was silent for a time, then went on, 'At least Roy's at the farm; he'll look after things while Richard's gone. It's reassuring that I can depend on him. He's a good boy, all things considered.'

Maria looked at her questioningly. '"All things considered"?'

'You're an intelligent woman, Maria. You must have wondered about . . . about Roy, his story.'

Maria smiled. 'Well, Donald and I have discussed him—'

'I know that he wasn't in the RAF,' Harriet said, surprising Maria. 'As soon as he came to the farm, asking Richard for work, I knew his story didn't quite add up. I *knew*, up here. My sixth sense, as Richard would call it.' She tapped the side of her head and smiled. 'Roy's stories, the way he told them – they weren't convincing.'

'So . . .?'

'So I checked. I have a friend in Bury whose husband is a military buff. Roy said he'd been stationed at Waddington, a rear-gunner with the Forty-Four Squadron, flying Lancasters. My friend checked the squadron records, and no one by the name of Roy Vickers ever flew for them – nor was he on the ground staff, an engineer or a technician or the like.'

'But he did work at the quartermaster's stores in Lincoln during the war?'

Harriet sighed. 'Not even that. My friend's husband contacted people who worked on the base at Lincoln, and no one knew anyone by the name of Vickers.'

'So he lied? Do you think it was deliberate; he knew that you . . .?' she faltered, staring down at her cup.

'Oh, I wouldn't have countenanced anyone who had deliberately lied and taken advantage of us like that, knowing about Jeremy. That would have been unconscionable, Maria. No, what happened was that he came to the door one day a couple of years ago and asked Richard if he needed anyone to help around the farm. He said he had experience, having worked on a farm in Norfolk for years. As it happened, we'd let someone go just that autumn, and Richard was working all hours to get things done. So he took Roy on for a few hours a day and let him live in the caravan in the meadow. And you see, young Roy was wearing that dirty RAF greatcoat and squadron tie, and Richard just assumed, without asking questions, that he was an ex-flier. As time went on, well . . . Roy never lied, outright, so much as never really told the truth, and it got to the point that everyone in the village assumed he was ex-RAF, so he played up to the part. I suppose he did lie, then, to keep up appearances, as it were.'

'But you knew the truth?'

Harriet nodded. 'Very early on. The way he looked uncomfortable, especially when the war was mentioned in Richard's company. I believe Roy felt uneasy at pulling the wool over Richard's eyes.'

'So Richard doesn't know?' Maria asked.

Harriet shook her head and smiled. 'My husband has many attributes – trust and loyalty among them – but imagination is not his strong point. He would find it hard to understand why Roy found himself forced to perpetuate the lie. He wouldn't understand the . . . the *psychological* pressure the young man must have found himself under for the past couple of years.'

'I see.'

'So please don't tell Richard anything about Roy. He would only be hurt, and Roy in turn would suffer. Things have been . . . well, for the past two years things have been going along very well.'

Maria sipped her tea, then smiled at Harriet. 'You must have known about Roy and Nancy?'

Harriet laughed. 'I saw the change in Roy last autumn. He'd always been very quiet, almost uncommunicative, and he'd rarely smile. Then, all of a sudden, he seemed to blossom, come out of himself. He was even quite chatty from time to time. "Harriet," I said to myself. "He's found a girl." Then I saw that young Nancy had changed the route of her walk and detoured down Crooked Lane, and five minutes after she passed by with that daft dog of hers, Roy would finish what he was doing and shoot off. Then Nancy started getting bold and meeting Roy some evenings at the caravan. Richard and I laughed about it.'

'You didn't disapprove?'

Harriet laughed. 'How could we? We were young once, Maria!'

'It's a pity others couldn't have been so understanding.'

'Oh, you mean the professor and that son of his?' Harriet said, sniffing. 'Nancy lived in fear of her uncle finding out. He was a miserable old soul, and no mistake. The girl's twenty, for heaven's sake – a young woman. He treated her like a child.'

'What about Xandra?'

'Despite the villagers hereabouts thinking her a bit snooty, I have a lot of time for Xandra. She's never fitted in, despite her

being here for ten years. I suppose it's because she's from
London and an actress. But I'll say this much for her – she
treats Nancy like a human being; they get on well.'

Maria refilled Harriet's cup. 'I must say, I don't understand
Randall's animosity towards Nancy. She thinks it's because
she's friendly with Randall's former wife – and knows what a
cheat Randall is.' She shook her head. 'But even so, his treatment of her seems excessive.'

Harriet smiled and tapped Maria's hand. 'There's more to
that than meets the eye, believe you me,' she said.

'Go on,' Maria said.

'Well, I think Randall is thinking about the future. When he
left his wife – or whatever happened – the professor was enraged.
He knew Randall wasn't the innocent party he claimed to be.
I suspect Randall feared being cut from the professor's will –
and what with Nancy looking after Xandra . . .'

'Ah,' Maria said, beginning to understand.

'Exactly. Randall thinks Nancy has inveigled her way into
his parents' affections, and fears that one day she'll take a cut
of what he thinks should rightly be all his.'

She stopped suddenly and exclaimed, 'Oh!', her eyes wide
open and staring into space.

Maria was startled. 'Harriet? What is it?'

'Richard! Oh, my word, Maria . . .' She reached out and
clutched Maria's hand. 'Jeremy was here, just a second ago,
and he told me that Richard is on his way home! Oh, the
relief!' She sank back into the sofa, her face suffused with joy.
'Listen,' she said, gripping Maria's hand even tighter.

Only then did Maria hear the sound of a car engine as
it approached the cottage. She stared open-mouthed at the
farmer's wife.

'What did I tell you!' Harriet called out.

Maria crossed the living room and peered through the
window. Donald and Richard climbed from the car, the latter
extricating his oversized frame with difficulty.

She hurried to the front door and pulled it open.

'You're back! And Richard . . .' She hugged Donald and
smiled at the farmer. 'Come in. Harriet knew you were on your
way.'

Donald stared at her. 'How on earth . . .?'

Richard smiled. 'Her old sixth sense.' The farmer laughed.
'It's unerring.'

They moved to the living room and Maria watched as
Harriet stood up, a tiny figure beside the sofa. Richard advanced
and embraced her.

'I've been worried sick!' Harriet cried, dabbing at her tears
with a tissue.

'You silly old thing.' Richard laughed. 'I told you there was
nothing to worry about, didn't I? She does fret so!' he said to
Maria.

'But you're home now,' Harriet said. 'That's what matters.'

'Anyone would think I've been at war! You do fuss, woman.'

'And rightly so, with a big lumbering clod of a husband
like you!'

'Can I get you some tea, Richard?' Maria asked.

'Do you know, I think I'd just like to get home and settled,
if it's all the same,' Richard said. 'There's work to be seen to.'

'Roy's got all that in hand,' Harriet said. 'You're coming
back with me and I'm making you something to eat, and then
you're putting your feet up for the rest of the day. You can get
back to work in the morning.'

Richard turned and shrugged at Donald and Maria, as if to
say who was he to argue? He thanked Donald and followed his
wife from the cottage.

As the door closed behind them, Donald said, 'Did she really
claim she knew he was coming back?'

'I'll say. It was creepy.' She described Harriet's sudden
pronouncement that Jeremy had appeared and told her of her
husband's return.

'And you were taken in?' he asked.

She punched him playfully. 'Well, she was right, wasn't she?
Seconds later you arrived back.'

He kissed her. 'Harriet merely has excellent hearing. She
heard the engine seconds before you did, and wishful thinking
did the rest.'

'You cynical old man!'

He moved to the kitchen. 'Have you been out this morning?'
he asked.

'No – why?'

'And have you had lunch?'

She shook her head. 'No.'

He raided the larder, pulling out two pork pies and a bottle of milk stout and stuffing them into the pockets of his overcoat.

'Donald?'

'I've been thinking of nothing all the way back but going for a long walk with you and munching on a pie at the top of the hill,' he said. 'All morning I've been talking to people I'd rather not talk to, and . . . and seeing things I'd rather I hadn't. Let's go, and I'll tell you all about it.'

Laughing, she found her hat and coat, pulled on her boots and followed him from the cottage.

TWENTY-ONE

They walked across the village green, turned along West Lane and cut through Culkin's Wood. The day was crisp and bright, and the earlier fall of snow had stopped. Even the wind had died down, making for perfect walking weather. The silence was broken only by the occasional cooing of wood pigeons, the cawing of distant crows and the sound of their own panting as they climbed the hillside path through the trees.

'Do you think poor Doctor Robertshaw tried to kill himself?' Maria asked when Donald had told her what he and Randall had discovered at the surgery.

He shook his head. 'It's impossible to say. I suppose only the doctor himself knows for certain. I suppose we can't rule out a suicide attempt.'

'Was the doctor close to his brother?'

'I asked him that the other day. He said they weren't especially close.'

'Did the medic say whether he'd survive?'

He shrugged, looking up the hill. 'It's touch and go, apparently.'

The crest of the rise was in view. She slowed down and gripped his hand, allowing him to haul her the rest of the way.

'I wonder how Nancy will take it?' she said. 'Do you know if she was close to Spencer?'

'She would have met him when he came to examine Xandra,' he said, 'and no doubt at family gatherings.'

'The poor girl; she's certainly been through it.'

They came to the top of the hill and stood side by side gazing down at the view.

The earlier snowfall had laid a fresh, dazzling patina over the land. The scene was monochrome, predominantly white, with buildings and drystone walls standing out in charcoal hues. The sun was lost now behind a pewter sky, betokening more snow to come. Smoke threaded from a hundred village chimneys, adding to the grey caul. In the distance, the low hills folded in behind each other to the tree-lined horizon. The scene appeared deceptively peaceful.

Maria made out Standing Stone Manor and the stark monolith sequestered in the empty, white-blanketed field behind the house.

'To think,' she said, 'that human beings have been making their homes here for thousands of years. Just think of all the many lives that have passed, unrecorded, forgotten now.'

'Steady, girl, that's waxing a bit poetical, isn't it?'

She nudged him. 'You unromantic realist.'

He said, 'Just think of all the intrigues, jealousies, hatreds and murders committed over the centuries. Think of the crimes that have gone undetected, the killers gone unpunished. I'm glad we're living now, Maria, when law and order prevail. I'd hate to have lived in the lawless times of the Neolithic age.'

'They no doubt would have had their own laws, though.'

'You're right. But what might have been less sophisticated was their means to uphold the law and capture the wrong-doers.'

'Spoken like a true private detective!' She laughed.

She gazed down at the village.

'What I'd rather think about,' she said, 'is all the love and happiness and good times spent across the centuries.'

He kissed the top of her head. 'And that's why I love you,' he said.

She pointed. 'Look.'

In the meadow behind Wellspring Farm, next to the gypsy caravan, Nancy and Roy Vickers, along with Bill the dog, were playing in the snow. Nancy launched a snowball at the young man. He dodged it and the dog leapt acrobatically through the air in a futile attempt to intercept the missile. Their happy cries eddied up the hillside.

Donald produced the pork pies and opened the bottle of stout with his Swiss Army knife, and they sat on a fallen log and ate their impromptu lunch.

Maria told him what Harriet had said about Roy Vickers. 'You were right – he didn't have anything to do with the RAF. He didn't even work in the quartermaster's stores at Lincoln.'

He passed her the bottle of beer.

'Do you know something?' he said as she drank. 'I can't dislike him for that. But I wonder why he felt the need to lie?'

She watched the young man chase after Nancy with a giant snowball which he launched at her retreating back. It exploded on her duffel coat, and she turned to him suddenly. They came together and embraced.

'Harriet doesn't think he deliberately lied, just never corrected the assumptions that he did have an RAF past.' She passed him the bottle.

He nodded. 'I like that,' he said.

She laughed. 'Listen to you! Under that cynical exterior, you're just as romantic as me.'

'That'd be going it some, girl.' He stood up. 'Come on, I'll race you to the foot of the hill.'

'But I can't run on this!' she cried as Donald set off at a sliding shuffle down the hillside and she picked her way carefully after him.

She caught him up as the hillside levelled out and became a meadow to the north of the stream that ran through the village. They pulled open the farm gate, passed through and latched it after them, then set off along the lane.

'My word,' Donald said. 'Is that who I think it is?'

Maria peered up the lane. In the distance, tall against the skyline between the high hedges, she made out the scarecrow figure of Xandra Robertshaw. She carried what looked like a shepherd's crook and proceeded slowly, picking her way over the snow-covered lane towards them with exaggerated care.

'Well, I never,' Donald murmured.

'Xandra!' Maria said. 'It's nice to see you out and about.'

The woman smiled. She wore a knee-length plum-coloured Burberry with the collar turned up, a woollen scarf, and a hat that looked more like a turban. Her face was pale, her cheeks sunken. She was breathing hard from the exertion, her breath rattling.

'It's such a wonderfully fresh day,' she wheezed, 'and as I haven't ventured out for weeks, I thought I'd take the opportunity while I'm feeling a little better.' She smiled at them. 'Have you been far?'

Maria pointed to the tree-clad hillside to their right. 'Up through the wood.'

The woman nodded. 'I think I'll turn around now and head back. I'll join you if I may?'

'Of course,' Maria said. They walked slowly as Xandra fell into step beside them.

Donald made a polite comment to the effect that he was pleased she was feeling a little better.

'I'm feeling alive for the first time in an age, Mr Langham. Oh,' she went on, 'Randall telephoned just before I set off.'

'Ah . . .' Donald said.

'He told me about your discovering Spencer.'

'Yes. I'm so sorry. Did he say—?'

'He's still unconscious – and if he does survive, Randall said, the medics fear that there might be some permanent damage to his liver or some such.'

'Let's hope not,' Maria said.

Xandra sniffed. 'I never liked the man, to be perfectly frank, though he seemed to feel something for me, which was a pain.'

'He did?' Donald said.

'I think he felt sorry for me – because I was married to Edwin. They were never that close. Or perhaps he pitied me, on account of my illness. Whatever the reason, he seemed to think there was a bond between us that I failed entirely to apprehend.'

'Did the medics know whether Spencer overdosed on purpose?' Donald asked tentatively.

Xandra shook her head. 'I asked Randall the same question, but the doctors couldn't tell. If it was accidental, then he was a damned fool. As he was a medico, one would have thought that he would have administered himself a safe dosage, wouldn't one?'

'Perhaps so,' Donald murmured.

'Randall has made an appointment for me to see a consultant in Cambridge tomorrow afternoon,' Xandra went on. 'He seems to think that a second opinion might be wise. I assume he's of the view that his uncle, under the influence of his addiction, might have been a far from competent practitioner.'

They walked on in reflective silence for a time, before Xandra turned to Maria and said, 'Is that beer I smell?'

Maria smiled. 'We had a picnic of milk stout and pork pies on the hillside,' she explained.

The woman looked down at her. 'Milk stout and pork pies?' she said with all the hauteur of an epicure. 'I must admit it's a combination I've never experienced.'

'I recommend it,' Donald said with a playful wink at Maria.

'And speaking of food, if you can call it that,' Xandra went on, 'when all this business is over, you really must come to the manor for dinner.'

'That would be lovely,' Maria said.

They came to the bridge on Crooked Lane, and Xandra paused. 'This is where our paths diverge,' she said. 'Oh, I saw Nancy earlier and told her that she was welcome back at any time and that she should ignore Randall's behaviour. I also told her that she'll no longer need to run after me like a nurse-maid. I think from now on I can look after myself.' She paused. 'Milk stout and pork pies? I wonder . . .'

She hoisted her stick in farewell and walked slowly over the bridge.

Donald watched her go, then raised an eyebrow at Maria. 'Well, she seems to have found a new lease of life.'

Maria threaded an arm through his and they set off along Crooked Lane.

They came to the meadow and the gypsy caravan; there was no sign of Nancy, Roy or Bill the dog, though a snowman stood lonely sentinel before the caravan.

As they were passing the meadow, the caravan door opened and Roy Vickers emerged, carrying a brace of pheasant. He hoisted them in greeting and called out, 'Half a mo!'

They paused while he hurried over to the wall. 'I was going to pop over with a message from Nancy,' he said. 'Richard and Harriet have invited us to stay for dinner, and Nancy wanted to apologize that she won't be in till later. She said she'll be back by nine. I hope that's all right?'

'Of course it is,' Maria said. 'Enjoy the . . .' She pointed at the dead birds.

Roy laughed. 'Oh, we won't be eating these tonight. They haven't hung long enough. They're a present for Harriet, in thanks for the meal.' He hesitated. 'I was going to say . . .'

'Yes?' Donald said.

'Well, I'm a bit worried about Nancy.'

'Go on.'

'After everything that's happened over the past few days . . . You see, we saw Xandra just now, and she told us about Nancy's uncle, the doctor.'

'And Nancy has taken it badly?' Donald said.

Vickers gave a crooked grimace. 'That's the thing, Donald. Quite the opposite, actually. She seems to be oddly happy-go-lucky, almost bubbly. I think she's bottling it up.'

'That's not uncommon,' Donald said, 'as a way of coping with such unpleasantness.'

'I'm just worried that it'll hit her at some point and there'll be a reaction – and she'll be correspondingly . . . I don't know . . . melancholy. I wouldn't know what to do if that happened.'

'There would only be one thing you could possibly do,' Maria said. 'Be there to support her, *if* it happens.'

'I'll second that,' Donald said. 'It's obvious that she thinks the world of you. Just be there for her through thick and thin . . . to coin a cliché.'

The young man nodded. 'Anyway, I'll be getting back inside. And thanks for everything – for making Nancy so welcome.'

He turned and hurried towards the farmhouse.

Later, back at the cottage, Maria prepared a quick meal from Wednesday's leftover casserole, mashed potatoes and boiled cauliflower. Rather than eat at the table in the kitchen, they sat on the sofa before the fire and ate while listening to the news on the wireless followed by *My Word!*

Afterwards, Maria mixed herself a gin and tonic, and Donald continued where he'd left off and opened another bottle of milk stout. He turned the volume down on some dance music and put more coal on the fire.

He told her about the plot of his next novel as the clock ticked towards ten and the wind blew noisily outside.

Warmed by the fire to the edge of sleep, Maria murmured, 'No sign of Nancy yet.'

'Didn't Roy say she'd be back by nine?'

'Probably having too good a time.'

'We could always go to bed and leave the back door unlocked,' he said. 'We're not in London now.'

She nodded.

A little later, she said, 'Do you think she'll be all right?'

'Of course. She's only a stone's throw away, after all.'

'Not in *that* way, you idiot. I mean after what's happened to the professor and Spencer.'

He thought about it. 'She's young and resilient, and she has someone who loves her. She'll bounce back. Hello, speak of the devil.'

The back door rattled open and Nancy called out, 'Sorry! Sorry! Sorry I'm so late!' The apology was accompanied by the sound of scrabbling claws on linoleum, and Bill burst into the room followed by Nancy, rosy-cheeked and glowing.

'I know I said I'd be back by nine, but Harriet was so kind and Richard made me drink some awful Scotch, and we had *such* a good time.'

Donald laughed. 'I think you're a trifle tight, my girl.'

Nancy pulled off her coat and stood swaying, beaming down at them. 'Just a teeny-tiny little bit. S'all right, though, 'cos Roy walked me home. I'm fine. I think I'll go to bed now.'

'Sleep well,' Maria said.

'C'mon, Bill!' Nancy commanded.

The dog had curled up on the rug before the embers and showed not the slightest inclination to budge. 'I said, come on, Bill. It's beddy-byes time. Up you get!'

'You'll be lucky.' Donald laughed.

'He's badly trained,' Nancy said. 'Or, rather, not trained at all. My uncle . . . he told me off for not training him properly. But then he would, wouldn't he? He had a thing about dogs being . . . being well trained. S'pose it was all to do with his first wife, wasn't it?'

Donald said, 'His first wife? Deirdre?'

Nancy nodded as she poked Bill in the ribs with her stockinged toe. 'That's the woman. Deirdre. She was a dog trainer, you see. Come on, boy, up you get.'

Maria looked at Donald. He was staring up at the girl. 'You mean,' he said, 'that she trained dogs?'

'That's right. A dog trainer. Quite an . . . an authority, by all accounts. Oh, Bill, you're *so* bad!'

Maria said, 'You go to bed, Nancy. I'm sure Bill will be fine down here. I'll put the fireguard in place before we turn in.'

'If you're sure,' Nancy said, then screwed her nose up at them in farewell and stumbled from the room.

Donald sat up, waited until the door clicked shut, then said, 'Well, blow me down!'

'The dog in the park?' Maria said.

'It was trained to fetch the blasted valise.' He screwed his eyes shut, then opened them and stared at her.

'But why would Deirdre blackmail the man she'd just got back with?' Maria asked, her head swirling.

'You know, I thought it odd that she should resume a relationship with someone who'd treated her so appallingly in the past. I wonder . . .' He tapped her knee. 'First thing in the morning, my girl, I'm going to pay the woman a little visit.'

'You do that, Donald, and perhaps you'd be a *wonderful* darling and make me another drink?'

Their drinks recharged, they sat in the glow of the fire, talking, as midnight approached.

TWENTY-TWO

At ten o'clock the following morning, Langham turned into Elm Lane and parked twenty yards from the Old Manse. He sat for a minute, watching the snow fall and considering Deirdre Creighton and her part in the life and death of Professor Edwin Robertshaw.

Rather than approach the front door, he made his way down the drive at the side of the house. He came to a double garage, a rickety weatherboard affair with a corrugated asbestos roof, and with his handkerchief wiped a clear patch in the frosted windowpane. There were no cars in the darkened interior. He glanced across at the house; no lights shone behind either of the two side windows. He moved cautiously to the rear of the building. Twenty yards away, at the bottom of the garden, he made out what might have been dog kennels and a long run enclosed in wire netting.

He checked the rear windows and, reasonably confident that he was unobserved, made his way down an asphalt path to the kennel. Like the garage, it was absent of any incriminating evidence it might once have contained.

He retraced his steps back down the drive and knocked on the front door.

The maid opened the door and frowned. 'Oh, it's Mr . . .?'

'Langham,' he said. 'Is Mrs Creighton at home?'

'If you'd care to come this way.' She led him to the drawing room and departed.

Langham moved to the settee and ran his fingers across the crushed velvet, finding pale hairs too thick to be those of a Persian cat.

'Mr Langham . . .'

He turned. Deirdre Creighton, as poised as he recalled from their first meeting, stood in the doorway with her fingertips resting lightly on the handle: she might have been posing for an interior shot in *Homes and Gardens* magazine. She wore a pale-green dress and pearls, and her hair was immaculately coiffured.

'Ah, you said you might be back, Mr Langham. Would you care to take a seat?'

He eased himself on to the settee as she took the Queen Anne chair opposite. 'The case is proving to be more than a little intriguing,' he said.

'Are you any closer to apprehending the person responsible for . . .?'

'We're getting closer by the day,' he replied, 'little by little, interview by interview. I assure you that it's only a matter of time before we have the affair cleared up.'

'That is more than gratifying to hear,' she said with a smile. 'How might I be of assistance, Mr Langham?'

He withdrew his notebook and spent half a minute leafing through his record of their first interview, not as an aide-memoire but as a ploy to keep her waiting.

He looked up. 'I'd like to ask you about your relationship with the professor.'

She sighed. 'As I think I mentioned last time, our marriage was far from satisfactory. Edwin thought nothing of—'

He stopped her with a raised hand. 'When I said "relationship", I was referring not so much to your marriage as to your more recent relations with the deceased.'

She swallowed. 'I see.'

'Well . . .?' he said, smiling across at her.

'What would you like to know, Mr Langham?'

'According to my notes,' he went on, making a show of consulting his notebook, 'you said you were lonely, and then Edwin appeared on the scene and provided a welcome distraction from the same old routine.'

She looked away from him and gazed through the window. 'That is correct,' she said in a quiet voice.

Langham sighed and sat back, crossing his legs and relaxing. He said, 'And now, if you don't mind, I'd like the truth.'

Her eyes flashed at him. 'The truth?' she said, her expression inscrutable.

'I don't buy it, Mrs Creighton. More than twenty years ago the professor was serially unfaithful to you, ending in his having an affair which, to employ a cliché, was the straw that broke the camel's back, and you threw him out. And then, a few months ago, you just happened to accidentally bump into him in the Midland and it proved to be the rekindling of your relationship. You took him back, albeit presumably on your own terms: he provided a welcome distraction from the same old routine.'

She nodded, but far from convincingly. 'That's correct, yes.'

He stared across at her, letting the silence stretch. 'I'm no psychologist, Mrs Creighton, but I don't think that it takes one to see your story for the flagrant fabrication that it is.'

She held his gaze. 'It's the truth, Mr Langham.'

He smiled at her. 'There are two ways we can go about this. You can tell me the truth, and it will go no further than these four walls – or you can persist in your lies and I'll hand over what I know to the police.'

Her eyes widened and she shook her head. 'But . . . but I thought you said *you* were from the police?'

'You are not the only one adept at stretching the truth,' he said. 'I'm a private detective, working on the case on behalf of the Robertshaw family.'

'I see.' She sat clasping her hands on her lap, gazing down at the carpet as if frozen. He found himself feeling sorry for the woman.

'I have no idea whether you decided to make the professor pay for his past misdeeds when you met him,' he said, 'or whether it came to you later. Whichever it might have been, you decided to blackmail him.'

She swallowed. Without looking at him, she murmured, 'What assurance do I have that you won't pass what I tell you on to the police?'

'Whether you believe me or not,' he said, 'I'm a man of my word. The police need to know nothing about the blackmail. However, if you insist on withholding the truth . . .'

'What do you want to know?'

'First of all, I'd like confirmation that you wrote to Professor Robertshaw on two occasions – on the second, demanding one hundred pounds.'

She leaned forward in the chair, wringing her hands. 'It wasn't to bed. He said it was a miracle that his brother managed to run his surgery, though I understand he had lost a number of patients recently, and the practice was suffering in consequence.'

'Presumably, Spencer was grateful for his brother's help?'

The woman thought about it. 'It's difficult to assess what Spencer thought of his brother from the little that Edwin mentioned. I . . . I suspect that if Spencer were cut from the same selfish, egotistical cloth as Edwin, he would be more likely to resent his brother for his assistance than be grateful.'

Langham made a note of this. 'Well, I think that covers everything.' He closed his notebook and slipped it into his breast pocket.

'Mr Langham,' she said hesitantly. 'About what I did . . .'

He leaned forward, resting his elbows on his knees. 'As far as I'm concerned, what you did was reprehensible. At the same time, I think I know what motivated you. Hatred is a powerful emotion, isn't it, and so hard to resist, and when you saw a way to gain revenge . . .' He gestured. 'I'm not condoning what you did, Mrs Creighton, but I think I understand.'

She sighed. 'I assure you that . . . that it would not have continued, Mr Langham. Edwin was becoming more . . . more insistent that we escalate the terms of our relationship, and I'd decided that in a month, maybe two, I would sever all contact with him—'

'Escalate the terms of your relationship?' he said, smiling at the euphemism. 'Did he say what he had in mind?'

Mrs Creighton almost winced as she said, 'He wanted us to remarry, Mr Langham.'

'Remarry? But . . .'

'He told me that his wife was ill – terminally ill – and he said that she would be dead within a month. After that, he said, he would be free.'

Langham stared at the woman. 'He said that – *free*?'

'He said we could marry, and that I could move into the manor.' She shook her head. 'I was, of course, horrified at the thought, and I decided that enough was enough and I would stop seeing him.'

Langham nodded, considering what she'd told him, then climbed to his feet.

---

just the money . . . honestly,' she said, almost pleading to be believed. 'I . . . I admit that . . . that I am living beyond my means here. Appearances can be deceptive. I rent this place, and the upkeep is exorbitant, and the annuity I received upon the death of my second husband hardly covers—'

'So you began the affair with the professor with the express intention of extorting funds from him?'

'No! No, that was only a secondary consideration. I admit that the money would have come in useful, but my primary motive was . . . was probably even more base than that: I wanted *revenge*. I wanted him to pay for how he'd hurt me all those years ago. Do you have any conception of what it is like, Mr Langham, to love someone, to genuinely love someone with all one's heart, and then to find out that they are being unfaithful to you? Can you begin to comprehend the pain, the mental anguish?' She shook her head. 'And more than that, one's trust in human nature is undermined, wrecked.'

'So you decided to exact your revenge.' He smiled to himself as he fingered a dog hair on the settee beside him. 'I must admit, it was a clever ploy, using the dog to retrieve the valise. Very clever indeed – or perhaps not. You see, when I discovered that you were once a dog trainer, it all fell into place.' He raised a finger on which sat a wiry hair.

He looked across at her. 'You really must have hated the man.'

She smiled bitterly. 'Hatred does not really describe the degree of loathing I felt towards Edwin Robertshaw. He almost destroyed my life all those years ago. Hardly a day went by when he didn't cross my mind, sour my thoughts, poison my happiness. When the opportunity came to avenge that hurt, I *took* it.'

'But did you hate Robertshaw sufficiently,' he said, 'to kill him – or to have him killed?'

She looked shocked. 'I . . . I swear, no – I might not be perfect, Mr Langham. I admit that I hated the man. But I am no killer, and nor would I have employed anyone else to kill him. It was sufficient to see him tortured by my blackmail demands.'

He let the silence stretch. 'There is one thing that puzzles me,' he said. 'In the first blackmail note, you wrote: "If you don't pay up, Nancy will find out.'" He shrugged. 'What did you mean by that? Why did you think that Nancy would be bothered about her uncle's conducting an affair with you?'

An odd light entered her blue eyes, and Langham took it for self-congratulation. 'My express intention was to hurt him, Mr Langham. He would be tortured by the secret of his affair becoming public if he didn't accede to my demands – but I wanted to torture him even more. I wanted him to worry himself sick as to who might know his *other* secret.'

Langham shook his head. 'His other secret?'

'Why do you think I left him, twenty years ago? What do you think pushed me over the edge? He'd had previous affairs, as I mentioned, and though they hurt me, it was the last one that almost destroyed me. You see, he was having an affair with his sister-in-law, Amelia Robertshaw – the wife of his youngest brother, George.'

Langham's mouth ran dry. 'But . . .?'

She nodded, smiling. 'Not only was he having an affair behind my back, Mr Langham, but he was betraying his brother. Can you imagine the kind of egotist who would do that without the slightest qualm? When Amelia fell pregnant with his child, the truth came out. You see, George was unable to father children. Amelia admitted the affair to her husband and begged him not to throw her out – and he showed more forgiveness than I did. They remained together, though George did sever all ties with Edwin. For me, it was the last straw, and I threw him out and didn't set eyes on the monster for twenty years.'

'But the child . . .' Langham began.

'A daughter,' she said.

He sat back on the sofa, staring at her. 'Good God – it was Nancy,' he said, rubbing his eyes tiredly. 'Nancy is the professor's daughter.'

She nodded. 'I read about her parents' death in the train accident two years ago,' she said, 'and when I was reacquainted with Edwin, he told me he'd taken her in. The least he could do, he said. Despite myself, I admired him for this – it was one of his rare acts of humanity.'

Langham sat in silence for a while, considering how Nancy might react to learning the truth about her parentage. 'My word,'

he said at last. 'Well, that came as something of a revelation, I must admit.'

She leaned forward. 'You don't think it has any bearing on . . .?'

'I can't see how it might,' he said. 'Even if she had somehow found out, she could have no reason to hate her father, surely?' He shook his head. 'We've come to know Nancy quite well over the past few days; she would never do such a thing.'

He sat back and closed his eyes, marshalling his thoughts. Then he leafed through his notebook, reading quickly and aware of her eyes on him.

'There's one other thing I wanted to ask you,' he said. 'Did Edwin ever mention his surviving brother, Doctor Spencer Robertshaw?'

'He did crop up in conversation, yes.'

'In what regard?'

She hesitated, fingering the pearls at her neck. 'They were never close – in fact, I gained the impression that Edwin disliked his brother, but at the same time he felt a certain . . . pity for him.'

'Did he say why?'

'I recall him saying that Spencer had a traumatic time of it in the war. He served in Africa, in a tank regiment, and his vehicle suffered a direct hit near Tobruk. Spencer was injured but was thrown clear of the wreckage. His fellow crew were not so lucky. They all perished, and Spencer witnessed their deaths. According to Edwin, he never got over what he saw that day.'

'That would account for it,' he said, more to himself.

'His addiction?' she asked.

'The professor told you about that?'

'Edwin said Spencer's receptionist would contact him when the doctor was having one of his "turns" – I don't think the woman was ever aware of her employer's addiction – and Edwin would go over to the surgery to "sort things out", as he said. A little while ago, it got to the point where he was going over a few times a week.'

'A little while ago? Can you recall exactly when this was?'

She thought about it. 'Just before Christmas,' she said. 'He would go over and find Spencer almost comatose and put

She stood also. 'Mr Langham, you promise you won't . . .'

'Not a word to the police,' he said. 'I'll see myself out.'

'Thank you, Mr Langham. Goodbye.'

He left the house and walked slowly along the lane to his car. He sat for a time, ordering his thoughts. So Professor Robertshaw had been confident that his wife would be dead within a month . . .

He drove south to Bury St Edmunds and made his way to Mrs Greaves's terraced house.

TWENTY-THREE

angham parked outside the small redbrick house, consulted his notes, then strode down the short path and rapped on the stained-glass panel of the front door. It was opened almost immediately by a portly middle-aged man in the uniform of the local bus company.

Langham showed his accreditation. 'Is Mrs Greaves at home, by any chance?'

'Else!' the man called. 'It's the police, come about poor Doctor Robertshaw.' He said to Langham, 'Come in, sir. I was about to go – my shift starts at twelve. You'll find Else in the front room. Terrible business. She's fair shook up still.'

'Thank you,' Langham said, squeezing past the man as they exchanged places. He moved along the short passage until he saw the glow of a standard lamp in the cramped living room.

Mrs Greaves was ensconced in a chintz-covered armchair drawn up to a two-bar electric fire, and the aroma of dust burning on the elements filled the room like incense. She clutched a mug of tea in her right hand and a balled handkerchief in her left; from time to time she dabbed at her reddened eyes and sniffed.

'I'm sorry to bother you at a time like this, Mrs Greaves,' he said, taking a seat opposite her. 'I just need to ask a few questions, if I may?'

'I still find it hard to believe, sir. I mean, I know he was bad and all, but I never thought he was that bad.' She stared at him. 'But he must have suffered something shocking, mustn't he, to do what he did.' She leaned forward. 'It *was* a suicide attempt, wasn't it?'

He noticed an effigy of the Madonna on the mantelpiece next to a wooden crucifix propped against the wallpaper. 'That remains to be seen,' he said.

She crossed herself. 'I've been saying prayers for him all

night, I have. Hardly slept a wink. He must have been suffering terribly, mustn't he? Pain is a terrible thing, sir.'

'It certainly is,' he agreed. 'Now, I wonder if you can help me with one or two things?'

'I'll do anything I can to assist,' she said, and smiled at him, woebegone.

'I understand that when Doctor Robertshaw suffered these . . . attacks, he contacted his brother, Professor Robertshaw?'

'That's right, sir. It started a year or so ago. I mean, that's when his illness got worse. There were times when he could hardly go on, if you get my meaning.'

'Of course.'

'Well, on these occasions I had to close the surgery and cancel all his appointments, and that didn't go down too well with some folks, as you can well imagine. I did my best to get him up to his room, but look at the size of me! Once or twice I was getting desperate, so I remembered he had a brother and called him up, desperate like. To his credit, the professor dropped what he was doing and rushed over and got Doctor Robertshaw into bed. He'd be a lot better by morning and would assure me he was well enough to see his patients.'

'How often did he have these turns?'

'In the early days? It was just an occasional thing to start with, but then it happened more often. A few months ago, they were happening a couple of times a week, regular as clockwork. Always on Friday afternoons, after the surgery closed, and quite often earlier in the week, always later on. Funny how that happened, isn't it? Sometimes I had to call the professor, but more often than not Doctor Robertshaw rang his brother himself.'

'And more recently?' Langham asked. 'Before Christmas?'

'Ooh, sometimes he fell ill three times a week, and I was fair worried. But what could I do, I ask you? I mean, I couldn't tell him to see a doctor, could I? I reckon he knew what was wrong, but there seemed nothing he could do to cure himself, poor soul. I wonder if it was that that sent him over the edge, sir, knowing that there was no hope?'

'It might well have been, Mrs Greaves,' he said. 'Over the

course of the past few months, and more recently, how often did the professor come over to assist his brother?'

'Well, it got to be such a regular kerfuffle that we decided it best if we got a spare set of keys cut for the professor. You see, often as not the doctor would fall ill when I wasn't around, and he'd be incapable of getting to the door and letting his brother in. So one day the professor suggested I give him the keys so he could have copies made, which was a good idea if you ask me. That way he needn't bother me when I was at home, and he could let himself in as and when he liked.'

'When exactly was this?'

'Oh, just before Christmas, I'd say.'

'And these keys,' Langham said. 'Were they just for the surgery and the apartment itself?'

'Well, he took the whole bunch, sir. Easier that way, he said, rather than taking individual keys off the ring.'

'So the keys were for the surgery's front door, his apartment . . . and where else?'

Mrs Greaves counted off the rooms on her fingers. 'The front and back door, the waiting room and Doctor Robertshaw's consulting room – that's four. His private apartment, five. The dispensing room, six. And there was a key for the drug cupboard, too. That's seven.'

Langham nodded, considering his next question. 'I know this might be inconvenient,' he began, 'but it would assist the investigation if you could see your way to accompanying me to the surgery. There are one or two things I'd like to check on the premises.'

'Of course, sir. But I hope you don't want me to go into *that* room, do you? His study, sir, where we found him. I couldn't set eyes on that place again, I couldn't, not for all the tea in China.'

'No, of course not. You do have your keys handy, I take it?'

'I do, sir. Locked secure in my bureau, they are.'

She crossed to a walnut writing bureau and withdrew a bunch of keys. 'Bear with me while I get my hat and coat, Officer. Perishing cold it is out there.'

She shuffled into the hall and busied herself donning a maroon overcoat and a hat like a tea cosy, then stuffing her feet into fur-lined boots.

They left the house and drove to the Willows.

She sat in silence when they pulled up outside the surgery, staring out at the darkened building. Then she said, 'Who would have thought it, sir, a week ago? It makes you think.'

'It certainly does, Mrs Greaves. In your own time.'

She took a deep breath. '"Be strong, and let us show ourselves courageous,"' she quoted. 'After you, Officer.'

Smiling, Langham led the way along the path to the front door of the surgery and Mrs Greaves let them in.

'Oh, the memories I have of this place. I worked here twenty years, Officer, first for Doctor Harper, and then for Doctor Robertshaw – God have mercy on him – when he took over ten years ago.'

'If you could show me to the dispensing room.'

'Of course. Follow me this way.'

She led him along the corridor, past the stairs that led to the upper floor, to a door at the back of the building. She fumbled with the keys in the dim light of a forty-watt bulb, then unlocked the door and switched on another light.

Langham entered, looking around him. It was an inner room without windows, with a worn navy-blue carpet and pale-green walls. Four tall grey filing cabinets stood against the far wall. To the left was a counter, behind which was the double door of a tall, white-painted cupboard set into the wall.

She looked around and sniffed. 'Many's the hour we spent in here over the years, sir, Doctor Robertshaw and me, sorting the deliveries and stacking them away.'

'In there?' Langham asked, pointing to the cupboard behind the counter.

'That's it, sir.'

'I wonder if you'd be good enough to open it, Mrs Greaves?'

She lifted a folding flap on the counter, unlocked the cupboard doors and opened them wide to reveal six long shelves divided into pigeon holes, each one stacked with a variety of glass bottles, vials and small cardboard boxes.

He turned and indicated the filing cabinets. 'And these are?'

'Patient records, sir, referring to personal prescriptions.'

The drawers of the filing cabinet were labelled from *A* to *Z*.

Mrs Greaves chattered away to herself reminiscently. 'Every Thursday morning it was, sir, the delivery. We'd have everything sorted and stacked within an hour.'

He said, 'I believe that Doctor Robertshaw was treating his sister-in-law, Xandra Robertshaw?'

'That's correct, sir. In a bad way, she was, too. She'd had tuberculosis, but the treatment fair knocked her back. Not long for this world, so I understand. Doctor Robertshaw would go over to the manor at Ingoldby every month to check up on her.'

'I understand that he changed her medication a little while back?'

She frowned at him. 'I don't know where you heard that, sir. I'd know about it if he had. You see, we went through each patient's prescriptions together, and when Doctor Robertshaw went out on a home visit, I'd have all the medicaments ready and waiting for him, I would.'

'And you're positive that Mrs Robertshaw's medication hadn't changed at some point around Christmas?'

Mrs Greaves nodded vehemently. 'I'd stake my life on it.' She pointed to the filing cabinets. 'If you don't believe me,' she sniffed, 'then take a look for yourself. You'll find Mrs Robertshaw's medical records in there, sir.'

He pulled up the drawer marked *R* and leafed through the manila files within; each was labelled with the patient's name, and within seconds he'd located the file belonging to Xandra Robertshaw.

The only drugs that Dr Robertshaw had prescribed for the treatment of his sister-in-law over the course of the past years were sedatives and painkillers, and the prescription had not changed a month ago.

He slipped the folder back into the drawer and pushed it shut.

'You've been more than helpful, Mrs Greaves. We can lock up now and I'll drive you home.'

'A pleasure to assist the investigation, sir,' she said, locking the cupboard and then the door of the dispensary. 'And rest assured I'll be praying for Doctor Robertshaw.'

'I'm sure he'll be reassured by this, Mrs Greaves,' he said, ushering her along the corridor and out to the car.

He drove her home, saw her into her front room, then motored from the town, lost in thought.

The snow had stopped, but the roads were covered with slush and the going was slow. For the last two miles into Ingoldby-over-Water, he was trapped behind a trundling coal wagon, and it was after one o'clock when he arrived home. He pulled into the drive, kicked the snow off his brogues and ducked into the cottage.

'In here!' Maria called.

He removed his overcoat and joined her in the welcome warmth of the kitchen.

'Homemade vegetable soup for lunch,' she said. 'I take it you're hungry?'

'Famished – but I wonder if it can wait?'

She stared at him. 'Donald, what is it? You look . . . shocked.'

'I am, and with good reason,' he said. He pulled out a dining chair and sat down. 'I need to get over to the manor, right away. Where's Nancy?'

'She went to see Xandra, perhaps an hour ago.'

'Good, I didn't want her to overhear what I have to say.'

'Overhear? Donald, what is it?'

'Sit down,' he said, 'and I'll tell you.'

Removing her apron, she pulled out a dining chair and sat opposite him.

'This morning I discovered that Professor Robertshaw was Nancy's father, and also,' he went on, 'I suspect that the professor switched his wife's medication in order to kill her.'

TWENTY-FOUR

Nancy was playing with Bill on the lawn when Donald and Maria arrived at the manor.

As they turned in through the gates and walked up the drive, Langham glanced at Maria. She was quiet after listening to the details he'd recounted on their way from Yew Tree Cottage.

'Could you stay out here with Nancy while I go and find Xandra?' he said. 'I don't want the girl interrupting.'

'Yes, of course.'

Nancy looked up and waved when she saw them, and Bill romped up and deposited his tennis ball at Maria's feet. She tossed the ball back on to the lawn, and they joined Nancy beside the snowman effigy of the late professor.

Her father, Langham thought.

'Good news!' Nancy said, smiling at them. 'Xandra told me that Randall is moving out at the end of the week and that I could come back then. Would it be all right if I stay with you until he goes?'

'Of course,' Langham said. 'We like having you around.'

'Thanks ever so,' she said. 'I must say, my aunt seems to have picked up a little. She isn't as miserable any more, and she's up and about. I just hope it lasts.'

'I have a feeling it might,' Langham said.

Bill dropped the ball at her feet, and Nancy picked it up and threw it in a high parabola through the air.

'Isn't it strange?' she said. 'After all my aunt's gone through over the past few days, you'd think she'd be down in the dumps!'

'Isn't it?' Langham murmured, squeezing Maria's hand. He gestured to the house. 'Where will I find her? I need a quick word.'

'She's in the conservatory, tending to her plants. If you pass the staircase and turn left, you'll find it at the very end of the corridor.'

Langham left them playing pig-in-the-middle with Bill.

He entered the manor, walked past the staircase and turned along the corridor, rehearsing what he would say to Xandra Robertshaw. He came to a door with glass panels in its upper half and peered through the condensation. Beyond, he made out a blurred figure amid the greenery.

He knocked and entered, the heat cloying after the sub-zero temperature outside. A vast, ancient iron radiator burbled in the centre of the glass-encased extension, and Langham wondered at the cost of the heating bill for the conservatory alone.

Xandra stood behind a trestle potting table, pruning a spider plant with a pair of secateurs.

She looked up and smiled as he batted his way through a mass of overhanging fronds.

'Ah, Mr Langham, I presume?' she said.

'Oh – I see, yes,' he said, belatedly understanding the reference. 'I wonder if you have five minutes?'

'Yes, of course. But it really must be five minutes. I was just finishing off here before changing to drive over to Cambridge with Randall. My hospital appointment, you see.'

'Quite,' he said, looking around for somewhere to sit. 'I must say, you're looking well.'

'I'm feeling well, Mr Langham. Over here.'

She pulled off her gloves and led the way across the conservatory to a rattan table and four wicker chairs arranged beneath the overhanging fronds of a tropical fern. He took off his hat and coat and deposited them on the table.

They sat down, Langham's chair creaking beneath his weight. 'For someone deprived of their painkillers,' he went on, 'I'd say you're looking remarkably chipper.'

She smiled at him. 'How can I help you?'

'This morning, in the course of my investigations,' he said, 'I called on Deirdre Creighton, and a little later I saw Mrs Greaves, your brother-in-law's receptionist.'

She gazed appreciatively at a nearby bromeliad. 'And?' she said.

He hesitated. 'On Wednesday morning, during the interview conducted by Detective Inspector Montgomery, you gave the impression that you didn't know the identity of your husband's mistress.'

She winced, ever so slightly. 'What of it?'

The way she avoided his eyes told him all he needed to know.

'I think you were being economical with the truth,' he said.

'What if I were, Langham? Who my husband was carrying on with was of little concern to me.' She hesitated. 'Very well – I did know he was seeing the damned woman. I found a note from her in his jacket, full of sweet nothings and anticipating their next tryst.'

'But you didn't confront him about it?'

'Of course not! That would have been quite beneath me.'

He opened his notebook and read a couple of entries. 'Going back to the interview with Inspector Montgomery,' he said. 'You were quite adamant that your husband wouldn't have taken his own life.'

'So?'

'In fact, you were sure that he'd been murdered. Was that,' he went on circumspectly, 'no more than a little game, Mrs Robertshaw?'

She looked away from him and examined the bromeliad more closely. She withdrew her right hand from the tabletop so that he could no longer see it shaking. 'A game?'

'To divert us from the chase,' he said, 'in a manner of speaking.'

She shook her head. 'I genuinely thought that a man like Edwin would not take his own life. Ergo, the only possible alternative was that he'd been murdered.'

He nodded and referred to his notes again. He felt a tension in the air and was aware of Xandra's unspoken desire for him to leave.

'During the interview with Montgomery, you admitted to detesting your husband.'

She swung her gaze to regard him. 'What of it?'

He refrained from replying. He read his notes, turning the pages slowly. Her impatience was almost palpable, a charge in the air that connected them like electricity.

He said at last, 'I wonder what made you hate him most: the fact that he was having an affair or that he was trying to kill you?'

She made no response to this, merely stared into the greenery as if frozen – and this, for Langham, was response enough.

He said gently, 'How did you find out?'

She returned her right hand to the tabletop and beat her long fingers in a slow tattoo, watching the operation with dispassion as if the hand did not belong to her. When she spoke, he had to lean forward in order to hear her murmured words.

'Just before Christmas I was feeling . . . *wonderful*, Mr Langham. I was very nearly free of pain, and if you've ever suffered like that, I think you'll know what I mean when I say that I was a new person, released not only from constant pain but from the mental agony that accompanies it. I even began to believe that I might survive for a few more years.' She smiled, as if chastising herself for such an optimistic notion. 'Then, after Christmas, over the course of a week, I began to feel dreadful again; the pain returned, and with it the demons, the spectre of death.'

'And this coincided with the change in the kind of painkillers you were taking?'

Xandra smiled at him. 'There was no change, according to my husband. I was on the same course of pills, as far as I could tell – the only change was that I took them in the morning, and they were administered by Edwin, not Nancy.'

'But did you notice whether the pills you began taking were any different to the previous ones?'

'As far as I could tell, they were just the same. Not that I took that much notice – I was always half asleep at the time.'

'But surely, when you began to take a turn for the worse, you mentioned this to Spencer?'

She smiled bitterly. 'I hadn't had a visit from him since the end of November. Edwin told me that his addiction was taking its toll and that he was incapacitated – and Edwin no doubt told his brother that I was getting along fine and didn't need his monthly visits.'

'And you weren't suspicious at this point – you didn't link the change of regime to your resumed ill-health?'

She hesitated. 'Not immediately, no. I'd suffered relapses before, you see. As far as I was concerned, this was just another one of them.'

'So how *did* you find out that Edwin was . . .?'

'It was quite accidental, I assure you. A little over a week ago, Edwin came in with my morning medication, gave me the pills and a glass of water and watched me take them. A matter of seconds after he left the room, I happened to choke and cough the pills back up, then spat the foul-tasting mush on to the carpet. I was feeling ghastly and couldn't summon the effort to call him back. The following morning, he brought the pills in with my breakfast, and I said I'd take them after I'd eaten the toast. In the event, I fell asleep, and by the time I awoke a little before noon, Nancy had been in and cleared away the tray. Later that day I began to feel a little better – clear-headed and not so nauseous – and I wondered if it might have anything to do with not having taken the painkillers for two days running – though, oddly, the pain was no worse than it normally was. The following day, I hid the pills under my tongue when Edwin gave them to me, and spat them out when he left the room. And the next day, I did the same, and the day after that, too.' She paused and smiled across at him. 'Within five days, I was feeling as well as I had been before Christmas, and a small, insistent voice began in my head: what if it was the painkillers that had been making me feel worse than usual? Then it occurred to me that my recent relapse coincided with Edwin's administering the pills in the mornings. And it was only a very small leap of supposition to the corollary: what if Edwin was . . . poisoning me?'

'How did you find out for certain?' he asked.

She smiled, but without humour. 'I overheard him in his study,' she said. 'I was on my way to the kitchen for some toast, and I heard him on the phone. To *her*. He told her that he'd be with her soon, for ever – that "soon Xandra will be dead". That's when I *knew* that my husband was slowly killing me.'

Langham asked, 'When was this?'

She held his gaze. 'On Friday afternoon.'

He framed his next question, watching her closely. 'And did you plan then to kill Edwin – or was it a later, spur-of-the-moment thing?'

She swallowed, regarding her fingers on the tabletop. The

only sound in the conservatory was the ticking of the radiator and the occasional dripping of condensation droplets from the glass roof on to the paved flooring.

She nodded at last, as if she'd finally made the decision to tell him everything.

'I was shocked, of course – stunned. There was no love lost between us, Mr Langham. I knew what kind of self-centred, self-obsessed man my husband was; I'd known all about his affairs in the early days of our marriage, but I had my son to think of, and a comfortable life in Oxford . . . And when I fell ill, it was all I could do then to hold my sanity together. I had no energy to waste on actively *hating* my husband. We led our separate lives.' She shook her head. 'No, I didn't revile Edwin until I heard him say that soon I would be dead. And then it all fell into place, and I understood what he'd been doing.'

'And you planned your revenge?'

She shook her head. 'Oh, no, Mr Langham. I'm not that kind of person. This was no cold, calculated murder aforethought.'

'Then what happened?'

'I decided to have it out with him, tell him that I knew of his affair and that he was poisoning me. And then I planned to leave him.' She smiled at Langham, bleakly. 'Of course, I was aware that this was just what he wanted – me out of the way so he could be with his mistress. But there was little I could do to . . . to *win*, was there? It would be enough to see his reaction when I told him that I knew and that he'd failed to kill me.'

'You could always have gone to the police and told them about the painkillers.'

She smiled at this. 'I doubt very much that they would have believed me – and anyway, what proof did I have? No, I decided that I would simply tell him what I knew, and what I thought of him.'

'And you did this?'

'On Tuesday evening, when Nancy was sleeping, and I knew that Edwin would be alone in his study, I came down and confronted him.'

'What did he say?'

She pursed her lips, as if in an attempt not to break down. She nodded very slowly to herself as she thought back to that fateful night.

'He laughed at me, Langham. The bastard laughed at me! I had expected . . . oh, I don't really know what I thought he'd do. Perhaps deny that he was poisoning me, tell me that I was imagining it all. But no, he simply laughed in my face, then said that he should have made sure of the job and poisoned me in one go. Then he took his torch and went out through the French windows to his beloved standing stone.'

'And you saw red, took his revolver from the bureau, and gave chase with the intention of shooting—?'

She interrupted. 'I took the revolver, yes, but even then, I had no desire to kill my husband. I wanted to frighten him, to . . . to make him see what an evil, egotistical monster he was. I followed him out to the stone and I told him this, and he countered with insults, calling me . . .' She gestured. 'It doesn't matter what he said, but his accusations hurt me. He reached for the gun, and we struggled . . . He hit me and I staggered back against the stone. Then he came at me again, and I moved aside to avoid him, and raised the gun and fired.'

He lifted a hand. 'One thing,' he said, recalling that only the professor and Richard Wellbourne's prints had been discovered on the weapon. 'Were you wearing gloves at the time?'

'I . . . I had a pair of lace gloves in the pocket of my dressing gown; I must have pulled these on before picking up the gun.'

He stared at her. 'I thought you said you had no desire to kill your husband – and yet you had the foresight to pull on the gloves before picking up the gun.'

'I don't know what I was thinking, at the time,' she said. 'I was *angry*, Mr Langham.' She shrugged wearily.

'Edwin fell back against the stone and slid to the ground,' she went on. 'Even then, I didn't believe he could be dead. It was only when I picked up his torch and shone it on him that I . . .' She fell silent, then said, 'I felt, then – and I am not proud of this – I felt at once elated and terrified at what I had done. I dropped the revolver and fled back to the house, fearing that the shot would have awoken Nancy. As it happened, I was in luck. She was still sleeping, and I returned to bed.' She smiled across at him. 'And oddly, Mr Langham, I slept very well for the remainder of the night.'

He looked to his right, through the glass. He made out the indistinct, blurred shapes of two people and a dog, playing on the lawn. Nancy's laughter reached him as if from far away.

Xandra interrupted his thoughts. 'What now?' she asked.

'If I were you, I'd phone Inspector Montgomery and make a full confession. Tell him all about the medication, and Edwin's unfaithfulness. Impress upon him the psychological stress you've been under during the past few months.' He sighed. 'And most importantly, tell Montgomery that you fired the revolver to protect yourself from his further violence.'

She sat across from him, upright and oddly proud, then inclined her head. She rose to her feet, murmuring, 'Yes, I'll do that now, Mr Langham. Thank you.'

'One more thing before you go,' he said. 'Did you know that Nancy was the professor's daughter?'

She nodded. 'He admitted as much, just before we took her in,' she said. 'Not that I let that affect my regard for the girl,' she went on.

She moved around the table and left the conservatory, and Langham sat in the cloying heat amid the tropical plants and listened to the innocent peal of Nancy's laughter.

TWENTY-FIVE

N ancy threw the ball in a great arc across the lawn and watched the dog scamper after it, her gaze far away. The girl had been lost in thought ever since Donald had gone inside.

She turned to Maria and smiled.

'What is it?'

'Last night, when I went to see Roy in his caravan,' Nancy said, 'he confessed.'

'Confessed?' Maria shook her head. 'To what?'

'I think you know. I've seen you watching him.' She smiled and went on, 'And I mean that in the nicest way.'

'Confessed to what?' Maria pressed.

'I did wonder about his past, about what he did in the war. You see, one or two of the things he said, the stories he told . . . Well, they didn't add up, or he contradicted himself. And then, of course, there was everything Randall said about Roy. I didn't believe him, but he went on so . . .' She shrugged. 'After a while, I began to wonder if there *was* something in what my cousin claimed, after all.'

'That Roy had never served in the RAF?'

Nancy nodded. 'So last night, I was a little drunk . . . Back at his caravan, I asked him. I told him to tell me the truth, that I'd love him whatever the truth was – but that I'd be hurt if he didn't trust me enough to believe that.'

'And he told you?'

Nancy sniffed and wiped the back of a mitten across her nose. 'He said I was right, that he'd never served in the RAF. He told me he'd lied about being the rear-gunner on a plane during the war. He said it all came about when he started working at Wellspring Farm, and he was wearing that old RAF greatcoat, and Richard and Harriet assumed he'd flown. And Roy didn't correct them about that right at the start. And later, when Harriet asked him about the war, he found himself telling lies just so . . . so that he wouldn't hurt her, he said.'

Maria nodded. 'I can understand that.'

'Then he told me what he had done during the war and that I'd hate him for it. He said he was a conscientious objector and worked for a chap called Middleton Murry who was a pacifist and ran a farm in Suffolk for conchies. And when he told me this, he started to cry. He said he was ashamed of himself when it came out later what terrible evil Hitler and the Nazis had committed. So he left the farm and moved around the area, looking for odd-job work and . . . and denying his past.'

As Maria watched Nancy, tears trickled down the girl's bright-red cheeks and sat there until she dashed them away with a mitten. 'Oh, Maria . . . when he told me this, I couldn't speak. There was something in here' – she touched her chest – 'that felt as if it was about to explode! Roy took my silence for condemnation, and he said he'd understand if I wanted to leave him and never set eyes on him again, but' – she shook her head – 'but even if he'd told me he'd been the bravest war hero in history, I couldn't have loved him more for telling me the truth. You see, he trusted me! And I told him this, and his relief . . . Oh, it was wonderful to watch, Maria. It made me feel so happy!'

Maria reached out. 'Come here,' she said. She pulled the girl to her and planted a kiss on her hot forehead. 'I've always liked Roy,' she murmured. 'He's a good person.'

Nancy nodded, sniffing. 'Isn't he? He's kind and gentle. He wouldn't do anything to hurt anybody, in any way. I suppose that's why he was a conchie, all those years ago.'

'I admire him for telling you the truth,' Maria said. 'It proves how much he thinks of you.'

'It does, doesn't it?' the girl said, laughing through her sniffles.

Bill nudged the ball closer to Nancy's feet, and she laughed and said, 'I know, boy. We're neglecting you, aren't we!'

She threw the tennis ball against the wall of the house, and it rebounded high up, bounced on the frozen snow in the drive and rolled beneath the professor's Daimler. Nancy laughed and, her gait impeded by her oversized Wellington boots, she galumphed across the lawn to retrieve it. Maria watched her reach under the car and grab the ball from the gravel.

She stared at the dry gravel beneath the car, suddenly aware of her heartbeat.

Nancy returned, peering at her. She halted, the tennis ball clutched in her mittened hand. 'Maria? Are you all right? You look as if you've seen a ghost.'

Maria forced herself to smile. 'It's nothing. Someone stepped on my grave, as the saying goes.'

Nancy laughed as Bill jumped up, trying to grab the ball from her hand. Nancy threw it across the lawn and Bill gave chase.

'Do excuse me,' Maria said, 'but I need a quick word with Randall. Do you know where I'll find him?'

'He was in the study, going over some legal papers or something. I say . . . you won't tell him anything about what Roy told me, will you?'

Maria smiled. 'Of course not. This . . . It's about something else entirely.' She reached out and took the girl's hand. 'I'll tell you what – later this afternoon, why not collect Roy and come round to the house, and I'll mull some wine and we'll sit before the fire and talk, all four of us. Promise?'

'I'll say.' The girl laughed. 'That will be wonderful. Mulled wine! Do you know, I've never had mulled wine before.'

'I shan't be long,' Maria said, turning towards the house.

'Good boy!' Nancy said as Bill dropped the ball at her feet.

Maria moved through the manor to the professor's study, her mind racing with the possibilities and the permutations. She dismissed the obvious assumption and examined those less obvious, and by the time she reached the open door of the study, she wondered if she had arrived at some approximation of what might have happened at the manor on Tuesday night.

Across the empty room, the French windows stood ajar. In the distance, next to the standing stone, Randall Robertshaw stood smoking a cigarette and staring down at where his father had met his end.

She crossed the room and slipped outside.

She walked across to the standing stone, her approach silenced by the snow. 'Hello,' she said as she came up behind him.

He started and swung around. 'Oh, it's you.'

'I didn't mean to startle you.'

He removed the cigarette from between his lips and smiled at her. 'You didn't,' he said. 'I knew you were here – at the house, I mean. I just wondered how long it might be before you sought me out. You have a habit of bearding me with awkward questions.' He gestured with the cigarette. 'I saw you out there, playing with *her*.'

'At least, this time, you aren't drunk.' She regarded him levelly. 'What's the real reason you dislike Nancy so?' she asked.

'The *real* reason? Isn't the fact that she's a clueless little nitwit enough?'

'She happens to be quite the nicest girl I know,' Maria replied. 'And she's been through a heck of a rough time over the past couple of years. Your treatment of her does you no favours, Randall, fuelled as it is by greed.'

He raised an eyebrow. 'Greed?'

'Oh, come on, now. You know the truth as well as I do. Did your father tell you, before he died – did he tell you the truth about Nancy?'

He feigned ignorance. 'The truth?'

'Surely, Randall, you know that she's his daughter?'

He held out his cigarette and regarded its glowing tip, considering her words. 'No, honestly, I didn't. But it begins to make sense now . . . Just before Christmas, I'd been beastly to her, and Pater blew his top. He hauled me into his study and told me that he intended to change his will and that when he eventually died – if my mother pre-deceased him – the house and everything he owned would be divided equally between Nancy and me.' He smiled. 'I must admit, it was something of a shock.'

'You must really have resented her even more then.'

'As if that were possible!' he muttered. He pointed his cigarette at her. 'But don't get it into that pretty head of yours that what he told me about changing his will had anything to do with his death.'

She returned his smile, without humour. 'Oh, I've worked

that out,' she said. 'To get at his assets would be too obvious
a motive. You're not that much of a fool.'

He leaned against the standing stone, affecting nonchalance.
'Then what kind of fool am I?'

'You're no fool at all,' she said. 'In fact, in some ways
you're a very clever young man.' She paused, then went on,
'How did you discover that the professor was slowly poisoning
your mother?'

He arched his eyebrows. 'My, you are perspicacious. How
did *you* find out, might I ask?'

'I didn't – that was Donald. But I asked you first.'

He finished the cigarette and flicked it into the snow, watching
it as it expired with a curl of smoke. 'Quite by chance, as it
happens. Last weekend, just after he'd rushed over to Spencer's
surgery, I found him in his study decanting some of my mother's
pills from one bottle to another. I quite startled him, and he
looked hellish guilty. I hardly thought anything of it at the time,
but then it came to me that my mother's recent decline dated
from the time he'd taken over administering her medication.
Nancy used to give my mother her pills of an evening, you see.'
He shrugged. 'I knew just what a self-centred, self-serving chap
he was . . . and I began to wonder if it was possible that he
was poisoning her. I knew he had the keys to Spencer's surgery,
and he went over there from time to time in order to check up
on him, or so he said. He would have been able to help himself
to whatever drugs he required. Of course, I knew nothing about
the type of medication my mother was on—'

'So you phoned your uncle?'

He regarded her coolly, then nodded. 'I told him of my
suspicions, and he said he'd run a check on his stock. He phoned
me back a couple of hours later, quite shaken. Two vials of
codeine were missing, and he said that this drug, to someone
in my mother's condition, depending on the dosage, would
prove fatal within a month or so. Her kidneys would have been
unable to process the drug, he said.'

'When was this?'

Randall thought about it. 'I discovered my father monkeying
with the pills on Sunday morning, and I consulted Spencer the
following day, on Monday.'

'And a day later, on Tuesday evening, your father was dead.'

Randall looked up into the sky, frowning. It had begun to snow again. Maria turned her collar up against the wind and wished she'd remembered her hat in the rush to leave the cottage.

She hunched her shoulders and dug her hands into her pockets. 'Randall, would you care to tell me exactly what happened here on Tuesday evening?'

He smiled at her and tried to bluster. 'Well, apparently, it was rather hectic,' he said, 'what with old Wellbourne barging in, all in a huff about the disputed land. He and Pater were at it hammer and tongs—'

'I mean after that,' she interrupted, 'when Richard had gone home. What happened *then*?'

He shrugged, avoiding her gaze. 'What on earth makes you think I know anything about that?'

She said, 'Because you didn't go over to your uncle's place at six o'clock on Tuesday evening. In fact, you were with him, in town, at no point that night. You were here at the manor all the time.'

He laughed, 'What makes you assume—?'

'Your car was parked in the drive all evening,' she said.

'You've no proof.'

'On the morning the body of your father was discovered,' she said, 'I came over here with Donald. Nancy's dog was playing with his ball, and I just happened to throw it for him . . . and it rolled under your car. I retrieved it from the *dry* gravel.' She shook her head. 'I didn't realize what it meant at the time – in fact, it was only just now, when Nancy was playing with her dog and I saw the ball roll under your father's car, that the memory of that morning came back to me. It had been snowing all night on Tuesday – the following morning it was white-over – and if you had indeed been at your uncle's for up to six hours, when you returned after midnight, as you claimed, you would have parked over fallen snow.' She smiled at him. 'Your car was parked beside the house all the time.'

'Quite the little detective,' he said. 'So you think I killed my father in rage over what he was doing to mother, then contacted Spencer to supply me with a foolproof alibi?'

'Well, it all fits, doesn't it? You had the motive – to avenge

your mother – and the opportunity. You knew where your father
kept his service revolver. All you needed was an alibi, and as
you say, Spencer could provide you with that.'

He shook his head. Despite the chill wind, he was sweating:
perspiration stood out on his high forehead.

'So are you going to go to the police with your little theory?'
he sneered.

She stared at him. 'Of course not,' she said, 'because I know
– just as you know – that it didn't happen like that.'

He swallowed. 'You *know*?'

'None of it fits with the type of person you are, Randall.
You're impetuous, impulsive. You act in the heat of the moment,
rashly, without thinking, without taking into consideration the
consequences of your actions. This was demonstrated the other
day when you threatened Roy Vickers with the shotgun. And
the way you hector Nancy – you're headstrong, heedless. On
Sunday, you discovered what your father was doing, and you
didn't find out for certain that he was poisoning your mother
until Monday, on hearing back from your uncle. It was *then*
that you would have confronted your father with what you'd
found, on impulse, in rage – if you'd been man enough to do
so. But you didn't do that.'

She watched him. He stared at the ground, biting his
bottom lip.

She went on, 'No, your father's killing was premeditated,
carried out by someone who knew just where he kept his revolver
– in anger, yes, at what your father was doing, but thought
through beforehand.' She hesitated. 'I was puzzled, though, why
your uncle should agree to provide *you* with an alibi. But then
it became obvious, after a little thought. Following your phone
call, Spencer knew what your father was doing. He realized
that his brother had taken the drugs from his dispensary, while
supposedly helping Spencer out when he was incapacitated.
And after stewing over the actions of his brother for a day,
Spencer came over here on Tuesday evening and . . . Well, you
probably know what happened far better than I do.'

He was leaning against the standing stone, no longer looking
nonchalant but almost defeated, staring at the ground between
them.

'Well?' she pressed.

At last, he said, 'It was about nine o'clock or so. I was upstairs, in my room. I heard a car approaching along the drive and looked out, but I couldn't make out who it was. I thought nothing of it at the time; my father often had friends over. About twenty minutes later, I heard a gunshot, and a few minutes later Spencer was hammering on my door. He looked ghastly. I don't know whether he was affected by drugs he'd taken, but he was hardly coherent. He said he'd confronted my father about the missing codeine, about poisoning my mother. They were in the study. Spencer said he took the revolver from the bureau and threatened my father . . .' Randall swallowed. 'He ordered my father outside, marched him across to the standing stone, and while his brother was still babbling his denials, he raised the gun and – in his own words – "executed" him.'

'What did you do when he told you this?'

Randall shook his head. 'I calmed him down, first of all. He was like a man possessed. I guessed that he knew the enormity of his crime, but at the same time he was righteous. He said that my father had deserved to die for everything he'd done.' He grunted. '*Everything*. I think Spencer resented my father for far more than attempting to kill my mother. He was the loneliest man I'd ever known, and he resented my father for the ease with which he seduced women. When Spencer discovered that my father was slowly murdering my mother, whom he thought the world of . . . well, I think that was the final straw.'

'How did your father know about the codeine? I mean, how did he know that it would have such a lethal effect on your mother?'

'That was another thing that filled Spencer with guilt. You see, he blamed himself for planting the notion in my father's head. At some point, he said that although my mother could take painkillers, at all costs she must avoid codeine and other opioids which would prove fatal to someone with such an advanced renal condition.' He shook his head, recalling the night in question. 'He actually told me this that night – it was another stick to beat himself with, along with the shame and the guilt of his brother raiding his dispensary for the drugs.'

'You didn't think of phoning the police at this point?'

'No. No, I didn't. You see, perhaps a part of me did despise my father, did think that he should have been punished for what he'd planned to do to my mother. Also, I admit I felt sorry for my uncle. I told him to return home, and impressed on him that the best way to give himself an alibi would be to provide me with one.'

She smiled. 'Which is what I meant when I said that in some ways you were a very clever young man.'

'I'll take that, all things considered, as a compliment.'

Maria sighed. 'Your uncle's recent overdose . . .' She shook her head. 'In the cold light of day, when he could look back on what he'd done, I would guess that the guilt proved just too much.'

Randall pursed his lips, and she was surprised to see that he was on the verge of tears. 'I should never have phoned him,' he said. 'I should have kept my suspicions to myself. If I'd only . . .'

She reached out and touched his arm. 'You had to find out for certain what your father was doing. You did the right thing. Can you imagine if you'd ignored your suspicions, and your father succeeded in killing Xandra? Imagine how you would have felt then.'

He drew himself upright, took a deep breath and nodded. 'What a bloody business,' he said. 'What a bloody awful, tragic mess.'

She said, 'The police need to know what happened, whether your uncle survives or not.'

'But if he dies, then surely . . . surely, then, the secret can die with—'

She interrupted. 'Letting you neatly off the charge of conspiring to pervert the course of justice?' she said. 'Randall, the police need to know everything – even the lie of your alibi. They need to know who killed your father so as to avoid the possibility of mistakenly convicting an innocent person.' She hesitated. 'You're always so keen to accuse Nancy of acting like a child – now you need to act like a man and tell the police *everything*.'

He thought about it for a few seconds, then pushed himself away from the standing stone. 'Very well, yes,' he said.

'One more thing,' she said before he moved off to the house. 'Does Xandra know what your father was doing to her?'

'I told her after I removed the tablets from the bathroom cabinet on Monday,' he said. 'That's why she thinks that *I* shot my father. You see, she knows my alibi was a lie. On Wednesday afternoon, when the police had left, she saw me move the car into the garage, revealing the dry gravel. She saw this through her bedroom window and, like you, realized that I'd been at the manor all night.'

'Did she confront you?'

'She asked me if I was guilty, and I swore I didn't shoot my father.' He shook his head. 'I rather think she didn't believe me.'

He stepped away from the standing stone.

'About Nancy . . .' she began.

'What about her?'

'Please don't tell her about the professor being her father, all right? I think it might be best for her if I did that.'

'Very well, I'll keep mum,' he said. 'I'd better go and phone that Montgomery chap.'

'Yes, you do that.'

She turned and watched him walk towards the house through the falling snow.

As Randall approached the French windows to his father's study, Donald emerged and spoke briefly to the young man. Then he looked across the snow-covered lawn and waved to her.

He hurried across, smiling. 'There you are! You'll never guess what . . .'

She laughed. 'Mmm. Now, let me try . . . I think,' she went on, 'that Xandra has confessed that she killed her husband – am I correct?'

'Well, blow me down,' Donald said, 'how on earth did you know that?'

She reached up and stroked his cheek. 'Let's go inside out of the cold, my darling. I have something to tell you.'

She linked an arm through his and walked him back to the house.

EPILOGUE

Langham carried a pint of Fuller's and a gin and tonic from the bar and crossed the room to where Maria was sitting before the blazing fire. Outside, twilight was descending, along with a new fall of snow. Through the mullioned windows, he could just make out the square tower of the church across the green.

'Good health,' he said.

They were due to meet Nancy and Roy a little later, along with the Wellbournes; he was looking forward to a quiet pint or two and a long evening of pleasant conversation with their new friends.

'You hardly slept last night, Donald,' Maria said, 'and all day you've been quiet.'

He smiled at her. 'I suppose I've been berating myself for not being able to see through Xandra's lies.'

'But you said she was convincing,' Maria said, 'and she had a motive and the opportunity, after all.' She shook her head. 'She was a brave woman, Donald – to willingly take the blame like that, in order to save her son. I always liked her.'

A log collapsed in the hearth, sending a flurry of sparks shooting up the chimney. A few more customers entered the bar, discarding overcoats, hats and scarves, and commenting on the inordinate snowfall.

Langham raised his drink. 'And you were correct in your initial feelings that the professor was not a very nice character,' he said, then laughed. 'I was wrong there, too – I thought he was a decent enough cove, at the time. It's only thinking back that I realize what an incredibly arrogant and self-centred chap he really was. Heck, I've just had a thought . . .'

'Go on.'

'There he was, merrily poisoning his wife so he could run off with his lover and start a new life. Then he receives the blackmail letter – and he was so safe in his assumption that he wouldn't be found out that he calls me in to look into the blackmail case. As far as he was concerned, the two were entirely separate. Oh, and I realized something as I lay awake last night.'

'What?'

'Deirdre . . .' he said.

Maria made the connection. 'If Deirdre hadn't decided to get her own back on her ex-husband and embark on a spurious affair with him,' she said, 'then it might never have entered the professor's head to get rid of Xandra.'

'Precisely.' Langham shook his head. 'As a consequence of what Deirdre did, Spencer killed his brother and then attempted to take his own life.'

'I wonder . . .' Maria began speculatively, swirling her drink. She looked across at him. 'If the professor *had* succeeded in poisoning Xandra, I wonder what he'd planned then?'

'You mean about reporting her death?'

She nodded. 'As Spencer was her doctor, he would be called on to examine her and issue a death certificate. As she was ill and her death wouldn't have been unexpected, then perhaps he would have issued a certificate without being too scrupulous? No doubt the professor was banking on this.'

'You're probably right,' he said.

The previous day, Montgomery had phoned Langham with the latest news regarding Spencer Robertshaw. The doctor had recovered consciousness and, following police questioning, had admitted to shooting the professor 'in the heat of the moment'. What the prosecution would make of this at his trial remained to be seen.

Montgomery also reported that they'd arrested Randall Robertshaw on a charge of perverting the course of justice: the young man could look forward to a custodial sentence of a few months.

That morning, Maria had been uncommonly quiet while unpacking boxes. When Langham questioned her, she said she'd been mulling over when to inform Nancy about the truth of her parentage.

'It might be for the best if you break it to her sooner rather than later,' he'd said. 'Are you OK with that?'

She'd broached the situation with Nancy when the girl came back to the cottage after taking Bill for a walk, and Langham had left them to it and retreated to his study.

Now Maria said, 'I'm surprised that she took it so well, though knowing what a tough cookie Nancy is, perhaps I shouldn't be. She's had a lot to endure over the past couple of years.'

The girl had cried to begin with, then brightened and said, 'Well, that's a bolt from the blue! Who would have thought? The professor, my father! He wasn't a very nice man, was he, all things considered?' She had blotted her eyes with a handkerchief. 'I knew my parents had been through a bad time at the start of their marriage. My father . . . George . . . he once told me as much. But they'd patched things up and stayed together. I wonder if George knew I wasn't really his daughter?'

'Apparently, he did, yes.'

That had brought about more tears. 'And yet he loved me as his own daughter,' she said. 'He was a wonderful person. You would have liked him, Maria. I'll always think of him as my real father, you know.'

'And so you should,' Maria said.

The door of the public bar opened, admitting a swirl of snow on the wind, along with the Wellbournes.

Richard crossed to the fire and beamed down at them. 'Drink up and I'll get them in,' he said, pulling off his overcoat and unwinding his scarf.

'No, let me get these,' Langham protested.

'No, you won't,' Harriet said. 'We've had some good news.'

Richard laughed. 'You don't know that, Harriet!'

'Yes, I *do*,' the little woman insisted. 'I'm *never* wrong when it comes to . . . well, you know what!'

Maria laughed and asked, 'Good news?'

'One of Harriet's hunches,' Richard said.

'It's more than just a hunch, you cynical old man!' she chided. 'Now, go and get those drinks, will you?'

Obediently, Richard took their orders and retreated to the bar.

Harriet settled herself into a seat beside the fire, and Langham asked, 'Now, what's all this about?'

'Well,' Harriet said, 'Nancy hasn't said anything, but I *know.*' She tapped her short, greying hair. 'Last night, it came to me suddenly – like a vision. I had a mental image of Nancy being very happy: she was smiling and there was something white falling all around her head and shoulders – and it wasn't snow – and she was with a young man. And then the vision ended, leaving me feeling all cosy and warm!'

Richard returned with the drinks and rolled his eyes at Langham.

'So you think . . .?' Maria began.

Harriet smiled triumphantly and sipped her sherry. 'I do!'

Richard said, 'She's picked up on Nancy's manner. The girl's been smiley and coy all morning – like a cat with the cream. Even I can see that!'

'But I knew *last night*, Richard,' Harriet pointed out. 'At seven, I saw her walk across the meadow with Bill and go into Roy's caravan. She was there an hour – and when she left the van and went back to your cottage, Maria, that's when I had my vision.'

Maria said, 'Well, over dinner last night she did seem rather dreamy and happy with herself.'

'You see,' Richard said, 'Maria picked up on it, too.'

'Yes,' Harriet pointed out, 'but I know *why* the girl's so happy.' She almost hugged herself. 'And I would be, too, in her position. But if you all doubt me,' she went on, smiling, 'then just wait until Nancy and Roy arrive – they have an announcement to make.'

'An announcement?' Langham echoed.

'Just you wait and see,' Harriet said.

They didn't have long to wait, as within minutes Roy and Nancy pushed through the door and entered the public bar with Bill on a short lead. Roy bought their drinks and they crossed to the fire. Nancy looked bright-eyed and elated, and Roy had shaved and changed into his best suit. Bill curled up beneath Nancy's chair, his tail beating the carpet in contentment.

Harriet leaned forward, wringing her hands. 'Well, you can't keep us in suspense any longer!'

Nancy beamed around at the expectant faces, then laughed. 'Well, the news is,' she began, 'that Uncle Spencer has been arrested for the murder of his brother, and Randall has been arrested, too – for telling lies to the police, apparently – and, oh, yes, Xandra has decided to sell the manor and move to the south of France, for her health. She promised to give me some money from the proceeds of the sale, and I plan to buy a cottage in the village.' She lifted her gin and tonic to her lips, playfully hiding her smile.

Harriet was beside herself. 'And?' she asked.

Nancy frowned. 'And?' She shook her head. 'No, I think that's all the news I can think of – what about you, Roy?'

The young man said, 'Well, there is one other thing . . .'

'Go on!' Harriet said.

Roy smiled. 'Last night,' he said, 'I asked Nancy to marry me, and she said yes.'

'There!' Harriet said, clapping her hands in joy and falling back into her chair.

Maria reached out and squeezed Nancy's fingers; Langham shook Roy's hand.

Harriet dabbed her eyes with a lace handkerchief, and Richard leaned over and kissed her.

'I think that calls for more drinks,' Langham said, and moved to the bar.